MURDER TAKE THREE

MURDER TAKE THREE

A Langham and Dupré mystery

Eric Brown

This first world edition published 2017
in Great Britain and the USA by
SEVERN HOUSE PUBLISHERS LTD of
Eardley House, 4 Uxbridge Street, London W8 7SY.
Trade paperback edition first published
in Great Britain and the USA 2018 by
SEVERN HOUSE PUBLISHERS LTD.

British Library Cataloguing in Publication Data
A CIP catalogue record for this title is available from the British Library.

ISBN-13: 978-0-7278-8709-2 (cased)
ISBN-13: 978-1-84751-817-0 (trade paper)
ISBN-13: 978-1-78010-880-3 (e-book)

Typeset by Palimpsest Book Production Ltd.,
Falkirk, Stirlingshire, Scotland.

ONE

F ridays were always quiet at the Ryland and Langham Detective Agency.

Langham sat with his feet lodged on the corner of the desk and his chair tipped back against the wall. He was going through the proofs of his latest thriller, as always wishing he'd been more drastic with the red pen. He scored a line through a particularly purple patch, then looked at the photograph of his fiancée on the desk. Maria smiled out at him, resplendent in a navy blue trouser suit and white sun hat.

He had another hour here, and then he was due to meet Maria at the Lyons' café in Notting Hill at five. The weekend beckoned, free from all obligations but pleasure. Spring had finally come to London; men were in shirtsleeves and women in flowery summer dresses. In one month he would marry Maria Dupré, and a week later – while they were honeymooning in Paris – his next novel was due to hit the bookshops.

He was thinking about shutting up shop for the day, and escaping early, when the bell tinkled above the street-level door and he heard footsteps on the staircase leading up to the first-floor office. He cursed his luck and hoped he could get the meeting over and done with and be away by four thirty.

He removed his brogues from the desk, righted his chair, and assumed a manner of brisk efficiency as he picked up a folder and gave it his spurious attention.

The door opened and a young woman stepped into the office, then paused and stared around her as if surprised to find herself in a shabby, down-at-heel detective agency on Wandsworth High Street.

Langham, for his part, was no less surprised that this strikingly attractive woman should have sought out the services of Ryland and Langham. She was perhaps thirty, a little over five feet tall, and had a small, perfectly proportioned face, brilliant crimson lips, and a head of tight, platinum-blonde curls. She wore a cream pencil skirt, a box-shouldered blouson, and carried a tiny red handbag that was obviously more for show than utility.

'Donald Langham,' he said. 'If you'd care to take a seat.' He indicated a rickety spindle-backed chair before the desk.

She remained standing, her nose wrinkling suddenly. 'What in God's name is that awful smell?' she asked in a distinct American accent.

'Ah. That's the singular redolence of three-month-old beef dripping.'

'Say again?'

'Stale fat. We're directly above a fish-and-chip shop. You get so that you don't notice it, after a while.'

'I'm sure you do,' she said, eyeing the chair dubiously before seating herself and crossing her legs. 'I must admit that this wasn't quite what I was expecting.'

In contrast to the woman's startling perfection, the office, with its peeling, thrice-painted green wallpaper, worn brown linoleum, and fly-speckled window, looked nothing like the headquarters of a successful detective agency.

Langham sat back. 'We like to expend profits on assuring that our clients receive the best possible service,' he said, parroting the line he'd heard Ralph Ryland use more than once.

She stared at him across the desk, appraisingly. 'I must say, you don't exactly fit the bill as a tough-guy private eye.'

'I'll take that as a compliment. Now, how can I help?'

'Do you mind if I smoke?'

'Feel free.'

She fitted a Pall Mall cigarette into a long holder, lit it from a tiny mother-of-pearl lighter, and eyed him through the resulting smoke. 'You new to this job?' She had a forthright way of expressing herself which Langham found a little disconcerting.

'What makes you think that?'

'You look more like a bank clerk, if you don't mind me saying.'

'Not at all.' Langham laughed. 'I first worked at the agency for a couple of years after the war, took a long break, then rejoined Mr Ryland just recently.'

She smiled. 'So you *did* work in a bank?'

'No, I wrote novels.'

'A writer. That'd explain it.'

Explain what? he wondered. 'Have you met many writers?'

'Dozens, back home. And they're all the same. Poor schmucks crying into their beer about how they're gonna write the Great American Novel, but for now making a fast buck knocking out screenplays. Not that I'm saying you're *anything* like that, Mr Langham.' She smiled sweetly.

'Of course not.'

She blew out a plume of smoke, regarding him. 'So, let me guess . . . Your novels didn't sell, right, so you're back to being a gumshoe?'

He bridled. 'They do sell, actually. Rather well. But you get a bit stale, sitting behind a typewriter month after month. I work here a couple of days a week and write the rest of the time. Anyway,' he went on, 'how might I help you, Miss . . .?'

'Reynard. Suzie Reynard.'

The name rang a faint bell.

'I can see that you're struggling. You've heard the name, but can't quite place it.'

'You've been in the papers?'

She sighed. 'I'm always in the papers, but never for the right reasons. Never glowing reviews of my last performance, but always—' She stopped. 'But that's not why I'm here.'

So, that was how he recognized the name: Suzie Reynard was an actress.

She said, 'Your agency was recommended, Mr Langham.'

'Might I ask by whom?'

'"By whom"? You English crack me up. By a guy called Hank Denby, an American businessman over here five years ago. Mr Ryland did some work for him, and when I phoned Hank the other day and explained things, he said I should get in touch with this Ryland guy.'

'I'm sure we can help. What's the problem?'

She tapped an inch of ash into a tray on the desk, considering her next question. 'First of all, Mr Langham, how much do you charge?'

'Our standard rate is two guineas an hour, with expenses extra.'

'Two guineas? What's that in dollars?'

He did the calculation. 'Approximately six dollars.'

'Six dollars? You know what they charge in LA?'

'I can't begin to guess.'

'Twenty-five dollars per hour, and expenses, plus five hundred on the successful completion of the case.'

'This is Wandsworth,' he reminded her, 'not Los Angeles.'

'At six dollars an hour . . .' she said. 'OK, I'll hire you for the next week, maybe longer.'

'Doing what, exactly?'

'I want you to come up to Marling Hall, that's in Norfolk, stay a while and poke about.'

'"Poke about"?'

'Something screwy's going on, and I don't like it.'

'If you'd care to explain . . .'

'Ever since we arrived at the hall for the shoot, there's been this atmosphere. I'm a friend of Douglas Dennison – you heard of him, the movie director?'

'I'm sorry, no.'

'Anyway, Dougy's been acting kind of strange lately. Antsy. And then I heard him on the phone yesterday. Heard him muttering something like, "You can't threaten me like that . . ."' She shrugged. 'I don't like seeing Dougy so uptight.'

'You didn't ask him—?'

'Of course I asked him. He told me to mind my own business.' She sighed. 'Look, I get the impression someone in the cast has got their claws into him. They're an odd bunch. I want you to come up to the hall, stay a while, and get to the bottom of whatever's going on.'

'You're shooting a film up there?'

'You're quick. *Murder at the Hall*, a mystery flick.' She fanned smoke from her face as if batting away an annoying fly. 'Anyway, you'll come up and take a look around, talk to people?'

He would have passed the job on to Ryland, but his partner was going to Southend for the weekend.

Suzie Reynard sensed his reluctance. 'You'll be staying at the hall, the guest of Edward Marling. The production company's hired the place for a bundle, and it's open house up there. You can socialize and get to know the cast.'

'Can I bring someone?'

Smiling, Suzie reached out and picked up Maria's picture. 'Who's the broad?'

'Maria, my fiancée.'

'Good-looking girl. She should be in the movies. What does she do?'

'She's a literary agent.'

She wrinkled her nose. 'She's too beautiful to be sitting behind a desk all day.'

'She finds the job rewarding.'

'I didn't think English girls were so good looking.'

He smiled. 'She's French.'

'That'd explain it. Class.' She pulled on her Pall Mall. 'So, sure, bring her along. The more the merrier. Perhaps Dougy'll be able to find her a part. Oh, one thing – don't tell him why you're there, OK? He wouldn't want me hiring someone behind his back.'

'Mum's the word.'

'Huh?'

'I won't say a word to him.'

'Fine. Dougy's a pussycat, but he has this temper, see? Things don't go the way he wants, he flies into a rage. It's part of being a director. They think they're God Almighty. They're so used to having everything their way, telling folk what to do. So, when things don't go to plan, or if I do something he doesn't like . . .'

'I get the picture. I'll be discretion itself,' he said. 'I wonder if I might ask a couple of questions?'

She sat back on the rickety seat. 'Fire away.'

'Do you know if Mr Dennison has any enemies?'

'Dougy?' She laughed, and Langham expected her to say that Dennison didn't have an enemy in the world. 'Listen, Dougy makes an average of six enemies a film. Set designers he's bawled out, actors he's angered, writers he's sacked. Comes with the territory. As Dougy says, you can't make a movie without hurting a few folk.'

'So, has he made any enemies so far on this film?'

'Well . . . on Tuesday – this was before the phone call – we had a cast meeting at the hall, and there was a cold atmosphere. I felt it was directed at Dougy.'

Langham reached for his notebook. 'Directed at him from anyone in particular?'

'No, just from the cast in general. As if . . . as if people had been talking about him, behind his back.'

'I must say, it all sounds rather nebulous.'

'Meaning, Mr Langham?'

'I mean, are you sure you want to hire me just because you have the impression that someone has something against Mr Dennison who, by your own admission, has an aptitude for getting on people's nerves?'

Suzie Reynard leaned forward. 'Mr Langham . . . to be honest I'm a little scared. I have a feeling – and I put a lot of store by my feelings – that Dougy's in danger, and I'd never live with myself if something happened to him.'

'Well . . .'

'Look, two guineas an hour is peanuts. I'll make it five, if you'll agree to take on the case.' She tipped her head and smiled at him. *'Please . . .'*

He sighed. 'Very well, I'll drive up to Marling Hall first thing in the morning and we'll take it from there.'

She stood and held out a small hand, which Langham shook. 'I'm ever so grateful, Mr Langham.'

He saw her to the door and watched her descend the dingy staircase as if it were a catwalk.

He returned to his desk and was packing up for the day when he heard Ryland's rapid-fire footsteps on the stairs.

The door burst open and Ryland entered, whistling. 'Was I hallucinating, Don, or did I see an angel leave the premises?'

'No hallucination, Ralph. The angel was Suzie Reynard, the movie star.'

'Don't tell me,' the weasel-faced cockney said. 'Hollywood's come knocking and they want to film one of your books?'

'Fat chance. No, Miss Reynard has hired the professional services of Ryland and Langham.'

Ryland made himself an extra-strong brew of Typhoo while Langham filled him in on what Suzie Reynard had said.

'So, while I'm with the trouble and strife and bawling kids in Southend, you'll be living it up with movie stars in some big nob's country pile?'

'As our friends across the pond say, that's how the cookie crumbles. But I have to be back at the writing desk on Monday, Ralph, so you can take over at the hall then.'

Ryland slurped his tea. 'And at five guineas an hour I'll string it out for as long as I can.'

'I'll fill you in on Monday morning,' Langham said. 'Right, I'm meeting Maria at five. Have a great time in Southend.'

Ryland saluted. 'See you later, Cap'n. And give me love to the little poppet.'

TWO

Maria finished the phone call to a commissioning editor at Chatto, cleared her desk and grabbed her handbag. Fridays were always the busiest day of the week, with publishers and writers alike attempting to settle affairs before the weekend, and she was ready for a well-earned break. She was about to escape and meet Donald when there was a knock at the door of her office and Molly poked her head through.

'Maria, Charles would like a word, if you're free.'

'I was just about to leave. I wonder what he wants.'

'I don't know, but he does seem rather pensive.'

'Pensive?'

'Withdrawn. Not his usual self.'

She followed Molly from the office into the reception area. Molly returned to her desk. 'Charles's chauffeur was in earlier,' the girl said. 'He's quite a dish, isn't he?'

Maria smiled. 'But perhaps a little old for you, no? He must be at least thirty.'

'The way he smiles, and he can hardly bring himself to meet my gaze . . . He's very shy, for his age.'

Maria laughed. 'I'd better see what his nibs wants,' she said, indicating Charles's office door.

She knocked and entered.

Charles Elder was seated behind his huge mahogany desk; he rose majestically and held out his arms as if to embrace her. 'My dear, my dear. You do have five minutes – or perhaps ten?'

She smiled. 'Of course, Charles.'

'Take a seat,' he said, waving to a buttoned leather armchair.

Maria sat down and watched Charles pace back and forth before the empty hearth.

Charles Elder was gargantuan; he was huge physically, though he deported his elephantine bulk with a certain nimble grace – and colossal too in terms of sheer charismatic *presence*. Like certain Shakespearian actors who possess the innate talent to captivate an audience – with his florid face, snow-white peak of hair and fruity, declamatory tenor – he played the cynosure wherever he might be. Maria loved him like a second father.

'Would you care for a little drink?' he asked. 'Brandy?'

'I'd better not, thank you. I'm just about to drive to Notting Hill to see Donald.'

'Then pray indulge me while I indulge myself, child!' he said, sloshing himself a huge brandy and continuing with his pacing.

He lodged his triple chin on to his chest and frowned at the carpet. Molly was right: he did seem unaccountably pensive today.

Maria decided to break the silence. 'I don't know if you've noticed, Charles, but Molly is rather smitten.'

He looked at her. 'She is? Smitten? With whom, might I enquire?'

'With Albert,' she said.

He bellowed a laugh. 'Oh, the myopia of innocence!' he cried. 'Albert did mention the other day that she'd been attempting to engage him in conversation. He was somewhat embarrassed by her attention.'

'Perhaps,' Maria said, 'I should have a quiet word with her and say that Albert is spoken for?'

Charles beamed. 'Would you, my dear? That would be divine of you. If you could say that Albert has a little lady down Bermondsey way . . . that might cool her ardour somewhat.'

'I'll do that.'

Charles nodded and continued his pacing.

A minute later, impatient to be away, Maria said, 'Charles . . . what did you wish to see me about?'

The frown upon his porcine face intensified, and he said at last, 'How long have I been running this agency, Maria?'

'Ah . . . twenty years?'

'Twenty-two, to be precise. Twenty-two. I built the agency up from nothing to the status it enjoys today – that of one of the finest smaller literary agencies in London; these past few years ably assisted, might I add, by your good self.'

Maria sat back and watched Charles as he strode in rumination up and down the length of the Persian rug; she wondered where this might be leading.

'My circumstances have changed somewhat in the past few months,' he went on. 'Not to put too fine a point on it, I have, at my late age, been fortunate enough to stumble upon the bounty of true love. Albert is a boon; everything a man might ask for, and his devotion is matched only by my own.'

Maria leaned forward. 'And yet . . .?'

Charles stopped to slurp his brandy. 'And yet I face a dilemma, my child. I find myself tied, nay anchored, you might say, to that which for years has been the focus of my existence, to wit: the agency.'

Maria opened her eyes wide. 'You're not thinking of selling it, are you?'

'Selling?' he thundered. '*Selling?* Perish the thought! Of course not. However, I have – how shall I phrase this? – been contemplating of late the idea of taking a . . . you might say . . . a *back seat* in proceedings.'

'A back seat?' she echoed.

He approached and loomed over her, a tweed-clad man-mountain topped with an unruly summit of white hair. 'How would you care, my child, to take over the sole responsibility of running the Elder and Dupré Literary Agency?'

She opened her mouth, but no words came.

Charles rushed on, 'I have watched the way you handle our affairs, and I cannot overestimate how impressed I am. You know the business inside out, have a winning way with both authors and editors, and an acute – might I say scalpel-sharp? – business mind.'

'But . . . but *run* the agency, Charles?'

'What I propose, Maria, is this: I shall take a back seat, perhaps popping into the office one morning every fortnight or so. You will be duly promoted to my role; to fill your position, I shall advertise for an experienced, up-and-coming fellow, or filly, to assist you.'

He stared, his tiny eyes boring into her.

'You will, of course, be more than adequately remunerated, financially. I see no reason why you cannot contemplate a pay rise of fifty per cent.'

'*Sacre bleu!*' she gasped, fanning herself. 'But, but . . . Charles, this is something of a shock, and to tell the truth . . .'

'Yes?'

'Well, I was thinking I might mention to Donald the idea of moving to the country. Somewhere close to London,' she hurried on, 'so that I could still work here . . . though perhaps work from home two or three days a week.' She pulled a face as she awaited his reaction.

Charles arranged his full lips into a contemplative rose bud. At last he said, 'I see no reason why our two objectives – my desire to hand on the reins, and yours to enjoy a country idyll – should be mutually exclusive. You will think about my proposal, I hope?'

She smiled. 'Of course, yes. I'll tell Donald. He'll be thrilled.'

'The Happy Highways beckon!' Charles declaimed. 'I was talking with Albert, just the other day, about the idea of purchasing a caravan and hitting the open road.'

She smiled to herself as the image of Mr Toad sprang to mind.

'And speaking of Donald,' Charles went on, 'he is the second reason why I summoned you to my sanctum.'

'He is?'

'For many years,' Charles said, 'Donald's sales figures have been well above average; despite the fact that he sees himself as a stalwart of the mid-list, his books do sell rather better than that. However . . . I received a phone call this morning that might change the situation. Might, I say, boost the fellow into the big league . . .'

'A phone call?'

'Early days yet, of course – and not a word to old Donald on the matter until things are finalized, but . . .'

He went on to outline the details of the phone call, and finished with the warning not to tell Donald a dicky bird for the time being.

Ten minutes later Maria left the agency and drove, in a pleasant daze of disbelief, across town to Notting Hill.

Donald was sitting at corner table when she arrived at the Lyons' tea room. She paused, watching him, before crossing the crowded café. He was miles away, absorbed in an old copy of the *Daily Herald*, and absent-mindedly stroking the scar on his right temple.

She felt a surge of love for the man as she threaded her way between the tables, pulling off her gloves and removing her hat. She bent to kiss him and fell into a seat.

'My word! The traffic is *terr-ible*, Donald. I was stuck in a jam for ten minutes in Knightsbridge.'

He looked up at her, his thin face breaking into a smile. Then he frowned, tilting his head as he regarded her. 'What is it?'

She laughed. 'What do you mean, "what is it"?'

Donald took her hand. 'You seem in rather fine fettle. Good news?'

'I am soon to marry the handsomest man in London – that's why I am in "fine fettle", Donald. But what is this "fine fettle", anyway?'

'You're not deflecting me that easily, girl – out with it!'

She laughed. 'I cannot keep anything from you! Very well – I have some rather interesting news.'

He ordered her a coffee and poured himself a second cup of black Earl Grey. 'Out with it, then,' he demanded.

She told him about Charles's plan to take a back seat in the running of the agency, and her potential promotion. She had to restrain herself, as she finished, from telling him about the other potential good news.

He clutched her hand. 'My word! I don't know what to say. You'll accept, of course?'

She sipped her coffee, beaming at him over the cup. 'I think perhaps I might,' she said.

'Then this calls for a celebration, Maria. Now . . . how would you like an all-expenses paid weekend at Marling Hall in Norfolk?'

She blinked. 'Are you serious?'

'Never more so.'

'Norfolk is so beautiful. But why Marling Hall?'

'Have you heard of a film star called Suzie Reynard?'

Maria was surprised. 'Heard of her? Why, I've seen many of her films. She's not a leading lady, but often plays best friend roles. But why do you mention her?'

He told her about his meeting with Suzie Reynard that afternoon, and the actress's worries regarding the director Douglas Dennison.

'If it's as I suspect, a storm in a teacup,' Donald said, 'then we're in for a pleasant weekend in the country, and we might even meet some interesting types.'

'How exciting. And I thought, when you began work at the agency, that it would all be following unfaithful husbands and boring work like that.'

'That's what Ralph's been doing all week. I think he's a trifle miffed that I was manning the desk when Reynard blew in.'

Maria sipped her coffee. 'Was she beautiful, in real life?'

'I wouldn't say beautiful so much as . . . as attractive in a fragile, brittle kind of way. And tiny. Not much over five feet tall.'

'That's surprising. It doesn't show in her films.'

'I suspect they have tricks to make the stars seem tall. Look at Audie Murphy. Oh,' he went on, 'she saw your photo on my desk and said you were so beautiful you ought to be in movies yourself.'

She laughed. 'Perhaps I'll be offered a part this weekend, Donald! Did you know that I was on the stage at school in Gloucestershire?'

'Were you good?'

'No, to be honest. I was *terr-ible*. So wooden. And I couldn't remember my lines! Miss Macmillan, our drama teacher, despaired of me.'

'Bang goes your film career, then.'

'That's a thought. I really should invite her and a couple of my other old teachers next month.'

'It'll be the best-attended wedding in London.'

Maria smiled, staring into the remains of her coffee. 'Just thirty days, now,' she said, looking up. 'You aren't getting – how do you say? – cold feet, Donald?'

'Cold feet? Me? Not on your nelly. I can't wait.'

She squeezed his hand. 'Thank you. I cannot wait, either. To think that soon I'll be able to look at you and say, "My husband . . .".'

Donald smiled. 'Look, how about a meal at the Moulin Rouge this evening, to celebrate your good news, and then an early night? We have to be up with the lark in the morning if I'm to drive all the way to Norfolk.'

Maria beamed. 'I would like nothing more, *mon cher*.'

THREE

Langham braked his Austin Healey on the crest of the hill and exclaimed at the view.

'And I thought all Norfolk was flat!' Maria said.

'It is to the east, but the north-west is green and rolling. We came here on family holidays, way back in the twenties. I had an aunt in Hunstanton. Look, you can just make out Marling Hall between the trees.'

The hall was a sprawling, red-brick Elizabethan pile set in extensive grounds and lush gardens, surrounded by woodland. The hills and vales receded towards the horizon, becoming ever fainter and hazier in the midday sun.

He released the handbrake and they coasted down the lane.

'And what did you find out about Marling Hall in your *Big Book of English Country Houses*?' Maria asked.

Her *Big Book* line was a running joke with Maria, ever since Langham had shown her his library of reference books, describing certain ones as 'my big book' of this or that. That morning, before setting off, he'd pored over his guidebook to Norfolk.

'Well,' he said, 'it was built by a Catholic nobleman, Sir Christopher Marling, back in 1580, and it's been in the family ever since. Apparently it's owned by one Edward Marling, and I recall reading somewhere else – not in the guide book – that he was badly injured in the war. I wonder if they've fallen on hard times, which is why they're hiring out the hall as a film location.'

'What kind of film is it?' Maria asked as they swept around a bend in the lane between high hedges.

'None of my books could inform me about that,' he said, 'but Suzie Reynard said it's a murder mystery.'

He slowed to admire the view as the hedges gave way to low stone walls and rolling farmland. He had the windows wound down and the scent of wild garlic wafted in on the breeze.

'Have you seen any of Douglas Dennison's films?' he asked.

'The name's familiar, but I don't think I've seen any of his films. I do recall that he's been married about ten times, though.'

He stared at her. 'You're exaggerating, surely?'

'Just a little. But he's had a few wives. Do you know if he and Suzie are . . .?'

'I'm not sure – but she was obviously concerned about him, and calling him "Dougy" might suggest a certain familiarity. Or perhaps I'm reading more into it than is really there.'

Maria removed a compact from her handbag and powdered her face. 'And her concern? Warranted, or is she worrying unnecessarily?'

'Let's hope the latter,' he said. 'All I want from this weekend is good company, the occasional walk, and plenty of time to relax. Ah, this must be the place.'

Two tall red-brick gate posts stood sentinel before a long, curving gravelled drive. Langham turned the car and puttered between stands of elm and oak. Dappled shade alternated with coruscating sunlight; after a bitter winter, summer was on its way.

A hundred yards down the drive, they negotiated a bend between riotous rhododendron and Marling Hall came into view. The house was built in the common Elizabethan E-shaped style. The multi-turreted, mullion-windowed façade, with an enfilade of tall chimney stacks silhouetted against the cloudless blue sky, might not have changed one iota in almost four hundred years. Langham half expected to see a nobleman in doublet and hose step through the studded oaken door and greet them on the steps that fanned down to the drive.

The person who did emerge to greet them, however, struck him as anachronistic against the backdrop of the ancient hall: she wore tight beige shorts, a skimpy halter top, and a huge floppy white sun hat.

She stood on the top step and waved with exaggerated excitement.

Maria said, 'Suzie Reynard – but she's as tiny as a child, Donald!'

'I told you she was small.'

To the right of the hall, beneath a stand of elm trees, a gravelled area served as a parking lot for a green van and half a dozen cars. Langham pulled in beside a Bentley saloon, and they climbed out and carried their cases towards the house.

Suzie hurried down the steps to greet them. She flung her arms around Langham as if he were her long-lost brother, kissed his cheeks, then smiled at Maria while Langham made the introductions.

'My, but you're even more beautiful in real life than in the photo!' Suzie said. 'No upstaging me, now. I'm the leading lady in this film!'

'I was just telling Donald, last night, how bad an actress I was at school. You have no need to worry on that score.'

'And I just love your accent, Maria. You'll have to give me lessons!' She gripped Maria's hand and led them up the steps and into the house.

'Evans!' Suzie sang out as they entered the cool of the chequer-board hall. A carved L-shaped staircase led up to a first-floor gallery along which a dozen suits of armour stood guard. A butler appeared from a side room and hurried to take their cases.

They climbed the stairs and Suzie chattered away. 'I'll show you to your rooms, and then you can join us out back. We're just about to have lunch. Since the weather's so divine we're dining al fresco.'

Suzie escorted them along the gallery to a bedroom, then explained, 'When I told Cynthia Marling that you were coming, she asked if you were married. I boobed and said you weren't, so she insisted you have separate rooms. Bit of a prude, our Cynthia. *Catholic,*' she whispered. She grinned as she pulled a small key from her pocket.

'For the communicating door to the next bedroom,' she explained with a wink at Maria, then said she'd see them outside in fifteen minutes.

'Oh,' she whispered before slipping from the room, 'and not a word to anyone about why you're really here. If Dougy found out, he'd blow a gasket. Tell people we met at some London party, right?'

When they were alone, Maria moved to the open window and stared out. Langham joined her and slipped an arm around her waist.

'Well, what do you think of our film-star friend?'

'I think she's very sweet, if a little – what's the word . . .?'

'Loquacious?'

She laughed and pointed down to the rolling greensward which extended for a mile or more behind the house; in the distance, a lake shimmered in the sunlight. 'Look, that must be the rest of the cast.'

The butler and a maid were ferrying salvers of food to a long table, and just beyond it, in the shade of a stand of beech trees, were four men and a woman, holding glasses and cigarettes.

As they watched, Suzie Reynard came around the corner of the house. She plucked a drink from a table set out with glasses of wine and approached a tall, sun-bronzed young man in a tennis shirt.

'I don't see Douglas Dennison,' Maria said.

The group comprised of two very old gentlemen seated on deck-chairs, a tall, dark-haired woman in her forties who struck the pose of a bored *femme fatale*, the young Adonis and Suzie. Another man stood off to one side, looking thoroughly bored with proceedings.

'My word,' Langham said.

'What is it, Donald?'

'The tubby little fellow with his pants pulled up high over his belly—'

'You mean the man who looks like a lonesome Tweedledee?'

'That's him. Terrence Ambler. I used to know him rather well. He knocked out a few thrillers for Hubert and Shale just after the war, then worked as a cameraman for the BBC. The last I heard, he'd just got into scriptwriting, but we haven't crossed paths for years.'

'He doesn't exactly look as if he fits in.'

Maria was right: he was gripping a glass of white wine and staring with morose determination at the lawn between his feet.

'No, old Terrence never did. Or should I say young Terrence? He must be in his mid-thirties now, though he always struck me as a rather curmudgeonly old man.'

'Did you like him?'

'Do you know, I did. Many people didn't, found him too miserable. But we always got along over a pint or two. That is, when we were both struggling, and could cry into our beers and rail at the perfidy of the publishing world.'

'Well, he's probably doing all right for himself now, if he's writing films.'

Langham grunted. 'He'll still find something to complain about, I'll wager.'

'I'll just freshen up and change, then we can go down and join them.'

Suzie skipped across the lawn when Langham and Maria emerged from the hall. She took Maria's hand and dragged her towards the group beneath the beech trees.

'Everyone! Everyone! Can I introduce my good friends from London, Donald Langham, the famous writer, and Maria Dupré, the well-known literary agent.'

One of the old men, who resembled an antediluvian tortoise, hoisted his glass, and croaked, 'Donald and Maria!' while running an appreciative eye across Maria's form-fitting summer dress.

Terrence Ambler, Langham noticed, had moved further away from the group and was kicking pine cones across the lawn like a reprimanded schoolboy.

Suzie led them over to the muscle-bound youth. 'This is Chuck – Chuck Banning. This'll be Chuck's first big role. All the way from rural Idaho, fresh-faced and still wet behind the ears.' She lifted her shoulders and grinned at Langham and Maria. 'I'm showing you the ropes, aren't I, Chuck? We're like brother and sister, hm?'

Chuck Banning towered over the diminutive Suzie, torn between blushing at her solicitude and frowning at being dismissed as merely her sibling. The result was curiously disarming expression that belied the young man's somewhat imposing physique.

Chuck shook hands with Langham. 'A writer? I'll have to look up some of your books.'

Suzie said, '*Murder at the Museum, A Cairo Affair, The Maximillian Gambit* . . .'

Langham eyed her with surprise. 'You've done your research, Suzie.'

'Shhh!' she hissed, then whispered, 'We're friends, remember?'

'So, this is your first film?' Maria asked Chuck, covering for Langham's faux pas. 'Have you been to England before?'

Banning shrugged modestly. 'It's my first trip to the mother country. I was actually born here, but my parents moved to the States when I was one. I can't believe my luck, Miss Dupré. A few months in LA and I land my first big film role. Would you believe that?'

'Chuck plays my leading man,' Suzie said. 'In the story, you see, he's fresh from the States, having inherited this country pile from a long-lost relative.'

Chuck laughed. 'Only there's a skeleton in the cupboard in the form of a disinherited nephew, and murder is in the air.'

'Da-da-dah!' Suzie intoned. 'Isn't it exciting? But we move along . . . Let me introduce the venerable – that's a word, isn't it? – Sir Humphrey Lyle.'

The wrinkled, reptilian gentleman struggled from the trap of his deckchair and presented himself with a snap of his heels before Maria, taking her hand and bestowing upon it a somewhat liquid kiss. Langham recognized the old man's long, equine visage from dozens of black-and-white British films dating back to the twenties.

'Charmed,' Sir Humphrey drawled in a voice as rich as tawny port, his rheumy gaze shuttling between Maria's hooded eyes and her cleavage. 'Up for the weekend, hm? Capital! We shall have plenty of time, *plenty*, to get acquainted, I daresay.'

Suzie disengaged Maria's hand from Sir Humphrey's claw. 'We shouldn't monopolize, Sir Humph. And as Mr Haggerston seems to be in the land of nod,' she said, glancing at the other old man who was snoozing in his deckchair, 'we move on.'

She escorted Langham and Maria across the lawn, murmuring as she did so, 'Did you know that Sir Humphrey's full name is Humphrey Lyle-Vetch? Can you guess what I call him?'

'Go on,' Langham said.

'Sir Humphrey Vile Letch. He can't keep his hands to himself. So be warned, Maria.'

They stopped before the tall, slim woman in her forties, a veil of raven hair eclipsing half of her pale face.

'And here we have the . . . the *vastly* experienced Varla Cartier,' Suzie said.

'Susan has the most cutting way with euphemism,' Varla said, gracing the younger actress with an acid smile. If Sir Humphrey Lyle's voice was redolent of old port, then Varla Cartier's was aged sherry fortified with brandy. Langham detected a slight foreign intonation behind the West Coast American drawl.

Her sable silk dress emphasized her spidery slightness, and she clutched an almost empty glass of sparkling white wine with hands that had not survived the ravages of time as well as her face.

Suzie went on, 'I was six when I first starred alongside Varla.'

'"Starred"? You had a walk-on part, and you only got that because your father was a high-up at RKO.'

'Oh, I'm *so* sorry, Varla. It's you who were the star then, wasn't it? And when was that? Twenty-five years ago?'

Varla gave Suzie a poisonous look, which the younger woman feigned not to notice.

'Varla has appeared in simply *hundreds* of films over the decades,' Suzie said. 'All of them—'

Maria interrupted. 'One of my very favourite films is *Choice of Evils*. I thought you were superb.'

'You're too kind,' Varla murmured, gratitude sparkling in her obsidian eyes. 'Would I be right in assuming that you're French?'

'Despite my being in England for more than twenty years, my accent is still a giveaway.'

'But from the north, *oui*?' Varla went on.

'That's right. Paris.'

'Ah . . . I was born in the south-east. Marseilles. Cartier is my stage name. My original surname was Novy, from the Occitan.'

'I didn't know you were French,' Suzie said, clearly surprised.

Varla's red lips twisted into an amused little smile. 'Since when have you taken it upon yourself to be my biographer, Susan? And anyway, I am not technically French any longer. I emigrated to the

States in my teens and became a American citizen ten years later, in 1924.'

'A year before I was born,' Suzie said. She pointed across the lawn to Terrence Ambler. 'And the dumpy little Englishman over there, playing football with acorns, is our immortal scribe who penned the script with, I must say, a lot of help from Dougy.'

'Speaking of whom,' Langham said, 'where is Dennison?'

'He doesn't do lunch.' She pointed along the side of Marling Hall to where a bulbous caravan – resembling a big silver toaster – stood before the high frontage of a box maze. 'That's his home away from home. He's refused to take a room in the house – he likes to live in his trailer during a film. You'll meet him at dinner.'

Maria and Varla were deep in conversation, in their native French, about European cinema. Langham caught Suzie's eye and indicated Terrence Ambler. 'I've actually met Terrence before. If you'll excuse me I'll go and say hello.'

'Go right ahead.'

Langham strolled from the shade of the beech trees and approached the short figure of the screenwriter.

'Terry,' he called out. 'I say, it's been rather a long time.'

Ambler swung round, clearly surprised at being unexpectedly buttonholed. His food-stained green shirt swelled over a pot belly and his baggy corduroy trousers were held up by a pair of frayed red braces. His sartorial sensibility – or lack of – hadn't changed in years.

'Langham? Goodness gracious me, it is.' Then his nascent smile was rapidly replaced by his default expression of lugubriousness. It was a transformation Langham recalled from years ago, as if he was unable to allow himself a moment's deviation from his characteristically morose demeanour.

'I suppose you've been brought in by Dennison to hack my script about? As if it hasn't been torn to shreds enough already.'

Langham tried not to smile at Ambler's pessimism. 'Don't worry yourself on that score. I'm here as a guest of Suzie Reynard's.'

'How do you know that little—?' He bit back what he had been about to say, and Langham suddenly recalled something about the writer that he'd forgotten: his misogyny. Ambler had an ugly man's resentment of the fairer sex.

'I've had to work with her on the rewrite for the past week,' Ambler muttered. 'I'm surprised you count her as an acquaintance, Donald; still less as a friend.'

Langham shrugged. 'You know how you meet all sorts at parties.'

They strolled across the grass, Ambler taking the occasional punt at pine cones as if venting his spleen on the natural world. 'Well, I must say I'm pleased she's not a bosom buddy.'

'You two don't get on?'

'You can accuse me of stereotyping, Donald, but she's your typical egotistical, empty-headed actress. You'll never guess—' He stopped.

'Go on.'

'It makes my blood boil even to think of it. By God, I worked hard on the script. And then Dennison gets his mitts on it and demands changes, and I do the rewrites like the craven hack I am. And then, if that's not bad enough, Dennison's little squeeze gives it a read through and objects to how I've portrayed her character. She wants a bigger part, and more lines. Donald, for pity's sake, she's the *lead*, as if her part wasn't big enough already! So she bangs into my room one morning and demands a rewrite, and I tell the little bitch where to go. The next thing I know, Dennison is hauling me over the coals and saying I'd better damned well increase her lines or face the sack. So – and I hate myself for the cowardly mercenary I've become – I bugger off with my tail between my legs and do the rewrite.'

'I'm sorry.' Langham was tempted to ask how much Ambler was being paid for the script, but restrained himself.

'You know, Donald, when I started on the film it was a murder mystery based on true events, but it's been watered down so much it's become a melodramatic farce.'

They walked on in silence for a time, then Langham asked, 'I take it that Dennison and Suzie are . . .'

'The little bitch is angling to become Mrs Douglas Dennison the fifth, or is it the sixth?'

Langham glanced at the writer. If anything, the years had worked to make Ambler even more embittered.

'Anyway,' Langham said, 'how did you get into script work? The last time we met you were a cameraman, and very proud of a cine camera you'd just bought.'

'I still have it. In fact, part of this job is to do some preliminary shooting for Dennison. Interior location shots to establish angles and all that.' He pointed along the side of the house to the van. 'The Morris Commercial's mine, a mobile dark room. I'll be developing the cine film before we begin the shoot in earnest.'

He remembered Langham's original question, and said, 'But how did I get into scriptwriting?' He shook his head. 'I was getting a pittance for my books, and I needed something that'd make me real money. I worked with the BBC for a few years, learned how to use a camera, and in my spare time wrote scripts and bombarded Boulting Brothers with scenarios until they relented and commissioned a thirty-minute filler. I've had regular script work for the past six years, mainly for the BBC, but with a few films along the way.'

'Good for you. It must pay well.'

'Do you know something, Donald? For all the money, I'd rather be writing my own books. At least that work is honest. I despise myself for prostituting what little talent I ever possessed.'

The same old Terry Ambler, Langham mused, at a loss to think of a suitable response. Ambler would be able see the bleak side of winning a hundred thousand on the pools. He smiled to himself as he recalled one of the young man's mordant epithets, 'Every silver lining has a cloud.'

'And don't get me started on the nauseating types that run the film world,' Ambler said.

The butler emerged from the house, approached a great bronze gong set up beside the laden table, and gave it three resounding blows.

'Ah,' Langham said, 'lunch.'

They crossed to the table and joined the diners.

FOUR

'It's a great story,' Chuck Banning was saying. 'I come over from the US of A to claim my inheritance, a country pile and the title that comes with it. Suzie plays the love interest. Then there's a murder attempt, and the plot thickens.'

Langham sipped his sparkling white wine. 'And what part do you play, Varla?'

Across the table from him, Varla Cartier leaned back in her chair. 'I suppose you could say that I play the older love interest. You see, my character was in love with Chuck's before the film opens.'

'And then little me comes along,' Suzie Reynard said, pressing splayed fingers to her chest, 'and Chuck is head over heels.'

Maria smiled. 'I can see where the murder comes in.'

Sir Humphrey Lyle, seated next to Suzie, ran a hand up and down

her forearm, and said, 'And I play the brother of the dead lord, the
evil Sir Henry Creech. In it for what he can get, don't you know?'

He removed his hand from Suzie's arm and slipped it beneath
the table; her expression froze, then she picked up her fork and
attended to the molestation. Sir Humphrey Lyle started, winced in
pain, then bent to his plate with the expression of a kicked dog.

Maria smiled across at the old man seated next to Sir Humphrey.
Well into his eighties, Desmond Haggerston had a long, jaundiced
face the colour of ripe cheddar and sad, bloodhound eyes. The old
man seemed barely to have woken from his earlier snooze in the
deckchair.

'And what part do you play, Mr Haggerston?'

'Me? Part? Play?' He blinked at Maria, confused. 'Oh, I'm no
actor. Perish the thought. I've no part in all this rubbish, thank God.
I'm a friend of old Marling's; invited meself over for the weekend
for a quick look-see.'

'Our host isn't joining us?' Langham asked.

Suzie said, 'Edward and Cynthia lunch alone in the house, Mr
Langham. Edward is an invalid, and can't do with much excitement.
They'll be dining with us tonight.'

Haggerston eyed Langham. 'Edward caught a bullet in the spine
in 'forty-four. War hero. Special Operations. All a bit hush-hush.
Rarely speaks of it. Wheelchair-bound. Suffers in silence. Cynthia . . .
she's a brick. The fortitude of the woman . . . You know what they
say, behind every great man there's a strong woman. Well, Cynthia's
that woman.' He fell silent and chewed on a chicken drumstick.

Suzie said, 'It's on account of Edward that we're all here at the
hall. During the last war, Dougy and Edward were in France together.
They've kept in contact ever since, and when Dougy raised the
funds to do the film, Edward suggested the production company
hire the hall.'

'What did Mr Dennison do during the war?' Chuck Banning
asked.

'You know something,' Suzie said, 'he's never told me that. We
met just after the war, when he got back to the States and started
directing again. You see, he just loved my work and wanted to cast
me in some of his movies. He talked about his time in England – he
really loved the place – but he never mentioned the war.' She beamed
around the table. 'We hit it off, even back then.'

Varla Cartier said, 'My word, you must have been barely out of
bobby sox. And how old was *Dougy* then? Fifty?'

Suzie shot Varla an icy smile. 'I was twenty-one, for your

information. And Dougy was forty. But when I say we hit it off, it wasn't until last year that we actually got together – in that sense.'

'Still,' Varla said under her breath, 'twenty years . . .'

Sir Humphrey knocked back his wine, groped around for a refill and declared, 'Twenty years? Why, that's nothing! I'll never see eighty again and just last year I was head over heels with a sweet little thing . . . Hetty, her name. An actress. Just twenty, I believe. Quite charming.'

Suzie rolled her eyes, then looked up and her expression changed rapidly. 'Dougy!' she cried, waving.

Langham turned in his seat and watched the director progress across the lawn. He was a short, squat man with the physique of a bullfrog, his bulky upper body tapering down to small feet. His face was careworn and craggy, his grey hair cut close to his skull. Despite the heat he wore a black leather flying jacket that had seen better days.

He kissed Suzie on the top of her head, pulled out a chair and dropped into it.

He nodded to Langham and Maria. 'Suzie told me you were coming, Donald and Maria, right? Didn't know the little floozy swam in literary circles. Welcome to the happy family.'

Langham raised his glass in acknowledgment.

'Hope my exalted cast has been entertaining you?' Dennison went on in his gruff Texan accent. He found a glass and poured himself a white wine. 'Here's to a fun weekend before the hard work begins.'

Dutifully, the diners raised their glasses and joined in the toast. Conversation had ceased at Dennison's arrival, and Langham received the impression that several of those who seconded the toast regarded the director with awe, while others cast a cold eye at Dennison, Varla Cartier and Terry Ambler in particular. Haggerston was attending to his meal, too abstracted to respond either way.

'Suzie tells me you're a writer. Send my people one of your books, huh, and we'll see if it's optionable.'

Langham smiled. 'I'll do that.'

'Any of your books ever been filmed?'

'I've never been so lucky.'

Dennison grunted. 'Your agent hasn't been working hard enough,' he said, then winked at Maria. 'That's a joke, by the way. Suzie told me you're Donald's Miss Ten Per Cent. I know how tough it is trying to sell film rights, especially over here. Your industry's dead on its feet.'

Varla Cartier raised her glass. 'But Dougy Dennison will breathe life into the old corpse single-handedly.'

'Too right, Varla – me and my illustrious cast, not forgetting the immortal words of my scriptwriter.'

Beside Langham, Ambler muttered, 'Thanks for sweet eff all.'

Dennison drained his glass and poured himself a second. 'How long're you staying, Langham?'

'Just for the weekend.'

'Pity. We don't begin the shoot till later in the week. That's when things'll really get interesting. All the enmities I've set brewing will come to a head and personal chemistry'll give the script some life.'

Langham regarded the director. 'Enmities?'

'A film is driven by chemistry, Langham. The story smoulders with hatred. We're talking resentment over money, sex and thwarted love. It's a rich combination.' He leaned forward, and murmured, 'So I've got together a cast which, between you and me, can't stand the sight of each other. Suzie and Varla fight like cat and dog – that goes back a long way. Remind me to tell you about it, someday. Sir Humph and Suzie don't see eye to eye, as I'm sure you've noticed. Varla resents Chuck for spurning her advances, and all Chuck wants is to get Suzie in the sack.'

'And you?'

'Me?'

'Who do you dislike?'

The director laughed. 'I'm above such concerns. I just stand back and observe, and when the time comes to light the touch paper – or rather, direct the whole show – then it's chocks away.'

Langham hid a smile at the director's mixed metaphors. 'And doesn't this approach run the risk of resentment?'

'Say again?'

'Who among the cast,' Langham asked, 'resents you for fostering the various enmities?'

Dennison laughed. 'No one resents me, Langham. They all think I'm God. I've got the entire cast eating out of my hand. Sir Humph's grateful for the chance to ham it up for one last time before he shuffles off. Suzie loves me for plucking her from a string of dud movies and letting her flaunt her ego. Varla—' He frowned, then went on in a whisper, 'Well, you might have a point there. Varla has a dark past, *mucho* insecurity. We had a thing, once, ten years ago. I got out at the first sign of her neuroses. But I've got her on a short leash, see. She's over the hill and knows it. No one else would give her a break, this late in her career.'

As the director was speaking, Langham glanced across the table at the actress. She was leaning back in her chair, smoking a cigarette and staring pointedly at Dennison as if she'd heard his every word.

Langham wondered if the director's opinion that no one disliked him – other than Varla Cartier – was a case of self-delusion.

He said, 'Suzie mentioned you were over here during the war.'

Dennison refilled his glass again. 'That's right. 'Forty-two to 'forty-five. Billeted for a time just up the road at Haggerston House.' He plucked at the sheepskin lapel of his flying jacket. 'I was a pilot, B-17s. Twenty-three missions and only three men lost. I put it down to a little skill and a hell of a lot of good luck. I wore the jacket on every mission and it saw me through, became a kind of talisman. Later I got into Special Ops and was dropped into the Cévennes in 'forty-four. I couldn't wear my lucky jacket then, of course, and that's probably why things went belly-up.'

Langham murmured, 'What happened?'

Still abstracted, Dennison shook his head. 'Mum's the word on that score, old boy,' he said in a mock English accent. 'Official Secrets and all that.'

Suzie was saying, 'And after lunch I'll show you the wardrobe and make-up room, Maria. You should see it! Talk about huge – it takes up almost all the ballroom.'

Maria smiled at Langham. 'You don't mind?'

'Of course not.'

Terrence Ambler said, 'I'll take Donald to a nice little pub down the lane, Maria, and we'll catch up on old times.'

'That sounds like an idea,' Langham said.

A little later the party broke up. Sir Humphrey and Desmond Haggerston staggered off towards the hall arm in arm, Sir Humph announcing that he had a bottle of fine brandy in his room. Suzie took Maria's hand and ushered her inside.

Langham noticed Douglas Dennison move around the table and stand over Varla Cartier, who was nursing a full glass of wine.

As Langham joined Ambler and crossed the lawn, Dennison's words drifted through the heavy afternoon air. '. . . And don't you think you've had quite enough of the sauce?'

Ambler expelled a heartfelt sigh. 'Saints preserve me, Donald! I sometimes think that if I spend another hour in their claustrophobic company I'll go stark, staring mad. Thank heavens I've found the Seven Sleepers.'

They left the grounds of Marling Hall and strolled along the lane.

FIVE

'I think I owe Donald an apology,' Suzie Reynard said as she led Maria to the ballroom.

'You do? Whatever for?'

'Yesterday I told him he looked like a bank clerk, not a private eye.'

'I'm sure he wouldn't have taken it to heart.'

'You think so? I hope not.' The young woman smiled at Maria. 'It's strange, isn't it, how wrong first impressions can be? I must have been in a bad mood, worrying about Dougy. Now that I've talked to Donald and got to know him a little, I understand what you see in him. He's very attractive in that quiet, reserved English way, isn't he?'

'Well, I certainly think so.'

'And handsome, too.'

'I thought so from the very first time I saw him – a photograph on the back of one of his books. Then I saw him in the flesh and he was even more attractive.'

'Was it love at first sight?'

Maria laughed. 'Goodness, no. But I liked him a lot. The thing was, Donald was *so* quiet I thought he'd never pluck up the courage to say more than two words to me.'

Suzie placed a hand on Maria's arm. 'I like the way he doesn't rush into replying when he's talking to you. He takes his time and thinks about what he's going to say. In a way it makes you feel as if what you've said is important.' She gave a dazzling smile. 'More people should be like that, instead of blabbing just to hear the sound of their own voices. Ah, here we are.'

Half the ballroom was given over to wheeled racks of costumes set out in rows, while the other half of the room was bare but for piles of stacked brown cardboard boxes and silver chests. More impressive, however, was the ballroom itself, with its polished parquet block flooring, rich oak panelling and an ornate gallery that ran around three sides of the room. A huge chandelier hung like a crystal stalactite, glinting in the sunlight that slanted through a line of tall windows to their left. Maria considered the thousands of formal events, balls and parties that must have taken place here over the course of almost four hundred years.

'My word,' she said.

'I just knew you'd like it!' Suzie sang, thinking that Maria was referring to the wardrobe. She floated down an aisle, running a hand along the line of hanging dresses. 'Show me a woman who doesn't like dressing up!'

Maria smiled to herself as she followed the actress.

'Dougy didn't like the original wardrobe we were offered,' Suzie said. 'You should have seen it! I mean, the Brits are so dowdy, don't you think?'

'Well, I do prefer Paris fashions.'

'All the dresses were grey and brown,' Suzie said. 'Dougy blew his top. We spent a week in London visiting all the wardrobe stockists, and Dougy took his pick. You see, cinema-goers want to see sparkling dresses and sharply cut suits.'

She pulled a red dress from the rack and held it against her tiny frame. 'What do you think?'

'It suits you.'

'I love to come in here and try things on, I must admit. And talking of dresses – have you chosen your wedding dress yet?'

'I think I have,' Maria said. 'It's white and simple, clean-cut. I don't go in for lots of lace and fancy bits.'

'Simple and clean cut sounds good, to show off all your curves.'

Maria smiled, and refrained from saying that she would be getting married, not parading down a catwalk.

'Are you nervous?' Suzie asked, selecting another dress and pressing it against her body.

'Not in the slightest. What's to be nervous about? I love Donald and I can't wait until we're married and living together.'

The actress looked at her with big eyes. 'You mean, you two aren't shacked up yet?'

'Not officially. I think my father would frown on that. We'll be sharing my flat in Kensington, after the wedding.'

'And until then you get away on fun weekends like this . . .' Suzie sighed. 'How romantic.'

They moved on down the aisle, turned and strolled down the next one, Suzie dreamily trailing a hand along a rack of dresses.

'The thing I don't understand,' the actress said, 'is how do you know when you've found the right man?'

Maria shrugged. 'I think,' she began tentatively, 'you try to stand back and think how you feel about this person, compared to other loves you have experienced. Which is hard, I know. And . . . and you just know when it feels *right*.'

Suzie twisted her lips, frowning. 'I don't know if I could do that. I mean, everyone I've loved has felt right at the time.' She glanced up at Maria. 'How many men have you been serious about?'

'Oh, I don't know . . . perhaps three, four . . . But they fade into insignificance compared to Donald. What about you?'

'I lost count after thirty or forty.' She halted, fingering the material of a silk ball gown. 'But it's different in LA. I meet simply dozens of men every week and they're all handsome and charming and they all want the same thing, like sharks in a pool hunting for the best meat. And, you know, it's hard not to be taken in by these predators. That's why it was great when I met Dougy.'

'He was different from the others?'

Suzie frowned. 'In a way. He wanted the same thing, and got it. But he's more considerate. Perhaps it's because he's older, he's more like a gentleman. I know he'd never look at anyone else while he's with me, but at the same time . . .' She trailed off.

'Yes?'

She sighed. 'Dougy's been married four times and has had countless other women. And I'm frightened that . . .' She shook her head. 'I'm sorry. I shouldn't be bothering you with all this.'

'That's all right.'

Suzie reached out and touched Maria's hand. 'You know something, you're so easy to talk to, it's as if I've known you for years. You're like my mom, or big sister.'

Maria smiled. 'Why, thank you, Suzie.'

They crossed the room and sat side by side on one of the big silver chests. 'What frightens you?' Maria asked.

'That Dougy will get tired of me, find someone else. That . . . that I won't be enough for him. I mean, I'm thirty-one, for God's sake, and his last few flings have been barely out of high school.'

'I wouldn't worry yourself on that score,' Maria said. 'You look about twenty yourself, and believe me you're beautiful.'

Suzie tipped her head, smiling, and murmured, 'It's odd, but before meeting Dougy it never entered my head that I might want to get married and settle down, but now it's all I can think about. I know it's stupid, but I just see us in a villa on the beach at Big Sur. I know I shouldn't dream, but I do.'

'You never know—'

'The thing is,' the actress swept on, 'when I first got involved with Dougy, I was warned he was bad news. Other women told me about him, and I'd heard rumours.'

'About?'

'His temper, his violence. You know, he beat up some of his old lovers, beat them up real bad, and he was hauled into jail a few times. His lawyers always got him off, and hushed up the stories. So . . . so when we got together, I knew all about his reputation. But do you know something?' She beamed at Maria. 'Never, not once, has he laid a hand on me – and we've been together nearly six months.' She shook her head. 'So I'm wondering . . . does it mean that because he's different with me, it's more serious? Or will he turn bad and beat up on me sometime down the line?'

'Perhaps all those stories,' Maria said, 'were exaggerations?'

Suzie worried her bottom lip with perfect teeth. 'I don't know, Maria. I talked to some of the women . . . He had this thing with Varla, just after the war, and she told me about how he treated her. But I don't know if that's just Varla, being bitchy because she's jealous.'

She sighed, pulled her plimsolled feet onto the chest and hugged her shins, her bare thighs pressing against her halter top. 'And then there's all this business . . . Dougy's made enemies, plenty of enemies, but I've never seen him like this. He's nervous. Always looking over his shoulder. The rest of the cast hate him.'

Maria recalled overhearing Dennison telling Donald how he encouraged enmity amongst the cast, and she wondered if their dislike of him might be justified.

'From what he was saying at lunch, he created the atmosphere to achieve . . . artistic effect,' she said.

'No, this is different. I've seen how he works on other films. There's always one or two people he winds up, but never *everyone*.'

'So your worry is,' Maria said, 'that you don't know quite where the threat is coming from?'

'That's about it. Anyone here could be threatening him, but I don't know *who* it might be.'

Maria squeezed the actress's hand. 'Well, Donald is here, and his partner will be coming up on Monday. I'm sure that between them they'll sort things out.'

'Do you think so?' She smiled, then gave Maria a hug.

'You know what we should do?' Suzie said with wide-eyed enthusiasm. 'We should get a bottle of gin and a bucket of ice . . . do you like gin?'

'I love it!'

'And we'll come here one night and get a little squiffy and get dolled up in all the fabulous dresses!'

'That sounds like fun,' Maria laughed.

'Just the two of us, no one else. I'll lock the door, because Varla likes to come here and try things on too. I've seen her.' She leaned towards Maria and whispered, 'She likes to wear men's suits, and floppy hats – she thinks she's Greta Garbo.'

Maria found herself liking this insecure, beautiful girl-child, despite the fact that they had nothing at all in common.

'Know what?' Suzie said. 'I feel like a little drink right now. I know the Marlings "keep a good cellar"—' this said in an impeccable imitation of an aristocratic English accent, 'but they don't have bourbon. You ever tasted bourbon?'

'Never.'

'Dougy keeps a bottle in his trailer. I'll just shoot along and get it and we can have a little drink in the drawing room. Come on.'

Suzie led Maria from the ballroom.

They navigated their way through a warren of panelled corridors until they came to a sumptuous drawing room in the west wing. Suzie left Maria there, promising to be back in two minutes.

Maria strolled to the far end of the long room where sunlight slanted in through the open french windows, illuminating galaxies of dust motes. She stood on the threshold, staring out over the landscaped greensward to where the lake shimmered in the distance like an expanse of silver lamé.

She was thinking about Donald, and wondering if he was enjoying his beer with his old friend, when the door opened. She turned, expecting to see the elfin-form of Suzie Reynard.

Instead, Sir Humphrey Lyle advanced the length of the room, the glint in his eye that of a predatory wolf glimpsing prey.

'My word, beauty admiring beauty, what?'

He stood beside her and caressed the small of her back. '*On va fair un petit tour ensemble, eh, ma belle?*'

'I think not,' Maria said. 'If you would excuse me . . .'

She escaped his clutches, stepped through the french windows, and hurried along the back of the hall.

SIX

'I must say, Donald, that's one rather smashing girl you've brought along.'

'Maria's a gem.'

'Is it serious?'

'Well, we're getting married next month; you can't get much more serious than that.'

They strolled along the lane, passing from pools of dazzling sunlight to patches of welcome shade. Birdsong shrilled in the warm air and from afar Langham heard the muffled drone of a tractor.

Ambler laughed.

'What?' Langham asked.

'I was just remembering . . . it must have been around 'forty-seven. We were in the Cittie of Yorke, drowning our sorrows. You were bemoaning your sales figures and I'd just had something rejected by Gollancz. I remember the conversation got on to the subject of women and you told me about your wife. I distinctly recall you saying, "Never again. Once bitten . . ." etcetera.'

Langham contrasted what he had now to his circumstances back then, and thanked his lucky stars. 'After so many years of being alone, I'd had enough. Not that I really knew that – or would admit it – until Maria came along. Then marriage made a lot of sense. Did I mention she's my agent, too?'

Ambler gave him a sidewise glance. 'Blimey, she'll have you lock, stock and barrel!'

Langham laughed. 'You haven't changed a bit!'

They rounded a bend in the lane and came to a collection of tiny thatched cottages and, set back beside a huge oak tree, the Seven Sleepers.

Langham glanced at his watch. 'It's not three yet. You think they'll be open?'

'We're not in London now, old boy. The licensing laws around these parts verge on the elastic. Especially when you're as good a customer as I am.'

'So, this is your refuge?' Langham said as they entered the cool environs of the snuggery and ordered two pints of bitter.

'My bolthole and unofficial office since Monday. The scenes I've rewritten here over the past few days! Cheers. Shall we sit outside?'

They sat in the shade of the oak tree at the front of the pub, with a huge tarred barrel serving as a table.

'Speaking of marriage . . .' Ambler said, wiping a moustache of foam from his top lip with the back of his hand. 'Did I tell you I was hitched back in 'fifty-one?'

Langham stared at his old friend. 'You're joking?'

'Gospel. You sound surprised.'

'I am. I never had you down as the marrying type.'

'No one would have me, and looking back on it I wish me and Gillian had never met.'

'I take it that you're no longer . . .?'

'Lasted six months, a bit less, before she packed her bags and walked out. Can't say I blame her. She was a secretary at the BBC, and I was cock-a-hoop when she first showed interest. That soon changed, once the knot was tied. She called me the most miserable bastard on God's Earth.'

'No?' Langham said. 'You?'

'Less of that.' Terry smiled. 'Well, she had a point. I was happy for a month or two, and then everything went pear-shaped. We never stopped arguing. Everything I said just escalated into a row, and the awful thing was I could see it happening but couldn't do a damned thing to stop it. Hell, was I miserable. Then she did the right thing and walked out, and I was like a man suddenly released from jail.'

Langham knew the feeling. To his eternal regret, on hearing that his first wife had died of a brain haemorrhage in 'forty-one, his initial feeling was that of liberation. Only later had come the guilt.

'What was Gillian like?' he asked, to staunch the flow of his thoughts.

'Dead ringer for Suzie Reynard, would you believe? Pretty, small, blonde. When I first clapped eyes on Suzie, I nearly passed out. Thought it was Gill, come back to haunt me.' He grunted a humour-less laugh. 'Haunts me in a different way, though, our Suzie does.'

Langham sipped his pint. 'If you dislike the industry so much, why don't you get back into novels?'

'Let's admit it, Donald, I was never any good. Fifth rate. And film work pays a hell of a lot better than books. Look, I'm not bragging, but I got a forty quid advance for my last book. What do you think I stand to make from this script?'

'A couple of hundred?'

'Double that and add a hundred,' Ambler said.

Langham whistled. 'One of them a year and you're laughing.'

'I can rely on one roughly every eighteen months, with the odd bit of TV and radio work. But like I said, for that I've got to put up with the egos that go hand in hand with the business.'

'If lunch was an example of the vanity and in-fighting that goes on in the industry . . .'

Ambler blew. 'You kidding? That was nothing. You've no idea. Now publishing . . . That's still a gentleman's game. Blimey, some deals I did just after the war were sealed on a handshake. Word of honour kind of thing. Writers and editors got along, with none of the spleen and backbiting that plagues the film world.'

'Dennison's an odd chap, I must say,' Langham said. 'He seemed proud that he's set the cast at each other's throats.'

Ambler was nodding. 'I overheard that. He's a wily old fox. I don't trust him as far as I can spit. And believe me, most of the cast feels the same about him.'

'Oh?' Langham lowered his pint. 'He said that – with the exception of Varla Cartier – they practically worshipped him.'

'There you go. Hollywood ego. He knows he's not liked – but could he tell you that, a stranger? No way!'

'Do you know why he's so unpopular with the cast?'

'Varla hates him because they had a fling way back. He treated her abominably, she says. Then our resident hunk, Chuck Banning, resents him because Chuck has the hots for Suzie who only has eyes for Dougy. Sir Humph told me that he thinks Dennison is a vulgar ignoramus, though he's as nice as pie to the director's face.'

'And you?'

Ambler drained his pint and stared at the dregs. 'I tolerate the man. It's thanks to him that I have the job, but he's a bastard to work for. I do the rewrites, bite my tongue and say yes sir, no sir, in all the right places.'

'For five hundred quid a pop, Terry, there has to be a downside.'

Ambler shook his head. 'Do you know something? This was a decent project when I started on it. I know you find that hard to believe – I saw your face when Banning was describing the story over lunch. Sheer dross, I could hear you thinking. But it wasn't always like that.'

Langham looked sceptical.

Ambler smiled. 'It's based on a true story. Something Dennison learned during the war, while he was staying at Haggerston House. There was a murder there, back in the thirties. Desmond Haggerston's wife was shot dead in the grounds of the house. Haggerston was there when the deed was done, along with his son.'

'What happened?'

'Well, it was finally pinned on Haggerston's son, Nicholas – who, to put it bluntly, was an imbecile. Mental age of about five.'

'Poor Haggerston,' Langham said. 'No wonder he looks so woebegone.'

'It's a terrible story, all right.'

'But one that doesn't bear much resemblance to the rubbish Banning trotted out at lunch.'

'Exactly,' Ambler said. 'I started this project all bright eyed and bushy tailed. I wanted it to be a penetrating psychological insight into a group of disparate characters thrown together over a long weekend, with enmities and resentments, thwarted love and simmering hatred. The fifth draft was the best thing I'd ever done. I was proud of it. And I can't say that about much of my script work, to be honest.'

'And then Dennison hacked it about?'

'Tore the heart out of the story, changed it completely. All the insight was ditched when he demanded a bigger part for Suzie. Bloody hell, even Haggerston himself wanted a hand in the script.'

'Haggerston? Why?'

'When he got wind that Dennison was making a film based – however loosely – on the events of 'thirty-one, he hot-footed it down to the Smoke and laid siege to Dennison's hotel room until the director relented and agreed to meet him. The old man did his damnedest to get Dennison to abandon the project, but of course Dennison was having none of it. Little wonder it's ended up a farrago of clichéd nonsense.'

'How does Haggerston feel towards Dennison now?'

'They're still at daggers drawn,' Ambler said. 'They were friends during the war, when Dennison was billeted at Haggerston House. I think the old man sees the film as a betrayal of his trust, even though it'll bear little resemblance to whatever happened back then.' Ambler lifted his empty glass. 'How about another?'

'I wouldn't say no.'

While Ambler was at the bar, Langham leaned back and contemplated the view across the rolling fields, ploughed with the precision of corduroy, to a distant farmhouse on the horizon. What with the wine at lunch, and the strong bitter he'd just consumed, he was feeling more than a little comfortable. He considered what Ambler had told him about the cast of the film, and came to a decision.

Ambler returned with two brimming pints and set them down on the barrel.

'You know, this is just like old times,' the scriptwriter said. 'We should meet up again back in London.'

Langham raised his glass to that. 'I'll tell you something now, and I don't want this to go any further than the two of us.'

'Cross my heart . . .' Ambler said.

'The real reason I'm here isn't because Maria and I met Suzie at some London party.'

Ambler pointed at Langham. 'I thought it odd that you were a friend of Suzie's, you know? It didn't seem quite right. For one thing, the Langham I knew didn't go to the kind of parties Suzie would attend, and she doesn't frequent literary soirées. So, out with it, Donald – why *are* you here?'

'You know how I worked part-time for a detective agency just after the war?'

'Sure, you once gave me some gen for one of my thrillers, remember?' Ambler said.

'Well, I recently started back at the agency, and yesterday Suzie Reynard waltzed in.'

'No kidding.' Ambler whistled. 'What did she want with a private eye?'

Langham told him about Suzie Reynard's concerns regarding Douglas Dennison. 'She thinks he's under some kind of threat.'

'Threat? What kind of threat?'

'She didn't really know,' Langham admitted.

'I can attest that old Dougy isn't well liked, but under threat?' Ambler shook his head. 'You want my opinion, our Suzie's worrying her sweet little head over nothing.'

'To be honest, that's what I thought – and what I think now that I've seen the lie of the land. But at least we'll get a weekend in the country out of it.' He hoisted his pint. 'And it's nice to meet up again, Terry. Cheers.'

Ten minutes later Langham checked his watch and said he'd better be pushing off.

Ambler regarded the last inch of his pint lugubriously. 'I might stay here and have a few more. Fortify myself for the ordeal of dinner this evening.'

'Catch you later,' Langham said, and made his way back to Marling Hall.

SEVEN

'Donald!' Maria called. She hurried down the steps of the hall, her face darkened by an expression of concern. 'What's wrong?'

'It's Suzie. She's in a state. We had a pleasant chat in the ball-room, and then she said she was going back to Douglas's caravan for some bourbon for me to try.'

'And?'

'And she found me in our room ten minutes later, hysterical.'

'She's there now? We'd better go and see what's the matter.'

They hurried into the hall and up to their room. The actress was sitting on the bed, sobbing into a lace handkerchief.

Langham knelt before her. 'Suzie? What is it?'

'It's awful, Mr Langham! Horrible!'

'What is?'

'I . . . I can't describe it . . .' Her face, running with mascara and tears, looked like an artist's messy palette.

Maria sat down beside Suzie and put an arm around her shoulders. 'It's all right now, Suzie. Don't worry. But we need to know—'

'Who'd do such a terrible thing?' the actress wailed.

Langham took the woman's upper arm and shook her gently. 'Look, we need to know what happened, Suzie.'

'Down . . . down there. Dougy's trailer—'

'What . . .?' Langham asked.

'Dougy went off when he saw – saw what someone had done! He stalked off into the woods.'

'Something happened down at the caravan?' He looked up at Maria. 'I'd better take a look. You two stay here.'

He made his way to the door, but Maria followed him and laid a hand on his arm. 'There's something else . . . Sir Humphrey is lost in the maze.'

He shook his head. 'What?'

'He's lost in the maze – and it's my fault.'

'This is getting more surreal by the second. Why is it your fault?'

'He came into the drawing room while I was waiting for Suzie. He was rather drunk, Donald, and suggestive. I went outside and he followed me. I ran into the maze, but he came after me. When he'd passed the turning where I was hiding, I dashed out again and made my way back here. Only . . . he is still in there, shouting that he can't get out, and I'm a little concerned for him.'

Langham suppressed a laugh. 'Very well, I'll pop down to the caravan and see what all the fuss is about, then I'll do my best to rescue Sir Vile Letch. Sit tight and I'll be back in two flicks.'

He hurried from the room and down the staircase.

Emerging into the sunlight, he turned right along the ivy-clad façade of the hall, came to the corner and turned again. Dennison's caravan stood to one side of the house, its silver bulk incongruous against the backdrop of the woods. He hurried across to its open door and stopped in his tracks.

Now he saw the reason for Suzie Reynard's distress.

A huge hare, its throat cut, hung from the door handle by its ears, which had been tied together to form a loop. A congealed smear of blood marred the silver metal door.

He removed the hare and laid it out on the gravel, kneeling to examine the carcass. Its pelvis had been crushed, obviously by a trap. He concealed the animal in the undergrowth, then made his way back into the house.

Suzie was still sobbing on the bed, with Maria consoling her.

'You see!' Suzie almost shrieked when she saw Langham. 'Dougy's in danger! I was right – someone wants to kill him! This is a warning . . .'

He pulled up a chair before the bed. 'When did you find the hare?' he asked, sitting down.

Maria said, 'A hare?'

'Hung on the caravan door,' Langham said.

Suzie sniffed. 'I found it right – right after I left Maria. I – I don't know when that was.'

Maria said, 'Just after four.'

'And you saw no one near the caravan?'

The actress shook her head and sniffed.

'Where was Douglas?'

'He was in the trailer. He was sleeping, but woke up when – when I saw the dead – the dead thing and screamed. He took one look at it, told me to go inside and – and pull myself together, then went off into the woods. Leaving – leaving me!' She wailed again and Maria squeezed her hand.

The actress looked up. 'Call the police!' she demanded.

'Well, it isn't actually a criminal offence, Suzie. In fact, in the country, it can be seen as a gesture of generosity,' he finished lamely.

'But . . . but that's *revolting*!' Suzie cried. 'It – it was meant as a warning, Mr Langham! A threat. *Please* call the police.'

'I don't think—'

'*Please!*' she implored.

He sighed. 'Very well, I'll do that, but I doubt—' He silenced himself, nodded, and left the room.

He descended to the hallway, found a telephone in a corridor leading to the east wing, and asked the operator to connect him to the local police station.

A minute later he was attempting to explain the situation to a taciturn desk sergeant.

'A hare?' the man said.

'That's right, a hare, hanging on the door of the caravan.'

'A hare? Its throat cut, you say?'

'That's right.'

'A big hare, you say? Big and fat?'

'Well, big enough, yes. And I think it was meant as a threat.'

'A threat?'

'A threat to Douglas Dennison, the director.'

'The director? And what does this Mr Dennison direct, sir?'

'Films.'

'Films? And he has a big, fat hare on the door of his caravan?'

'That's right.'

'Know what I'd do if I were him, sir?'

'No . . .'

'Pop it in the pot, sir. Fat hares make a nice meaty broth, they do.'

'But I think it was meant as a threat,' Langham said. 'It wasn't the first time.'

'What, he's had more hares hung on his door?'

'No. No, but he's had other threats, apparently.'

The sergeant sighed. 'Tell you what I'll do, sir. I'll send a constable over in the morning. Not too early, sir, it being Sunday, and he'll have a nice chat with you about this here hare.'

'Thank you, that's much appreciated.'

Langham replaced the receiver and leaned against the wall, beginning to regret having had a second pint at the Seven Sleepers.

He returned once again to the bedroom. Suzie was sniffing and dabbing her eyes with a tissue. Maria sat on a chair before her, patting the actress's knee.

'They'll send someone over in the morning,' Langham said, 'and if we get no joy from the boys in blue, Suzie, my partner will be here on Monday. Don't worry, we'll get to the bottom of who did this.'

She sniffed again and nodded, looking for all the world like a small child placated by the promise of sweets.

Langham walked to the window and stared out. 'Maria, what time did we leave the table after lunch?'

'A little before three o'clock.'

'Dennison went back to his caravan then, and obviously the hare wasn't there or he would have seen it. So someone must have left it there between three and four, when Suzie found it. It might have been anyone.' He shrugged. 'I know it's easy for me to say, but try not to worry, Suzie.'

She nodded bravely.

Maria said, 'Come on, we'll get you cleaned up, and then we'll dress for dinner, shall we?' She looked across at Langham. 'Sir Humphrey?'

'Dammit. I forgot all about the old goat. Right, I'll go and attempt to rescue him – though a couple of hours in the maze might sober him up and cool his ardour at the same time.'

Langham searched the house before finding the butler and requesting a map of the maze.

Evans returned with a folded plan and Langham hurried around the corner of the house. As he did so, he saw Dennison emerge from the woods and stalk across to the caravan, head down. The director climbed the steps and slammed the door without registering the removal of the carcass.

Langham continued along the side of the house, paused before the entrance to the maze and unfolded the map.

Faintly, issuing from the labyrinthine corridors of the boscage before him, Langham heard the old actor's distinctive tenor declaiming in Shakespearean tones. The words were too faint to make out, but their cadence rose and fell as if playing to a West End audience.

Langham called, 'Sir Humphrey?'

''Tis I, lost, lost amid nature's infernal bounty . . .' came the reply.

'I'll have you out in no time.'

'That would be most splendid, my boy. I have walked miles, veritably miles, seeking egress. But egress there was none. I need to see him!'

The old duffer, Langham thought, sounded more than a little drunk – even though he'd had an hour in which to sober up.

'Him?'

'Of course, him! Dennison, who got me into this mess!'

'I thought you were chasing Maria, Sir Humphrey,' Langham called.

After a brief silence, Sir Humphrey said, 'I think, my boy, we are at cross purposes. Now, do you intend to save my life, or not?'

'I'm on my way – just keep talking and I'll find you.'

'The Bard!' cried the knight. 'Any requests?'

'Whatever comes to mind,' Langham called back, stepping into the maze and turning left, towards the sound of Sir Humphrey's soulful lament.

'Under the greenwood tree, who loves to lie with me . . .'

The ground was planted with camomile, and the plant released a heady musk as Langham turned first right, then left, following the sound of the tenor.

'And turn her merry note, unto the sweet bird's throat . . .'

The box maze was vast – thirty yards on each side – and Langham took a couple of wrong turns, Sir Humphrey's dulcet tones diminishing as he did so, before he back-tracked and found the right turning.

'*Come hither, come hither, come hither . . .*'

Langham turned a corner and found the old actor seated on the ground, leaning back in the embrace of the privet hedge, his legs outstretched before him.

'*Here she shall see no enemy . . .*' The knight punctuated his soliloquy with a gulp from a hip flask, which he hoisted in greeting when he saw Langham.

'My boy, my boy! Now I know how Crusoe felt upon sighting the galleon's sail upon the blue horizon! Help me up and return me to civilization!'

Sighing, Langham took the old man's tweed elbow and hauled him to his feet.

They wended their way back through the tortuous turns of the maze, stopping from time to time for Langham to consult the map.

At last they emerged into the sunlight and Langham said, 'There, and let that be a lesson.'

The old man blinked like a dim-witted tortoise. 'A lesson?'

'Think twice before you chase young ladies into mazes.'

'Ah . . . the French filly! Quite a peach, that one. I say, do you know if she's by any chance *single*?'

Langham smiled, enjoying this. 'Do you know something, I do believe she is.'

'My word!' Sir Humphrey clapped his hands and fairly drooled.

'For another month, and then she's due to wed.'

The actor looked devastated. 'She is? What foul luck! Not for the lucky blighter who's plighted his troth, of course. Know the cove?'

'As a matter of fact I do. It's me.'

Sir Humphrey blinked at him. 'You? By God, sir! I think congratulations are in order! I shall shake you by the hand!' Matching action to the words, he went on, 'Now, if you'd be so kind as to assist me yonder to the vulgarian's tawdry chariot!'

'I don't think, all things considered, that that would be very wise, sir.'

'You don't?'

'Dennison's not in the best of moods at the moment.'

Sir Humphrey digested this, then barked, 'Good! And he'll be in an even worse mood when I've had me little say!'

The old man attempted to totter off towards the caravan but only succeeded, with Langham acting as an anchor, to describe a circumscribed arc. Langham held him upright and steered him, protesting all the way, across the gravel and around the corner of the house. He found a bench in the shade of the ivy and sat down beside the old man.

'Now, what's the contretemps between you and Dennison?' he asked.

'Contretemps? Speaking French now, are we? Ah, your little Parisian filly. Got her claws into you and giving you lessons, hm? Ha! French lessons . . . I'll bet she is! *Contretemps?* Bugger that, my boy. Plain old-fashioned animosity, more like.'

'What seems to be the problem?'

Sir Humphrey blinked his rheumy eyes and appeared crestfallen. 'Seventy years . . .' he murmured.

'Seventy . . .?'

'Seventy years I've trod the boards. Seventy years, man and boy!' He lifted his right arm and shot a scrawny wrist from the frayed cuff of his tweeds. 'Slit me veins and d'you know what you'll find? Blood 'n' greasepaint, that's what!'

'I'm sure I would.'

'I was playing to packed audiences before that . . . that ignorant little *shit* was even born. Understudy to Olivier at Stratford in 'thirty-five! And in 'thirty-eight, Gielgud was understudy to *me* – now, what d'you think of that!'

'I'm impressed.'

'I've starred in more films than Dennison's had women, and that's a hell of a lot, by all accounts.'

'I'm sure it is.'

'And then Dennison, *Dennison* . . .' he pronounced the director's name with venom, 'has the audacity to tell me how to act!'

'He did?'

'Just yesterday, a run through of the first scene. I was with that flibbertigibbet, Reynard, who was hamming it up something shocking. I delivered me lines and . . .' he spluttered with indignation, 'and Dennison had the temerity to tell me he wanted more feeling! Feeling? The line called for understatement, not feeling! The fool was plain wrong. Wrong!'

Langham murmured consolatory platitudes while Sir Humphrey patted his tweeds until he located his flask. He pulled it out and appeared bereft on finding it empty. He shook it next to his ear, then tipped it upside-down, and not a drop emerged.

'And if that were not bad enough, you know what he announced on Monday?'

'I dread to think.'

'Y'see, we'd agreed on a fee a couple of months ago. Two thousand, plus residuals.' He reached out and clutched Langham's arm. 'And then, as calm as you like, he tells me the budget's been slashed and all he can offer me is a flat fee of five hundred! Five hundred? The cheek! The infernal cheek!'

'Couldn't your agent—' Langham began.

The old man grunted. 'Sacked me agent years ago when she couldn't get me a West End run.' He sniffed. 'Haven't worked since. This . . . this *rubbish* was the way back. To show the world I could still do it, still had it in me.'

Langham thought the old man was about to burst into tears. 'It still can be, sir. You know, if I were you, I'd battle on regardless. Dismiss Dennison and his paltry fee and show that you can still act with the best of 'em. You can do it.'

'You think so?'

'I know it.'

Sir Humph sighed, looking far from convinced. 'What time is it, my boy?' he said wanly.

Langham consulted his watch. 'Just after five thirty.'

'Time for a quick one before dinner, methinks.'

The exact sentiment had evidently passed through Desmond Haggerston's mind, as at that very second the geriatric tottered down the steps from the house and, on finding Sir Humphrey, exclaimed, 'There you are! Been scouring the place for you. How about a spot of the cup that cheers before din-dins, hm?' Haggerston's characteristic melancholy had evaporated at the thought of alcoholic replenishment.

'Capital idea!' Sir Humphrey agreed, staggering to his feet. He turned to Langham, and said, 'And your kind words have assuaged my ageing heart, my boy. I'll bear them in mind. And remember me to that filly of yours, you hear?'

'You'll be seeing her again at dinner,' Langham reminded him.

'I will? Of course I will. Capital! Until then!' he cried, grasped Haggerston's arm, and sallied forth into the hall in search of a preprandial snifter.

Langham sat awhile in contemplation, then rounded the corner of the house, approached Dennison's caravan, and rapped on the door.

'Who's that?' the American called out.

'Langham.'

'About what?'

'I'd like a quick word.'

'Come in, then.'

Langham opened the flimsy door and blinked as he stepped from the sunlight and entered the Stygian gloom. He made out Douglas Dennison stretched full length on a double bed, legs crossed at the ankles. He was leafing through what Langham assumed was the shooting script.

The director tossed the sheaf aside as Langham approached the bed and sat down on a three-legged stool.

Dennison hitched himself into a sitting position and picked up a bottle of bourbon. 'Care for a hit?'

'I'll pass, thanks all the same.'

The director sloshed a shot into a cut glass and downed it in one. 'Don't tell me, young Suzie came running into your arms about that damned animal.'

'Not into my arms. Maria's.'

'Same difference.'

'She was distraught—'

'City girl. Brooklyn. Only dead thing she's seen before now was on a butcher's block.'

'She was upset – concerned about you, Mr Dennison.'

'Doug, for Chrissake. And she has no need to be upset. Trouble with that girl, she feels too much.' He sighed. 'Go on, what's she been saying?'

'She's worried about you. She . . . she thinks you're under some kind of pressure. And then the animal . . .'

'Pressure? I'm directing a damned film, for pity's sake. If that ain't pressure . . .'

'I think you know what I mean.'

Dennison poured himself another shot, eyed Langham, then asked, 'What concern is it of yours?'

Langham shrugged. 'I'm a friend of Suzie's. And I don't like it that someone's desecrated your caravan with a carcass.'

'Just some tomfool stunt,' the director muttered.

Langham tipped his head to one side. 'Are you quite sure about that?'

For a brief second Langham thought that the director was just drunk enough – or desperate enough – to divulge something. He caught a quick light of contemplation in Dennison's eyes, as if he were considering opening up.

Then the light died and Dennison snapped, 'Quite sure, buddy.

Like I said, some prankster playing the fool. Now, if you don't mind, I've a script to go through before dinner.'

EIGHT

That evening at dinner Langham made the acquaintance of Edward Marling and his wife, Cynthia.

Marling sat at the head of the table, Cynthia the other end where she regaled the film people with anecdotes of her childhood in India. She was a handsome, upright, grey-haired woman in her early fifties, older than her husband whom Langham took to be in his mid-forties.

To Langham's right was the somewhat inebriated Terrence Ambler who slurped his consommé and listened to what Douglas Dennison was muttering – something about yet another rewrite – with the occasional taciturn nod.

Maria sat across from Langham; Desmond Haggerston was seated between her and Sir Humphrey, who occasionally leaned past Haggerston and tried to engage Maria in conversation.

The dining room was long and low, boxed in by blackened beams and ancient mahogany panels. Oil paintings of glum-looking Marling patriarchs, dating back to the sixteenth century, stared down on proceedings with the pinched, peevish expressions of Puritans at a bacchanalia.

Edward Marling noted Langham's interest, and said, 'My great-great-etcetera grandfather onwards, with an uncle or two thrown in for good measure. That sly-looking cove, there, ended up in the tower for treason during the reign of Elizabeth.'

'And . . .?'

Edward brought his hand down on the back of his neck. 'And it's been downhill for the family ever since. It's a miracle we managed to hold on to the hall until now.'

Edward Marling was a big, heavy man imprisoned in a glistening chromium-framed wheelchair. He had a fleshy, sallow face – clearly inherited from the male line of the family, if the oils were any indication – and receding hair turning to grey. Despite his disability, and bouts of pain which evinced wincing expressions from time to time, he was affable and easy-going. Langham found himself warming to the man – all the more so when he said, 'It's good to meet you, Donald. I've enjoyed a few of your novels over the years.'

'That's kind of you.'

'I love a good crime yarn. I've plenty of time on my hands, these days. Cyn—' the way he contracted his wife's name, as he stared at her down the length of the table, made him sound like an arch-bishop about to expound upon the Ten Commandments – 'calls them rubbish and upbraids me for wasting my time. I see nothing wrong with a good detective novel, so long as it *is* good, well-written and well-characterized.'

'I'm with you there,' Langham said.

'Cyn has a thing about "self-improvement",' Edward went on. 'She seems to think that education, especially in the arts, fosters good morals and ethics in the individual and society at large.'

'And you contest that?'

Edward reached out and adjusted his wine glass. He had the odd habit of arranging everything before him – his cutlery, plates, and glass – with minute precision. 'Some of the most highly educated men in Europe,' he said, 'scions of the "finest" families and the product of the best universities, were responsible for the most outra-geous acts of barbarism the world has ever known. I speak, of course, of the Nazis.'

Before Langham could object that Hitler and Goering were not exactly scholars, and that several of Hitler's opponents had been members of great German families, Edward went on, 'And did you know that there's a tribe of pygmies – in the Congo, I think – who have no god, no concept of the arts, and it goes without saying aren't at all "educated", and yet they enjoy a society in which theft and murder and such crimes are unknown? Makes you think, doesn't it?'

From the far end of the table, Cynthia called out, 'Don't let Edward browbeat you with his ridiculous pet theories, Mr Langham. If it were down to my husband, we'd all be living in the jungle wearing grass skirts and eating monkeys.'

Suzie piped up, 'I wore a grass skirt, once. In *Aloha Hawaii*, remember, Dougy? All I recall is that it was mighty itchy.'

Sir Humphrey raised his glass. 'And I'll wager you were a verit-able vision, my dear. There's nothing, in my opinion, like a grass skirt for displaying a gal's derrière to its best advantage.'

Cynthia murmured, 'Would someone *please* be good enough to move the claret from Sir Humphrey's reach?'

Varla Cartier obliged, and refilled her own glass.

Edward eyed Langham, and murmured, 'What I experienced in the war opened my eyes, Donald. I saw supposedly civilized men behave like beasts – on both sides, I hasten to add.' He refilled his glass, then topped up Langham's. 'Saw service yourself, did you?'

'Field Security, Madagascar and India.'

'So you were spared the front line?'

'For the most part, though I did end up in a skirmish or two against the Vichy French in Madagascar.' He refrained from mentioning that in one bloody battle, to take the town of Diego-Suarez, he'd shot a French soldier who had been about to lob a grenade at Ralph Ryland.

He said, 'You were in France, I understand?'

Edward nodded. 'Special Operations. My French was fluent and I could pass as a native. Dropped into Brittany in 'forty-two. I was there for six months before things became a tad hairy. Managed to get out by the skin of my teeth. I went back in 'forty-four, this time to the Cévennes.'

He stopped, eyeing his glass with a far away expression. 'Wasn't so lucky, then.'

Despite his curiosity, Langham remained silent.

'To cut a long story short, I was captured by the Gestapo. The officer in charge of trying to extract names from me was a charming chappie, one of Cyn's highly educated sophisticates. He quoted Rilke and Goethe between ordering his henchman to slip burning brands under my fingernails.'

Langham winced. 'And you survived . . .'

'Without spilling the proverbial beans, too. Though God knows how long I could have held out. Three days after I was captured, the local resistance raided the Gestapo headquarters, shooting the verse-quoting officer and his henchman in the process, and managed to get me out in one piece. Smuggled me over the border into Spain, and the rest is history.'

'What a story.' Langham smiled. 'Makes my war seem like a walk in the park.'

'I'm writing my memoirs at the moment. There's a lot I can't go into, of course. I'll be looking for a publisher pretty soon.'

'If there's any way I can help . . .' Langham said. 'War memoirs are popular these days.'

'If you're doing nothing tomorrow afternoon, pop along to my study and I'll show you the manuscript, see if it's up to scratch.'

'I'm sure it will be,' Langham said.

Across from him, Maria had been attempting to engage Desmond

Haggerston in conversation, but had succeeded only in eliciting the occasional grunted monosyllable. Haggerston seemed interested only in competing with Sir Humphrey in seeing who could imbibe the greater quantity of red wine. So far, if the former's taciturnity and the latter's suggestive garrulousness was any indication, it was neck-and-neck.

Maria leaned forward, and said to Edward, 'As it happens, my agency has just taken on the manuscript of an officer who escaped from one of the Stalags. As Donald says, war memoirs are popular at the moment.'

'There you go,' Langham said, 'an interested agent already.'

'We'll certainly take a look,' Maria said.

'That's kind of you,' Edward murmured.

Cynthia's crystal-cut falsetto rang out along the table, 'Is that sort of thing really popular, these days? I would have thought the market was flooded with accounts of bravado in the face of the Hun.'

Langham glanced at Edward, who pursed his lips and positioned his fork with fussy exactitude on the table before him.

Maria smiled at Cynthia. 'There is always a market for well-written accounts of war exploits.'

Chuck Banning paused with a forkful of venison before his mouth. 'Say, weren't you and Doug together in France, Mr Marling?'

'That's correct, Chuck,' Edward said.

Dennison laughed. 'I was hiding in a hayrick, a day after being dropped. Only, you see, the navigator got his co-ordinates haywire and I came down ten miles east of where I should have. Place was swarming with Jerries. I was lucky. Ed's people came and rescued me in the nick of time. Boy, I'd never been so grateful to see a friendly face.'

'As I recall, Douglas, you were more concerned about a cut on your face than being captured.'

Dennison smiled. 'Gotta keep up appearances, Ed. Truth was, I was scared shitless – excuse my French.'

Suzie laid a hand on Dennison's arm. 'Dougy's French is excellent, isn't it? You see, his mom was French.'

'And I spent a lot of my childhood in the country north of Marseilles,' Dennison said. 'So, when I'd completed twenty-odd tours of duty with my squadron, a good word from Edward got me into Special Ops.'

Cynthia asked, 'And have *you* ever been tempted to write your memoirs, Douglas?'

Dennison grunted. 'Don't like ploughing old ground, Cynthia. The war's over. I'm looking ahead.'

Chuck Banning said, 'I might have been called up to fight in Korea, if the war had gone on longer.'

To Langham's right, Edward muttered, 'As if we haven't learned a lesson from the last one . . .'

Douglas Dennison heard him, and said, 'But the Korean War was necessary, Ed. You heard of the domino effect? We had to get in there and stop the reds, or they would've just kept on coming. They had to be stopped.'

Cynthia said, 'Isn't Douglas right, my dear?'

'That depends on how much of an economic threat you deem a communist Asia to be,' Edward said. 'Myself, I can't see the Soviet Union or their cronies posing much of a danger to the West, in the long run.'

Dennison pointed a fork at his host. 'And that's just where liberals like you are plain wrong, Ed.'

A heated, if reasonably good-natured, political debate followed, with Langham, Maria and Varla Cartier coming down on Edward's side, and Douglas Dennison, Cynthia and Chuck Banning speaking up for the opposition of communism wherever it might raise its ugly head. Suzie remained silent, and Sir Humphrey and Desmond Haggerston were too inebriated to contribute anything coherent to the debate.

A little later Cynthia suggested that coffee and port should be taken in the billiard room, and the guests drifted from the table in ones and twos.

While the women moved to the end of the room and conversed amongst themselves, Edward suggested a game of billiards. Douglas Dennison and Chuck Banning were paired against Langham and Edward – the latter, to Langham's surprise, managed to haul himself from his wheelchair and stand for long enough to complete his shot. He proved a more competent player than any of the other three.

Sir Humphrey and Desmond Haggerston sank into a leather sofa and passed the port between themselves for the remainder of the evening. The french windows were open to admit a warm evening breeze freighted with the scent of honeysuckle.

An hour later, the billiards contest completed with a British rout of the Americans – thanks to Edward's steady eye and calm potting – the men joined the women and sat around in desultory conversation. Langham noticed that Cynthia had seated herself on the sofa next to Chuck Banning, and while not openly flirting with the young American, her interest was obvious. Varla Cartier sat alone, her legs crossed, sipping brandy and eyeing the gathering with what looked like superior amusement.

Towards midnight the company broke up as the guests retired; Cynthia yawned and excused herself, followed by Chuck Banning. Dennison went next, with Suzie following him a few minutes later. Edward Marling said how pleasant it had been chatting to Langham and wheeled himself from the room.

Langham caught Maria's eye, and murmured, 'I don't know about you, but I think a turn in the garden would be just the ticket.'

Maria finished her coffee and linked her arm through his; they said their goodnights to the remaining guests and stepped out into the scented night.

'I needed to get away from there,' Maria said as they crossed the greensward behind the house.

'Too smoky for you?' he asked.

She pushed him. 'No, silly. I mean I couldn't bear the atmosphere in there for another second.'

'You mean the animosity between Edward and Cynthia?'

'Yes, but didn't you notice all the other ill-feeling?'

A full moon was out, silvering the grass and lighting their way. Langham heard far off birdsong and wondered if it were a nightingale.

'Go on . . .'

'Sometimes, Donald, for a writer I think you're very unobservant.'

He smiled. 'Just not as eagle-eyed as you, my sweet.'

'For one, Chuck ignored Suzie all night – miffed that she's rebuffed his advances, I think. Two, Varla Cartier was staring at Dennison as if she wanted to shoot him dead. Three, Desmond Haggerston was derisive to Dennison about one of his films. And did you hear him badgering Dennison about his current project?'

'I must admit I didn't.'

'You were talking to Edward,' she said.

'Whom I rather like,' Langham said. 'He's obviously long-suffering, with a wife like Cynthia.'

Maria frowned in the moonlight. 'I must admit that I didn't take to her,' she said. 'But then again we don't know the full story. We don't know why Cynthia might resent Edward so much.'

'I can pretty much guess,' he said.

She stopped and looked at him. 'Go on.'

'What if, and I'm speculating here, what if Edward's condition prevents him from, ah fulfilling his conjugal duties?'

Maria pulled a face. 'You're right.'

Surprised, he said, 'I am?'

'About the fact that you're speculating.'

'Oh.'

'There might be many reasons that Cynthia is so cutting to her husband,' she said.

They walked on in silence for a while, then Langham said, 'What do you make of Varla?'

'Mmm,' Maria said, contemplating. 'She is a dark horse, Donald. I think she has a secret past, and is hiding something, and is plotting *terr-ible* deeds.' She hung on his arm and laughed, almost pulling him off his feet, and belatedly Langham realized that she was jesting.

He said, 'No, seriously, she is a bit odd, don't you agree?'

She shrugged. 'It's hard to tell, until I know her better.'

They veered left and approached the side of the house where the maze and Dennison's caravan were situated.

'Do you think Chuck Banning and Cynthia are doing anything more than some innocent flirting?' she asked a little later.

He found the idea, if it were so, a little disturbing.

Maria went on, 'Because I think we might soon find out, Donald.'

'What makes you think that?'

She pointed. 'About fifteen seconds ago, Cynthia disappeared into the maze. Shhh!' she hissed.

Abruptly she pulled him behind the trunk of a monkey puzzle tree and peered out. A hundred yards away, a figure appeared around the corner of the hall. In the inky shadow cast by the building, it was impossible to make out who it might be.

Then the figure stepped from the shadows, into the light of the moon, and Langham saw that it was Chuck Banning. He hurried across from the house and disappeared into the maze.

'I don't understand,' he whispered. 'Why doesn't Cynthia simply go along to his room, if she wants to—?'

'Because,' Maria hissed into his ear, 'Banning's room is right next to Edward's.' She stifled a laugh.

'What?'

'Bad planning on Cynthia's part when she was allocating the rooms, I think!'

'You're terrible,' he said.

'Come on.'

They hurried from the cover of the monkey puzzle tree. To reach the house, they had to pass the maze. Langham increased his pace, unwilling to eavesdrop on what might be taking place between the older woman and the young actor.

As they were creeping across the grass, Maria stumbled. Langham took her arm, and the sound of voices issued from behind the high hedge of the maze.

'Have you told him?' the American said.

Cynthia's reply was too low to hear.

'Dammit! You know you've got to . . .' The remainder of the sentence became indistinct as Banning lowered his voice.

'Very well, I will,' Cynthia replied. 'But give me a little time.'

'How do you think he'll take it?' Banning asked.

'I . . . I don't know,' Cynthia said. 'It might . . .' The rest was lost, and a silence ensued.

Langham whispered, 'Let's get going.'

Maria nodded and they crept away from the maze like cat burglars.

They rounded the house and approached the steps, and Langham said, 'What on earth was all that about?'

'It sounded to me as if Banning wanted Cynthia to tell her husband about their affair.'

'Poor Edward,' Langham muttered.

They entered the hallway, where a low night-light shone, and hurried up the staircase.

Another surprise awaited them before they reached their room. At the top of the stairs Langham made out a shadowy figure on the floor, propped up between two suits of armour.

'Who is it?' Maria asked.

Langham stepped forward. The slumped figure was issuing a series of stertorous snores like those of a stranded walrus.

'Haggerston,' he said. 'We can't leave the old duffer out here. Isn't his room next to ours? Come on, we'll take an arm each.'

Between them they managed to manhandle Haggerston upright – the old man still only half-awake – and steer him along the corridor to his room. They tipped him onto his bed, turned him onto his side, and left him snoring fit to wake the dead.

Sleep was a long time coming for Langham. He'd had a little too much coffee in the billiard room, and the events of the evening, and the various conversations, were swirling around in his head. It didn't help that Haggerston's snores cut through the wall like a buzz saw.

He awoke in the middle of the night to find that Maria was sitting at the far end of the room, reading a manuscript by lamplight. The snoring from next door continued unabated.

On the way to the bathroom, he asked, 'What time is it?'

'Almost four. I cannot sleep.' She thumbed at the wall in disgust.

On his way back to bed he kissed her forehead. 'Don't stay up too long.'

'I won't, *mon cher*.'

He was dead to the world almost as soon as his head touched the pillow, despite the best efforts of their neighbour to deny sleep to the entire household.

Later, much later, something dragged him from his dreams. He awoke, startled, and sat upright. Someone was rapping on the door.

Beside him, Maria was fast asleep, oblivious to the frantic summons. The snoring from Haggerston, he noted, had ceased. He rolled out of bed and moved to the door, wondering if he might find a hysterical Suzie Reynard in need of consolation.

He pulled open the door and stood back.

Douglas Dennison leaned against the door frame, wild-eyed. 'Thank Christ!' he cried. 'You gotta come, Langham!'

'What?' he said, still dazed with sleep.

'She's dead . . .' the director said.

'Who's dead?' Langham asked – but Dennison had already turned and was reeling off along the corridor.

Langham dressed quickly, careful not to wake Maria, then left the room and hurried after the director.

NINE

The sun was up and the lawn was spangled with scintillating dew. Far off, a cuckoo called, its throaty muffled double note conjuring notions of a countryside at peace – which was wholly at odds with Langham's thoughts as he followed Dennison along the front of the house and around the corner towards the caravan.

The director paused before the fold-down steps and reached out to brace his arms on either side of the open door.

Behind him, Langham said, 'Suzie . . .?'

Dennison sobbed, his head hanging. 'Christ . . . Christ, who could have done this?'

The director took a breath, pulled himself up into the caravan, and stood aside as Langham followed him. Dennison indicated the bed.

In the light slanting through the window beside the double bed, Langham made out the body. Suzie Reynard was sitting upright, wedged into the corner of two walls, her legs drawn up to her chest as if she had been attempting, futilely, to scramble away from her assailant. She'd been shot two or three times, and what remained of her head was a sight that Langham wished he'd been spared. He turned away, his stomach churning.

Dennison said, 'Goddammit.'

He knelt and reached out to pick something up from the floor, but Langham said, 'Don't!'

The director jerked as if electrocuted and stood up. Langham squatted and examined the handgun lying on the worn carpet beside the bed – a British service revolver fitted with a long, cylindrical silencer.

Dennison voiced what Langham was thinking. 'But why the hell would someone shoot Suzie and then drop the weapon?'

Langham climbed to his feet. He pushed back the cuff of his jacket to look at his watch, then realized that in his haste to dress he'd left it on the bedside table. 'What's the time?'

Dennison glanced at his watch. 'Six forty-five.'

'Have you called the police?'

The director was staring back through the doorway, as if to avoid looking again at the body on the bed. 'I . . . For some damned reason, the first person I thought of was you.'

Langham wished that the director had spared him the dubious honour.

'I'd better go and call . . .' Langham indicated the house. 'Don't stay here alone. Come with me.'

Dennison rubbed his face. 'You don't need to go back into the hall. I had a phone rigged up out here.'

He snatched a bulky Bakelite telephone from a desk and left the caravan. Langham followed him and saw that a cable stretched from the phone, across the gravel, and up the side of the house.

Dennison found a folding canvas seat – a director's chair with his name stencilled across the back – and dropped into it. He stared at the phone in his lap, shaking his head. 'I . . . I don't even know the damned number.' His hands were shaking with delayed shock.

'Here, let me.' Langham took the phone and sat down on the caravan's steps.

He got through to the local police station and spoke to a yawning desk officer. 'I'm calling from Marling Hall,' he said, 'and I'd like to report a death.'

A silence greeted his words, followed by a shocked, 'A death?'

'In fact, it looks like murder.'

'Murder . . .' The officer swore, remembered himself, and said, 'Right-o. I'll jump on my bike and go wake up the sergeant. Shan't be long. Who's speaking?'

Langham gave his name and replaced the receiver.

Dennison slumped forward in the director's chair, his head in his hands.

Langham said, 'I presume you and Suzie spent the night here together?'

'That's right.'

'So, where were you when . . .?' He pointed over his shoulder into the caravan.

'I couldn't sleep. Around three thirty I got up and went out.'

'Where did you go?'

'Just . . . out. I walked.' In reaction to Langham's querulous expression, the director explained himself, 'I don't sleep. I'm lucky if I can grab a couple of hours' shuteye a night. I often get up and walk.'

'And this was around three thirty?'

'Three thirty-five. I checked my watch.'

'Did you go far?'

Dennison pointed beyond the maze. 'Through the woods, around the lake and through the pine plantation.'

'It must have been hellish dark for you to have seen your way.'

'There was a full moon. It was a beautiful night.'

'And you didn't see anyone, or anything, suspicious? A parked car?'

The director shook his head. 'No. No one, nothing. I was totally alone. I heard an owl. I thought how wonderful it sounded.' He lifted his head and looked bleakly at Langham. 'I often take a hike in the middle of the night, especially just before a shoot. It's a tense time. I have a lot to think about.'

'How long were you out walking?'

'I got back at six, then just sat out here . . .'

'For how long?'

'Forty minutes or so.' He took a deep breath. 'Then . . . then I thought I'd better hit the sack, went into the trailer and found . . .'

'But you didn't see the revolver on the floor in front of the bed?'

Dennison shook his head. 'No, just—' He stopped, then went on in a whisper, 'I just saw Suzie.'

'So, at around six forty you came straight into the hall and upstairs to my room?'

'That's right.'

'You didn't think to call the police?'

Dennison was silent for a time, then looked at Langham, and said, 'I wasn't thinking straight . . .'

'Why did you think of me, Douglas?'

He shook his head. 'I don't know. Maybe I thought there was something solidly dependable and British about you. The man to rely on in a crisis. I really don't know.'

For a second, Langham wondered if Suzie had admitted to Dennison that she'd hired him to look into the supposed threats against the director, but dismissed the idea. Dennison would have mentioned the fact.

'I take it that the door was unlocked?'

'That's right. I never lock it. For Chrissake, we're in the middle of the English countryside, and anyway there's nothing valuable—' He stopped suddenly as if hit by the thought that perhaps, if the door had been locked, Suzie Reynard might not have been shot dead.

He went on, 'What gets me, Langham, is how did the killer know Suzie was out here?'

'Why shouldn't they? Doesn't she usually . . .?'

Dennison was shaking his head. 'When we arrived here, Cynthia gave Suzie and me separate rooms. I told her I'd be bunking out here, in my trailer, and Suzie said she'd be sharing with me. Cynthia took it badly. She said she'd prepared a room, and that Suzie would use it.' Dennison shrugged. 'So, rather than offend Cynthia's religious sensibilities, Suzie agreed but snuck down to the trailer every night around one, then went back to her room at dawn.'

'And are you sure no one knew about this?'

'We thought it best to keep schtum.'

Langham massaged his eyes. 'But the killer *must* have known Suzie spent the night with you . . .'

'Unless,' Dennison said, 'they went to her room, saw she wasn't there, and guessed that she'd be down here.'

'So the killer came down here, knowing that you'd be here too . . .? Why didn't he just kill her in her room before one o'clock?' Langham frowned. 'There's another explanation of course.'

'There is?'

'The killer didn't enter the caravan meaning to shoot Suzie. Their intended victim was you.'

Dennison stared at him, his expression haggard. He shook his head, as if bewildered. 'So . . . so why the hell did they shoot Suzie?'

Langham thought about it. 'She was shot between just after three thirty, when you left the caravan, and six, when you returned. From three thirty until around five thirty, it'd be dark. If the killer came here between those times, he must have turned on the light in order to see his victim – she was backed up against the wall, and none of the shots missed her. If she were killed between five thirty and just before six, it would have been light . . .'

'So, what are you driving at?'

'Just this: if the killer came here to kill you, why did he kill Suzie when he saw her in the bed? Maybe it was because he was holding the revolver, and she saw him . . . And as he came here intending to kill you – *and still wanted you dead* – then Suzie had to die, too.'

'My God . . .'

'It's a working hypothesis,' Langham said. 'Of course, we can't rule out the possibility that Suzie was the intended victim after all.'

Dennison stood suddenly, staring down the drive as the sound of a car engine broke the silence. A black Rover rolled up the drive, crunching gravel. Langham walked to the corner of the house and signalled to the driver.

Two policemen climbed from the car, a walrus-moustached sergeant in his fifties and a gangling youth who appeared to be no older than twenty.

'Mr Langham?' the older man said. 'I'm Sergeant Briscoe, and this is Constable Dawson.'

Langham introduced Dennison and indicated the caravan. Sergeant Briscoe entered first, followed by Dawson, who had to duck through the low doorway. Dawson emerged seconds later, his face deathly pale, muttered something and hurried around the back of the caravan. Langham heard the sound of retching.

Sergeant Briscoe stepped from the caravan and sat down heavily on the steps, mopping sweat from his brow with a handkerchief. Dawson returned, looking sheepish.

Briscoe said, 'Been a copper nearly thirty years, gentlemen, and I thought I'd seen it all.' He pulled out a notebook and licked the end of a stubby pencil. 'Now, if you'd be so kind as to tell me who discovered the body and what time that was?'

From his director's chair, Dennison supplied the sergeant with the details. Briscoe finished writing. 'Dawson, get onto Norwich, there's a good chap, and tell 'em we'll be needing Inspector MacTaggart.'

Langham indicated the phone on the gravel beside the steps, and Constable Dawson picked it up and got through to divisional headquarters.

While his subordinate was speaking to Norwich, Sergeant Briscoe said, 'Mr Langham, I suspect MacTaggart and his men will be with us in an hour or so. I wonder if you'd be so kind as to get everyone in the hall up and out of bed, and then I'll have a word with them about staying put until the top brass get here.'

Langham made his way to the kitchen where he found the butler seated at a table, eating bread and jam and drinking a big mug of tea. He apologized for interrupting, said that there had been an incident in the caravan, and that very soon the police would be here to conduct interviews.

Evans looked shocked. 'An incident, sir?'

'A death,' Langham said, and left it at that. He told Evans to ask everyone to gather in the dining hall, then left the kitchen and made his way upstairs.

Maria was still asleep. Her head lay on the pillow, turned slightly to him, with her lips parted and her breath coming easily. He positioned a chair beside the bed and sat down.

Unbidden, he saw again the remains of Suzie Reynard, and something caught in his throat.

'Donald?'

Her soft voice startled him. 'You're awake?' he said.

'No, I'm still asleep and dreaming of my wonderful husband-to-be, who looks as if he has seen a ghost. You too could not sleep, thanks to Mr Haggerston's terrible snoring?'

He reached out and cupped Maria's cheek. 'You really are the most beautiful creature on Earth,' he said, 'and I'm the luckiest man alive.'

'Donald! What is it? Don't cry . . .'

'I'm sorry.' He took a deep breath. 'I'm sorry, but Dennison woke me earlier . . . It's Suzie, Suzie Reynard. She's dead. Someone shot her dead.'

TEN

The only person in the dining hall when they entered was Cynthia Marling, who rushed towards them from the far end of the room. Sunlight fell through the line of windows to the right, and the alternating patches of intense light and dark shadow gave her approach the halting, staccato movement of a silent movie heroine. She wore a green tweed two-piece, a worried expression, and was tugging on a string of pearls as she halted before Langham and Maria.

'Mr Langham, what *is* going on? Evans has just informed me that you told him something about a death and when I tried to see what was happening outside, I was turned back, insistently, by a police constable.'

'I think you'd better sit down,' Langham said, and pulled a dining chair out from under the mahogany leaf of the dining table.

Cynthia remained standing. 'Enough of the amateur dramatics, Mr Langham. What on earth is going on?'

Maria said, 'I'm afraid that Suzie Reynard is dead, Mrs Marling.'

Langham said, 'It appears that she was murdered.'

'No!' The news seemed to remove the woman's ability to remain upright, and it was just as well that Langham had readied the seat. He took Cynthia's elbow and lowered her to the brocaded cushion.

'Murdered? But . . . how?'

Langham, seeing that Maria was about to speak, got in first. 'That remains to be seen. The police are handling the situation and soon there should be a detective arriving from Norwich.'

'Dead? Suzie?' Cynthia shook her head, seemingly able to utter only gasped monosyllables. 'Who . . .?'

Langham crossed to a sideboard and poured a stiff measure of brandy. He left the bottle and several glasses on the table, as he suspected others beside Cynthia would be seeking its comfort.

Cynthia clutched the glass and took a swallow, thanking Langham, and then stood quickly and moved to the window. She stared out in silence.

The door opened and Chuck Banning strode in. 'Say, what are the cops up to? There hasn't been a robbery . . .?' He saw that Cynthia was weeping and rushed to her side. 'Hey, there, there . . . No need for tears.' He touched her shoulder, then looked back at Langham and mouthed, 'What gives?'

'Oh, it's terrible . . .' Cynthia said. 'Suzie . . . little Suzie has been killed. Murdered.'

Chuck assisted Cynthia to a chaise longue and sat down heavily beside her. He looked across at Langham. 'Suzie?'

'I'm sorry. Dennison found her in his caravan.'

Cynthia said, 'In his caravan? But what was she—?'

Before she could finish, Sir Humphrey Lyle entered the room. 'What's all this, then? What the blazes is going on?' His small reptilian eyes took in the tableau. 'Evans says there's been a death? Not old Desmond, forsooth?'

Langham said, 'I'm afraid Suzie Reynard was murdered at some point during the night.'

The old man seemed to stagger. He fell into the chair recently vacated by Cynthia and stared at Langham, his mouth hanging open. 'Suzie? Murdered? But . . . but she was so young!'

Cynthia looked up, and snapped, 'What in God's name has age got to do with it?'

'But . . .' The old man's jaw trembled. 'She was young, with everything to . . .' His voice trailed off as he shook his head. 'Young and beautiful,' he said to himself.

'It would be just as tragic if she were twice her age and ugly,' Cynthia remarked caustically.

'I say, is that brandy?' Sir Humphrey asked. 'Langham, be a jolly good chap and pour me a snifter, would you?'

Langham obliged.

Varla Cartier was the next to enter the dining hall. She looked around the gathering, and said, 'Is no one having breakfast this morning?'

Cynthia said, 'Didn't Evans tell you?'

'No one told me anything. I heard someone knocking on my door, but I was bathing.' She looked around, taking in the shocked expressions of those present. 'What's happened?'

Maria said, 'Suzie Reynard has been found dead in Dennison's caravan.'

Varla sat down quickly. 'Alcohol poisoning or an overdose?'

Chuck Banning said, 'What did you say?'

'Well, she liked to knock them back, and she was well oiled last night . . .'

'You, if I might say, have little room to speak,' Cynthia said.

'At least—' Varla smiled back at Cynthia with icy disdain – 'I'm not a drug addict.'

Langham asked, 'Was Miss Reynard?'

'She certainly liked the snow,' Varla said.

Sir Humphrey said, 'According to Mr Langham, Miss Reynard was murdered.'

Varla turned her head towards Langham, her veil of midnight hair swinging. 'Is that right?'

'I'm afraid so,' he said. 'Can I get you a drink?'

'I wouldn't say no.'

He poured her a glass, decided that he was in need of a shot and poured himself a measure.

The door opened and Edward Marling wheeled himself in, stone-faced, followed by a shocked Terrence Ambler.

'I suppose you've all heard,' Edward said. 'Suzie's dead. Found in Dennison's caravan . . . I was just talking to Constable Dawson. She was shot.'

Langham looked around the gathering as Edward said this. Cynthia was drying her eyes on a handkerchief. Chuck Banning, with Edward's arrival, had moved away from Cynthia on the chaise longue, and looked back at the woman as if desperate to console her.

Sir Humphrey reached for the brandy and sloshed himself another generous measure.

'After you,' Varla Cartier said.

Edward went on, 'We're to remain here until a detective arrives from Norwich. We're all under suspicion, it appears.'

Cynthia said, 'But Dennison never locked the caravan door. He told me so. It needn't have been anyone here.' She glanced desperately around the room. 'Anyone from outside could have got in and . . . and—'

'Be quiet, Cyn,' Edward Marling snapped. 'The police think it was one of us, and I wouldn't disagree.'

Chuck Banning said, 'Why do you think that, Ed?'

Edward considered replying, thought better of it, then turned to Langham. 'I'd like a quick word, Donald.'

He spun his chair and propelled himself to the far end of the dining hall. Langham, with a glance at Maria, followed him.

Edward parked his wheelchair in a parallelogram of sunlight. 'First of all, I know why you're here.'

'Do you mind if I ask who told you?'

'Suzie herself,' Edward said, 'after dinner last night. She was hitting the bottle rather and appeared upset. I asked her what was wrong. She told me about the hare business, then admitted that she was concerned about Douglas's safety and told me she'd hired you to investigate.'

'I didn't mention it as I didn't want to compromise my position. I hope you understand.'

Edward inclined his head. 'Of course.'

'And I'd appreciate it if you'd keep it under your hat for the time being. I'll inform the police about the situation, of course, but I'd rather the others were left in the dark.'

'I understand.' Edward hesitated. 'There's one other thing. I was speaking to Constable Dawson, demanding to know what had happened. The thing is, Donald, I think it was one of my guns which was used to kill her.'

'Ah . . .' Langham said.

'Look,' Edward went on, 'if you'd care to come along to where I keep my guns . . .'

'Lead the way.'

Aware that the eyes of everyone were on him and Edward, he followed the invalid from the dining hall. They passed through the hallway and along the passage, Langham accommodating himself to Edward's slow progress as he spun the chromium rims on the outside of the wheels. He noticed that Edward was wearing a pair of golfing gloves to lessen the risk of blisters.

Edward said, 'Where's Dennison?'

'Still at the caravan, with Sergeant Briscoe. He found Suzie and sought me out.'

'So you saw poor Suzie?'

'And I wish I hadn't.'

'So, where was Dennison when the shooting occurred?' Edward asked.

'He told me he couldn't sleep and took himself off on a hike through a pine plantation. When he got back, he found her.'

Edward looked up. 'And do you believe him?'

'For what it's worth, I do. He seemed pretty grief-stricken out there.'

Edward gestured to a door. 'Here we are.'

He turned the handle and pushed. Langham followed him into a small room lined with mahogany cupboards and cabinets. 'Where I keep my rifles and such, along with ammunition. I did a bit of hunting, before the war.'

'Is the door kept locked?'

'No, but all the cabinets are. However . . .'

He pushed himself across the room and stopped before a cabinet the size of a wardrobe. The brass lock had been jemmied, and the timber split. Langham pulled out his handkerchief and carefully, so as not to mar any fingerprints, opened the door.

A few old rifles were racked in the cabinet, above which was a shelf bearing several revolvers. 'My service revolver, and the silencer, are missing. Constable Dawson described the weapon they'd found. I have no doubt it's one and the same.'

'But who knew about this?' Langham indicated the cabinet. He looked around the room. 'It's the only one damaged . . . as if the killer knew exactly where to look.'

Edward bit his lip. 'I know. It would indicate, I'll say candidly, that the killer was very familiar with this room and specifically where the revolvers were kept.'

'Could you have been in here, with the cabinet unlocked, with the door open so that someone passing might have seen you and the weapons?'

Edward was shaking his head. 'I haven't been in here for years.'

'Who knows about this room?'

'Myself, of course, Cynthia, Evans – oh, and Desmond Haggerston. We went hunting together before the war.'

'No one else?'

Edward thought about it. 'No. No one.'

'Do you have any idea when the revolver might have been stolen?' Langham asked.

'Evans makes a round of every room daily,' Edward said. 'He reported nothing amiss here at noon yesterday. As soon as Dawson told me about the weapon, I came here and found this.'

'So someone came in here, forced the cabinet open, and took the weapon between midday yesterday and the early hours of the morning.'

Edward murmured something about the possibility of fingerprints.

Langham shook his head. 'I doubt the killer would have been stupid enough to leave prints, here or on the weapon, but it's something the forensic team will check. I'd make sure the room is locked from now on.'

Edward pulled a bunch of keys from his pocket. 'Will do.'

He locked the door and they made their way back to the dining hall.

Everyone looked up as they returned. 'Where have you been, Edward?' Cynthia asked.

'I was showing Donald the gun room,' Edward said. 'It appears that the weapon used to shoot Miss Reynard was my own service revolver.' He paused. 'So you see, Cyn, why I said that the police have every right to suspect one of us?'

Chuck Banning laughed uneasily. 'Not me, buddy. I don't even know where the gun room is.'

Cynthia reached out and laid a calming hand on the young man's arm.

'Are you saying,' Varla Cartier addressed Edward, 'that you think someone in this room stole one of your guns, crept out to the trailer and shot Suzie in the head?'

Cynthia said, 'But who said anything about Miss Reynard being shot in the head, Varla? Only the person who found the body would have known that – and the killer, of course.'

Varla kept her composure and smiled across the room at Cynthia. 'I was surmising when I asked the question, Cynthia. After all, wouldn't an assassin shoot his victim in the head, just to make sure?'

Chuck Banning looked around the room. 'Say, there's someone missing.'

Langham said, 'Douglas is still at the caravan, with the constable.'

'No, I mean the old man, Haggerston,' Banning said.

Beside Langham, Maria said, 'I think he might still be the worse for wear. We found him last night, collapsed in the corridor upstairs. We helped him to his room.'

Cynthia said, 'Perhaps it would be wise to see if Desmond is all right. Edward, would you ring for Evans?'

Edward pushed himself across the room and hauled on a tasselled bell-pull. A minute later Evans ghosted in with the sangfroid of his calling. 'Sir?'

'Would you pop up to Mr Haggerston's room, Evans, and ask him to join us?'

'I tried earlier, sir, received no reply and assumed he was still asleep.'

'Try again, Evans, there's a good chap.'

A silence followed the butler's departure. Langham took Maria's hand and gave her a grim smile.

Evans returned minutes later and announced, 'Mr Haggerston's door was locked, sir, so I thought it wise to find the spare key and check on him myself.' He cleared his throat. 'But when I entered the room, sir, I found it empty.'

Langham turned to the window at the sound of a car engine, and watched as a racing green Humber rolled up the drive. 'And this must be the detective from Norwich,' he said, 'right on cue.'

ELEVEN

Fifteen minutes after the detective inspector's arrival, Langham looked up as the door to the dining hall opened to reveal a tall, cadaverous man dressed in black, who looked more like an undertaker than a detective. He was flanked by a short plain-clothes officer in a raincoat and trilby.

The detective introduced himself as Inspector MacTaggart. 'I've just finished interviewing Mr Dennison,' he said, 'and I'll be seeing the rest of you one by one over the course of the next hour or so.' He consulted a sheet of paper in his hand. 'I'll see Donald Langham first, as you and Mr Dennison were the first people on the scene of the incident. The interviews will be conducted next door in the library. Mr Marling, could you get the butler and the maid in here, so they can take their turn? Mr Langham, if you would be so good as to accompany me.'

Langham squeezed Maria's hand and followed MacTaggart and his deputy from the room.

The library was a large room overlooking the driveway, with the two longer walls stocked with shelves of old morocco-bound volumes. MacTaggart and his younger colleague, whom he introduced as Detective Sergeant Ferrars, seated themselves in a sumptuous leather sofa before a low oak table piled with papers and old periodicals. At MacTaggart's invitation, Langham took an armchair opposite the two men.

'What I don't understand,' MacTaggart said, referring to his notebook, 'is why Mr Dennison, on finding Miss Reynard, decided to summon you rather than phone the police.'

'That occurred to me, too, and I asked Dennison about it. I think it was less a conscious decision than an impulsive action. He was in a state of shock, and for whatever reasons I was the first person he thought of contacting.'

'Sergeant Briscoe informs me that you contacted him yesterday, concerning—' MacTaggart peered down at his notes – 'a dead hare.' He looked up, skewering Langham with steely grey eyes.

Langham said, 'I think it would help if we got off on an even footing and I told you why I'm here, Inspector.'

'And why might that be, Mr Langham?'

'On Friday afternoon, Miss Reynard came to my office in London, where I'm a partner at the Ryland and Langham Detective Agency, and hired our services.' He went on to detail Suzie Reynard's concerns for the safety of the director Douglas Dennison.

'She invited me and my fiancée to the hall for the weekend,' he finished, 'to examine the lie of the land, as it were.'

'"The lie of the land",' MacTaggart repeated, his long grey face looking even more corpse-like. 'And what are your conclusions after examining the lie of the land, Mr Langham?'

'I'm not at all sure that Suzie Reynard was the killer's intended victim. I think the killer entered the caravan expecting to find Dennison there, disturbed Suzie Reynard – who was obviously awake when the killer appeared, as she was curled up in the corner of the caravan as if attempting to get away – and killed her, thus eliminating a witness.'

'And if you're wrong,' Ferrars said, 'and the killer intended to shoot Reynard all along?'

'If the killer's intended victim was Reynard, why would he have tracked her down to Dennison's caravan when the chances were that the director would be there as well?'

'Perhaps,' MacTaggart mused, 'the killer saw Dennison leave the caravan at—' he referred to his notes again – 'just after three thirty, and took his chance?'

Langham nodded. 'That's always possible, I agree.'

MacTaggart said, 'But if you're right, Langham, then Dennison is still in danger. I'll have a word with him about being on his guard.'

'That would be a wise move,' Langham said. 'Of course, there's another scenario.'

'Go on.'

'That everything Douglas Dennison has told us is a lie. He killed Suzie Reynard for reasons known only to himself.'

'And Reynard's concern that Dennison was under some kind of threat?'

Langham shrugged. 'She misinterpreted Dennison's behaviour – he was stressed, but it was because he was planning Suzie Reynard's murder.' He paused. 'But for what it's worth, I don't think Dennison did kill Suzie. From what I saw of him this morning, he didn't look like someone who'd just murdered his lover.'

MacTaggart looking up from his notes. 'And the murder weapon was found at the scene of the crime. That's odd.'

'I agree,' Langham said. 'I can't see why the killer would deliberately shoot Miss Reynard and drop the weapon on the floor.'

'Unless he intended to incriminate someone . . .' Ferrars mused. 'The revolver's owner, for instance?'

'The revolver belonged to Edward Marling,' Langham said, 'and it was stolen from a locked cabinet in his gun room.' He described his examination of the gun room with Edward Marling that morning. 'Edward said that his butler, Evans, made daily checks and reported nothing amiss at noon yesterday.'

'So it was taken between then and this morning . . .' MacTaggart said.

'The chances are,' Ferrars said, 'that the gun was taken by someone resident at the hall.'

'There's also the possibility that someone from outside entered the hall unseen and stole the gun,' Langham pointed out.

MacTaggart mulled this over. 'It's a possibility. I'll keep my options open, but I'll be concentrating, first and foremost, on the people resident in the hall this weekend.'

MacTaggart thanked Langham for his assistance and asked him to send in Terrence Ambler.

Langham returned to the dining hall. Edward and Cynthia and their guests were gathered in sepulchral silence at the far end of the room, watched over by Constable Dawson.

Ambler was standing by himself by the window, his short, portly figure silhouetted against the sunlight. He looked more than ever, Langham thought, like Maria's description of him as Tweedledee, disconsolate at being separated from his twin.

Langham told him that his presence was required in the library, and Ambler nodded grimly and hurried from the room.

Langham joined Maria at the table. 'How did it go, Donald?'

'Pretty much routine. They'll no doubt be questioning us all again over the course of the next few days.'

Cynthia was plucking at her pearls. 'They don't seriously think that it was one of us, do they, Mr Langham?'

'We are the prime suspects,' he said.

'But that's ridiculous!' She turned and glared at her husband. 'And I haven't forgotten what you said earlier about your gun – but why *couldn't* a stranger have entered the hall and taken it? And anyway,' she went on in what sounded like desperation, 'who amongst us, other than Edward and myself, knew where the gun room was situated?'

Sir Humphrey, his thin lips stretched in a lizard's inscrutable smile, leaned forward, and said, 'But there's a plan of Marling Hall hanging in the hallway, with every room in the place captioned. It would have been simplicity itself to have slipped into the gun room and taken a weapon.'

Varla Cartier said, 'A more pertinent question, rather than who had the opportunity to take the gun, would be who had a motive?'

A silence greeted the question, and as if to forestall further inquiry into the matter, the double doors to the kitchen swung open and Evans and a maid rolled a bain-marie into the room.

'Don't know about anyone else,' Sir Humphrey said, 'but I couldn't eat a thing. I wouldn't mind another dash of Napoleon's finest, though . . .'

One or two of the others helped themselves to bacon and toast and sat at the table, eating desultorily. Langham and Maria helped themselves to coffee and moved across to an oak settle by a window.

Chuck Banning looked up from his plate. 'I wonder what's happened to old Haggerston?'

Edward Marling was seated before the great empty hearth. Above him, hanging on the wall, one of his ancestors glared down at the assembly; the resemblance between the current incumbent of Marling Hall and the Elizabethan was remarkable.

Edward said, 'Haggerston likes to walk off his hangovers. He's no doubt taken a turn around the grounds. He'll be back at any time.'

Nervously, Cynthia glanced at his watch. 'But it's well after eight, now. He's always back in time for breakfast.'

'He'll turn up, I tell you.'

'I don't like it, Edward. What if – what if he was out early this morning and he saw, or disturbed, whoever it was who – who killed poor Suzie? What if he's at this very moment lying—'

'I think you're being overly dramatic, dear,' Edward snapped.

Langham sipped his coffee in silence. There was a brittle atmosphere in the room, a sense of barely contained desperation; from time to time he caught individuals glancing at their neighbours.

Cynthia pushed herself from the table and strode across to the window, murmuring, 'This is intolerable.'

Maria moved to Cynthia's side and placed a hand on her arm, murmuring something that Langham was unable to make out.

The doors opened and Terrence Ambler entered. He crossed to where Chuck Banning was sitting at the table, spoke to him, and the young man rather self-consciously got to his feet, wiped his mouth on a napkin and strode from the room.

Ambler poured himself a coffee and joined Langham.

'How did it go?' Langham asked.

The man's pudding face was dewed with sweat. He mopped his brow with a soiled handkerchief and tried to smile. 'Why do I always feel guilty at the very sight of a copper?' he said. 'They asked me all the usual questions – what I was doing between three thirty and six this morning? All I could say was that I was dead to the world, sleeping off the vino I'd had rather too much of last night. Didn't wake until Evans hammered on the door at some ungodly hour.'

'Well, the interrogation is over with, for now.'

'There'll be more?'

'Mark my word,' Langham said. 'Several sessions, until MacTaggart gets what he wants.'

Ambler sipped his coffee, then turned to glance around the room. 'Still no sign of Haggerston?'

'Not yet. Edward says he often goes for an early constitutional.'

Langham looked through the window at the gloriously sunny spring day; the lawn almost pulsed with colour and the sky was clear of cloud. It was a day for strolling through the countryside, not being cooped up inside wondering who might have murdered Suzie Reynard.

Beside him, Ambler said, 'Just a sec . . .'

'What is it?'

'Under the trees, where the vehicles are parked.'

Langham peered across the drive to where Ambler's Morris Commercial van and half a dozen cars stood. 'What about it?'

'Haggerston came in his car, a beat-up pre-war Bentley.'

'Well, it's not there now.'

'Bloody hell, Haggerston must have left . . .' Ambler looked at Langham. 'He couldn't have done for Suzie and hopped it, could he?'

'Haggerston?' Langham shook his head. 'I seriously doubt it. Do you have any idea where he might have gone?'

'Well, Haggerston House is only four miles away.'

'Curiouser and curiouser. I wouldn't mind finding out why he skedaddled like that.'

Langham glanced over his shoulder at the constable stationed before the door. 'What would you say to a quick spin over the Haggerston House, to fetch the old man back for questioning?'

'I'm game if you are.'

Langham crossed to where Maria was still consoling Cynthia Marling, drew her to one side, and said he was popping out for a breath of fresh air with Ambler.

Maria indicated Cynthia and mouthed, 'I'll stay with her, Donald.'

In due course, having gained Constable Dawson's permission to leave the hall, they hurried across the drive to Langham's Austin Healey.

TWELVE

Langham drove from the grounds of Marling Hall and turned along the lane, passing the Seven Sleepers and motoring through the village into the rolling countryside.

'Someone mentioned that it was you and Dennison who discovered Suzie's body,' Ambler said after a minute.

'Dennison made the discovery,' Langham said, 'then came for me. To be honest, I wish he hadn't.'

'Not pretty?'

Langham sighed. 'You know, it's one of those sights which you wish you could unsee – something you'll recall for the rest of your life.'

Ambler pulled a face. 'I'm sorry.'

'I thought I'd seen the last of things like that in the war. I recall—'

Ambler glanced at him. 'Yes?'

'No. It doesn't matter.' He hesitated. For some odd reason he felt compelled to tell Ambler about the incident. 'I was involved in a skirmish in Diego-Suarez, Madagascar. We were mopping up, after the battle, and I came across a Vichy soldier who'd taken a direct hit from a Sten gun. All that was left of him was his spine emerging from a pair of camouflage trousers. That's always been my defining image of war. The horror and the terrible indignity of it.'

'I had it easy, Donald. Pushing papers for the RAF on account of my dodgy kidneys.'

'I never knew that, about your condition.'

Ambler grunted. 'Blokes in the squadron soon had a nickname for me – Kidney Trouble. KT for short. It's stuck, and to this day old acquaintances still call me KT, without knowing what it stands for.'

The scriptwriter was silent for a time. 'It's just occurred to me. The film. With the leading lady dead . . . I'm sorry. You'll think me crass.'

Langham shook his head. 'Not at all. What will happen to the shoot?'

'There's been a lot of money and time invested so far, and I don't know whether insurance would cover any losses. My guess is that Dennison will find a stand-in. There are plenty of American actresses in London, or actresses who could fake an accent. And to be honest, it isn't that demanding a role.'

Langham hesitated, then asked, 'What do you know about Dennison's relationship with Suzie?'

'I must admit, I don't know whether it was just a physical attraction, or if there was anything deeper. There was a twenty-year age difference. It can't have been that easy to relate to someone young enough to be your daughter.'

Ambler indicated a fingerpost point to the village of Hambling. 'Take the turning and it's a couple of mile away. Haggerston House is a mile out of the village on the other side.'

Langham took the turning and wound down the window. He glanced at Ambler. 'You said you were stationed there during the war.'

'For almost a year.'

'Did you have much to do with Desmond Haggerston?'

'No, not much at all. He was pretty much a recluse. He must have been in his early seventies then, and remote . . . depressive.' Ambler shrugged. 'On the few occasions I did meet him, I got on rather well with him. You know what they say, Donald?'

'What's that?'

'Misery likes company.' Ambler stared ahead. 'Though to be honest I'm not surprised he was depressed. I can't begin to imagine what it must be like having to live through the murder of one's wife.'

'Did he ever speak about it?'

'Not a word. Dennison pieced together something of what happened and gave me the gist to work on. It's strange, but I've been writing the script on and off for so long, and it's undergone so many changes – in terms of events and characters – that I find it hard to know what the actual facts were.'

He pointed through the windscreen. 'Take a left here and follow the lane around to the right. We'll pass through a village, there'll be a red-brick-and-timber windmill to your right, and beyond it you'll see Haggerston House.'

They motored through a collection of tiny cottages, swung right, and a windmill – without sails – came into view. A mile or so beyond the weatherboard mill, Langham found the gateway to Haggerston House and negotiated a potholed driveway through a jungle of overgrown rhododendron. The house came into view, and it was evident that the building itself was in the same state of disrepair as the drive. Ivy shrouded much of the façade, growing over windows and creeping up over the roof.

'Looks as if it's seen better days.'

'It was falling down even during the war,' Ambler said. 'Haggerston, his wife, son and daughter lived in a few rooms in the west wing.'

Langham pointed. 'Looks as if we've struck lucky.'

Desmond Haggerston's aged Bentley, as battered as a stock-racing jalopy, stood in the moss-embroidered driveway. Langham pulled up behind the car and climbed out.

Ambler joined him, removed his jacket and stood staring up at the sad façade. 'We won't stand on ceremony, but pile straight in,' he said. 'They long ago dispensed with such luxuries as butlers and servants.'

They climbed a flight of crumbling steps and Ambler pushed through a creaking door.

'Who lives here now?' Langham asked.

'Just Haggerston and his daughter, Mary, who was a bit bats in the belfry back when I last met her during the war.'

A greater contrast to the restrained opulence of Marling Hall could not be imagined. The hallway was covered in a layer of dust and the carpet that covered the stairs was worn through to its weft and weave. Langham heard a scurrying, and turned in time to see an overweight mouse – or it might have been a rat – race along the skirting board and vanish into a crack in the wall.

'And people still live here?' he asked rhetorically.

Ambler led the way along a corridor to the west wing. A musty twilight prevailed, and the adenoid-pinching reek of damp and fungus filled the air. Langham saw a light switch and flicked it, with no effect.

Ambler whispered, like an explorer treading the sacrosanct precincts of an ancient temple, 'They should have sold it ages ago. The government made an offer just before the war, but old Haggerston couldn't bring himself to sell the country seat.'

He pushed open a door at the end of the passage and they entered a living room in minimally better state of repair than the rest of the house. An old sofa sat before the hearth, and beside the sofa stood a big radiogram.

'Desmond's room,' Ambler said.

'He doesn't seem to be at home.'

'We'll try upstairs, where his daughter lives.'

Ambler crossed the room and opened a door. A flight of narrow stairs disappeared into darkness. Here the light-switch did work, and the weak illumination of a low-wattage bulb lit a dog-leg staircase. They climbed, turned along an uncarpeted landing, and came to a door.

Ambler knocked and, on receiving a querulous, 'Who's there?', pushed open the door.

Langham's first surprise was the dazzling sunlight that burst into the room from a pair of long windows, illuminating a spartan living room not dissimilar in layout to the one below: a mangy sofa sat before the hearth, and in place of a radiogram stood a big television set.

His second surprise was the appearance of an old woman seated in an armchair by the window. Ambler's mention of Haggerston's daughter had brought to mind a woman in her fifties, but the diminutive woman ensconced in the high wing-backed armchair appeared to be much older. She wore an ankle-length lace dress that might have once been white but was now grey with dust, and she peered at her unwanted guests through a pair of half-moon reading glasses. Langham was reminded of no one so much as Miss Haversham.

Langham gripped Ambler's arm. 'His daughter?' he whispered.

Ambler nodded. 'I know.'

The woman lowered the book she was reading. 'Who're you?'

Ambler advanced, smiling. 'We're friends of your father, Mary. I'm Terrence, Terry Ambler. This is my good friend Donald Langham. We're looking for Desmond.'

'My father's not here. Try over at Marling. And when you find him, tell him that I want some money. Five shillings will do. Then I can go down to the village and buy some bread and milk and a bit of cheese. We're all out of groceries and I haven't eaten since yesterday. Tell him I need five shillings, Mr . . . Mr . . .?'

'Ambler. We met a long time ago, Mary, during the war. I was stationed here.'

She peered at him. 'Ambler? I recall an Ambler. KT! They called you KT for some reason. You always wanted to be a writer.'

Ambler smiled. 'That's right, I did.'

'And did you succeed, might I ask?'

Ambler smiled. 'Well, I've written a few things, a few books, the odd radio play and a film or two.' As if to deflect attention from what he perceived to be his own lack of success, he said, 'My friend here is a well-known writer. Donald writes crime novels.'

Mary Haggerston transferred her scrutiny to Langham. 'Crime novels, hm? So no doubt you'll be wanting the story?'

'I'm sorry? The story?'

'Don't come the innocent with me, young man. The story. The only story. The murder of my mother.'

'No, not at all. We came to see your father.'

'Don't lie, young man. I know what you want. I've had your type here before. Writers and reporters from the papers, raking over the past.' She smiled at Langham, a crafty light in her eyes. 'I'll tell you the tale, for five shillings. Five shillings for bread, milk and cheese. I'll tell you what happened.'

'I don't really—' he began.

'I'll tell you anyway, but I'll want the money!'

'Humour her,' Ambler whispered.

Langham nodded. He smiled at Mary. 'Very well.'

He moved to the window as Mary Haggerston began speaking, her words providing a soundtrack to the sunlit scene of the over-grown garden and a rambling, dilapidated greenhouse.

'We were never a happy family, Mr Langham. My mother and father always seemed to be bickering about something or other. The house didn't help, of course. It was falling down around our ears. As soon as my father had repaired one part of the place, another would collapse. He was all for selling the place, but my mother wouldn't hear of it.' She drew a sigh. 'I think that when I came along I was a great disappointment to my parents. My father wanted a boy, you see, a son and heir, and they got me. But then, a few years later, imagine their joy when my brother Nicholas was born.'

Langham glanced at the old woman. She was dabbing her eyes with a silk kerchief.

'And imagine their heartbreak,' she went on in a frail voice, 'when Nicholas turned out as he did. The pregnancy had been difficult, and Nicholas was premature. It was a miracle he survived. This was back in 1900, so to say that healthcare was basic would be an understatement. My parents were devastated. As for me . . . children don't have the prejudices of adults, or the concerns about what people think. I loved my brother for what he was, a beautiful, loving child.'

She paused again, for longer this time. Down in the riotous garden, a lone magpie hopped along a weed-choked pathway between overgrown beds, pecking at insects. The bird reminded Langham of his dead wife, Jane; she had been superstitious to a fault. Every time she had seen a lone magpie, she had called out, 'One for sorrow,' saluted it, and added, 'Good day, Mr Magpie,' in order to ward off bad luck. If she saw two magpies she would be overjoyed. 'Two for luck!'

Langham had reviled her superstition but had held his tongue.

'My childhood here was idyllic,' Miss Haggerston went on, 'playing with my brother in the garden during the long summers. When the Great War came, my father went away, and when he returned he seemed even more . . . morose, withdrawn. Anyway, he came back and got a job in London, in insurance. I went away to college, then found a job as a legal secretary in London. I was working when . . . when it happened.'

Langham saw movement down in the garden. The grounds were divided into what, long ago, must have been separate gardens divided by laurel hedges and bisected by gravel pathways. Over the years the gardens had become overgrown and had merged into a single, unkempt jungle. A figure appeared on one of the paths, briefly, before disappearing behind a bank of shrubbery.

'It was a bitter winter's day, just before Christmas,' the old lady went on. 'My mother was in the knot garden – it's still there, even now: it's away to the right, beside the towering oak.'

Langham found the oak, with a hexagon of ornamental flower beds beside it.

'It's the only part of the garden,' she said, 'that my father keeps up with, in memory of my mother.'

She dabbed her eyes, then went on. 'Apparently my mother and father had been in the garden that Saturday morning, discussing something about the house. As ever, they disagreed: father wanted to turn the house into a hotel, but my mother – she was rather a shy, insular person – really didn't want a horde of guests traipsing around the place. My father left her in the garden and returned to the house to work in his study. Nicholas must have overheard my mother and father arguing. He always took my father's side in any argument, trying to win his respect, his affection. Might as well have attempted to get blood from a stone. Nicholas must have taken a rifle from the room beneath the stairs, went out into the garden and confronted my mother. They argued and . . . and then he shot her once, in the chest. She died instantly. Nicholas was found a little later, playing with the rifle in the woods behind the house, and singing to himself.'

She drew a breath. 'Such a long time ago,' she said. 'What, over twenty-five years? I returned from London immediately to find the house . . . transformed. My mother dead, my brother arrested, my father beside himself and refusing to come out of his study. Nicholas, my poor, gentle little brother, was found guilty of murder and – and taken from me. My father was never the same again.'

Langham could only murmur, inadequately, 'I'm sorry.'

'It was obvious that my father was unable to look after himself, so I resigned my job in London and came back to Haggerston House to run the place and look after him, and I have been here ever since.'

Langham again detected movement far below, and someone appeared in the knot garden beside the oak; he recognized the tall, stooping, melancholic figure of Desmond Haggerston. The old man sat down on a wooden bench beside a rose bush, leaned forward and held his head in his hands.

Langham gestured to Ambler, who joined him at the window. Langham pointed to Haggerston in the garden, murmuring, 'We'd better go and ask him to return with us.'

Mary Haggerston said, 'There, now that you have the story for whichever scurrilous little rag you scribble for, might I trouble you for the promised five shillings, Mr Langham?'

He knew the futility of trying to persuade her that he wasn't a reporter, and withdrew a ten shilling note from his wallet. He handed it to the old woman, who clutched the note to her chest with bony fingers.

'And now, if I hurry, I can catch the village shop before it closes. Can you see yourselves out, gentlemen?'

Ambler led the way downstairs to a conservatory and out through a shattered glass door into the wilderness of the garden.

Langham said, 'Poor woman . . . to lose her mother, and then her brother. I take it he received a death sentence?'

Ambler nodded, pointing to a tunnel that burrowed through masses of hawthorn. 'A death sentence – commuted to life imprisonment due to diminished responsibility.' He tapped his head. 'He served a few years at Broadmoor, then was transferred to a loony bin near Hunstanton, where he's been to this day.'

They emerged on a pathway and Ambler looked left and right. 'This way,' he said, pointing to their right. He plunged down an overgrown path.

Langham batted a frond aside. 'This reminds me of reconnaissance missions I made in Madagascar, Terry. Only back then we had machetes.'

They came to the thick-boled oak tree and Ambler led the way into the knot garden. Langham looked across to the seat Desmond Haggerston had occupied – but there was no sign of the old man.

'He's vamoosed,' Ambler said.

Langham shielded his eyes from the sun and turned around. 'He could be anywhere in all this.'

'He's probably gone back to the house,' Ambler said. 'Let's sit down a while. I need a breather.'

Langham sat on a bench beside the scriptwriter and looked around the garden. 'So, this is where Victoria Haggerston was shot, back in 'thirty-one.'

Ambler indicated a bed, bursting with overgrown herbs, at the far end of the hexagonal garden. 'Right there, with a massive gunshot wound to her chest.' He pointed beyond the grounds to the distant treetops. 'And Nicholas Haggerston was found in the woods, fondling the rifle.'

Something caught Langham's eye a few yards away. He crossed the garden and picked up a small silver hip flask, its front dented.

'That's Desmond's,' Ambler said.

'Empty. Looks as if he was drinking, maybe flung it across the garden . . .'

He slipped the flask into his pocket and resumed his seat beside Ambler. He was about to remark how beautiful the garden could have been, with a bit of care and attention, when he heard the sound of a car engine starting up. 'Dammit. That can only be Haggerston's Bentley.'

Ambler slapped his palms down on his corduroys. 'Just when I was enjoying a rest . . . The old duffer's certainly giving us the run around.'

They left the knot garden and battled through the undergrowth until they came to the house, then found a pathway and followed it around the building, emerging at last into the sunlight.

Haggerston's Bentley was no longer parked in the drive.

'Come on,' Langham said. 'Let's get back to the hall.'

They climbed into his car, its interior sweltering from having stood in the sunlight. Langham wound down his window and gunned the engine. Halfway down the drive, he slowed as a tiny, tottering figure came into view.

'Mary,' Ambler said. 'Off to fetch her bread and cheese.'

'But it's a mile or more to the village . . .' Langham slowed down and called through the window, 'Hop in. We'll give you a lift to the shop.'

She beamed at him, clutching a hessian bag to her chest. 'Why, that's very kind of you, young man,' she said, climbing into the back seat.

Langham drove into the village, then said he'd wait for her while she did her shopping and drive her back to the house.

'That is most considerate of you. I've been dreaming of my cheese on toast all morning.'

Five minutes later she emerged with her bag full of provisions and Langham drove her back to Haggerston House.

She was silent until they turned into the driveway, then said, 'Of course, I don't think for a minute that Nicholas shot my mother, Mr Langham.'

He glanced over his shoulder at her. 'You don't?'

'Of course not. Would you like to know what I think happened?'

'By all means.'

'I think my mother took her own life, what with the worry about the house, her failing marriage and Nicholas's condition. I think it all became far too much for her, and one morning she took the gun and shot herself. Then Nicholas found her body and, beside himself, picked up the rifle and took it into the woods.'

They arrived at the house and he braked.

Mary Haggerston smiled, thanked him for the ride, and tottered up the steps.

'Well, well . . .' Langham said, turning the car and moving off down the drive.

'Fantasy,' Ambler commented. 'She might like to think her brother is innocent, but it certainly wasn't suicide. The experts agreed that Victoria Haggerston was shot at a distance of a few feet.'

Langham accelerated along the lane to Marling Hall.

THIRTEEN

Maria's interview lasted not quite five minutes. She could tell them nothing other than the fact that she had spent a night interrupted by Mr Haggerston's snoring and had read her manuscript from three o'clock until six, when she had finally returned to bed and slept until awakened by Donald a little after seven.

Later, when the detectives had finished questioning everyone and vacated the library, Maria returned and installed herself in a deep armchair with the manuscript she was working on. The novel was a serious treatise on the iniquities of colonialism by a distinguished lady author in her fifties, well-written but full of continuity errors. It was Maria's job to go through the manuscript and spot all the inconsistencies, but she found her attention wandering.

She thought back to her conversation with Suzie Reynard in the ballroom yesterday. The girl – as Maria thought of her, despite the fact that Suzie had been barely five years her junior – had exuded a life-affirming vitality, and Maria found it impossible to believe that anyone could have wanted to murder her. The fact that the killer was more than likely resident in the hall only added to the atmosphere of apprehension that hung about the place.

She recalled Suzie's breathless suggestion that they should liberate a bottle of gin and dress up in the ballroom like a pair of naughty schoolgirls, and fought unsuccessfully to hold back her tears.

The door at the far end of the room opened and Maria quickly pulled her compact from her handbag and powdered her cheeks.

She turned to see the tall, broad-shouldered figure of Chuck Banning standing with endearing diffidence halfway down the room. 'I'm sorry . . . I didn't mean to interrupt—'

'You're not interrupting.' She gestured to the manuscript on the table before her. 'I couldn't concentrate on work, anyway.'

Banning drew up an armchair and indicated the manuscript. 'You wrote that?' he asked in a tone suggestive of awe.

'One of my clients,' she explained. 'I'm her agent.'

He smiled self-deprecatingly. 'I trained as a carpenter back in Idaho, but I always wanted to act. To be honest, I'm not big on books. I was never that good at school. I must admit I even find it hard to read scripts. You must think I'm a real bozo.'

'We all have our strengths. I can't act to save my life.'

He shrugged his vast shoulders. 'It comes naturally to me, so in a way I feel a fraud. Anyway,' he went on, 'I just came to thank you.'

'To thank me?'

'For being so kind to Cynthia earlier. All this . . . it's hit her really hard.'

'It was the least I could do,' she murmured. 'You're close to Cynthia, aren't you?'

Banning stared down at his big, carpenter's hands and shrugged. 'She's a fine woman, Miss Dupré. I don't think she's appreciated.'

Maria watched the young man, wondering whom he thought might not appreciate Cynthia. She ventured, 'In what way?'

'Oh, in every way. In the way she runs this house, almost single-handedly, the way she bears Edward's—' He stopped suddenly, reddening. 'I'm sorry. I shouldn't speak out of turn. Edward's been a fine host. It's terrible that something like this has happened.'

Maria said, 'Did you know Suzie very well?'

'We met for the first time in London a couple of weeks back. I didn't know she and Douglas were . . . that is, that they were together. I made a fine chump of myself, asking her out for a drink.'

'What did she say?'

Banning half smiled at the recollection. 'I think she found it amusing – found my naivety amusing, that is. She let me down gently and said that if she were ten years younger she'd have taken me up on the offer, but that if she had a drink with me now, "Dougy" would probably have something to say about it.' He went on, almost wistfully, 'She was awful sweet about it, though.'

'She seemed a terribly sweet girl,' Maria said.

Banning was shaking his head as if in bewilderment. 'I don't understand it, Miss Dupré. Beats me who could have killed her like that. Shot dead while she was lying in bed? Who would've wanted her dead?'

'I'm as shocked as you are. I – I was talking with Suzie just yesterday afternoon . . .' She was unable to go on.

'Jeez.' He sighed. 'And I thought when I got the part and flew to England . . .'

'Didn't you say yesterday that it's your first time back here since you were a child?'

'That's right. Not that I remember anything about the place. I was a babe in arms when we left for the States.'

'So, what do you think of England?'

'After California, it's kind of small and cramped. And the people . . . well, they seem so small and cramped, too, and grey. You know, I was on the Underground last week, and I looked around trying to see a smiling face, and I didn't see a single one.'

'The war might have ended more than ten years ago, but people are still trying to get over the collective trauma.'

'Don't get me wrong,' Banning hurried on, 'I love the place. Everyone's been so kind and friendly, and this pile . . .' He gestured at the house, shaking his head in wonder. 'I keep thinking once I'm rich and famous I'll buy a pad like this, maybe closer to London, though.'

She smiled at his gauche optimism.

He climbed to his feet, and she was conscious of him towering over her. 'Well, I'll let you get back to work. And thank you again for being so considerate with Cynthia. It's been nice chatting, Miss Dupré.'

'It's been nice talking to you, too.'

She watched him stride from the room, reflecting on what he'd said about Cynthia, then picked up the manuscript and continued reading.

Half an hour later, having completed a chapter in which one character talked to another for fifteen pages about foreign policy in Kenya, Maria admitted defeat and set the novel aside.

It was dark and cool in the library, and beyoned the mullioned windows the sunlight beckoned. She returned the manuscript to the bedroom, then made her way outside via the conservatory.

She strolled through the kitchen garden – twice the size of any garden she had seen in London – and out the other side to the greensward that rolled towards the distant lake. She'd seen Donald head off in his car earlier with Terry Ambler, and suspected they were escaping for another pint at the local pub.

She found a great fallen tree trunk and sat down, crossing her legs and staring at the shimmering lake.

She laughed when she thought of Donald returning later, perhaps a little tipsy, and slowly filling his pipe and puffing it until it caught, then smiling across at her and winking in quiet amusement.

'Care to tell me what's so funny?'

The sudden question made her jump. 'Oh! I was miles away!'

Varla Cartier smiled. 'Sorry for sneaking up on you like that. I saw you sitting there, smiling to yourself . . .' She raised a big, expensive-looking camera on a strap around her neck. 'Mind if I take a snap or two?'

Maria self-consciously pushed a hand through her hair and arranged her cashmere cardigan. She never liked having her picture taken – unable to look at the result, even though others told her she was photogenic – but she relented now and did her best to smile as Varla moved around her and took half a dozen shots.

'Is photography a hobby of yours?' she asked when Varla finished and sat down beside her.

'I've been snapping for so long it's a part of my life. Back home I have a photographic record of my existence that'll prove a treasure trove for my future biographer.'

Maria glanced at the woman; something in her tone suggested she was being ironic.

Varla smiled. Her thin white face might once have been beautiful, but these days a liberal application of cosmetics was required to make it presentable. The woman's dark eyes, Maria thought, harboured a cynical light.

'Has anyone said that you should be in the movies?'

Maria smiled. 'Oddly enough Suzie told me that just yesterday.'

'But I mean it,' Varla said. 'Hollywood's full of women with Suzie Reynard's kind of good looks – anaemic, waif-like blondes. But sultry, smouldering glamour is quite another thing. You should take acting lessons and get yourself an agent.'

'From everything I've read about Hollywood,' Maria said, 'I think I'd be happier as a literary agent in London.'

'Maybe you're right. Hollywood is a cesspit. Look where it got Suzie.'

Maria stared at the woman. 'But surely her death had nothing to do with Hollywood?' She must have sounded shocked.

Varla laughed. 'No? Think again. She was aiming to get hitched to Dennison, right? That was her big mistake.'

'In what way?'

'Dennison's a gold-plated sadist. He eats women for breakfast – and strays like Suzie especially – spits 'em out and moves on to the next one. Only,' she went on, 'he's drawn the line at shooting them dead, until now.'

'Surely you don't think . . .?'

Varla held her hands up, palms outwards. 'I'm only conjecturing. But doesn't it look a bit odd to you? Dennison goes off for a midnight hike, claiming insomnia, and someone enters the trailer and shoots Reynard? C'mon. Suzie must have riled Dennison and good, the way I see it.'

The actress turned and stared back at the house. 'Look at it. Idyllic in the sunlight. But you know what? I'm beginning to hate the place. It's, what's the word, malign?'

Maria frowned at her. 'Surely you can't blame the venue for incidents enacted within it?'

'No? I'm not so sure, girl. There's a nasty atmosphere among the cast that wasn't there when we met up in London.'

Maria said, 'I think that might be down to you all getting to know each other . . .' and she wondered if Varla's cynicism was rubbing off.

'And what about our hosts, the fallen war hero and his

long-suffering, pious wife? Hatred positively crackles between them. I feel sorry for Edward. Cynthia acts all holier than thou, but there's no hypocrite like a religious hypocrite, right?'

'You mean how she is running after young Banning?'

Varla laughed and climbed to her feet. 'Let's stroll back to the house, and I'll tell you a little story all about our Mother Superior.'

Maria stood up. Varla linked arms with her – an intimacy Maria found discomfiting – and said, 'Cynthia's fling with Chuck isn't the first time she's bedded a Yank, you know?'

FOURTEEN

'Look who got here before us,' Terrence Ambler said as they motored up the drive.

Langham swung into the parking area beneath the elms and braked beside Haggerston's Bentley. They climbed out and strolled towards the house.

The Bentley was not the only recent arrival. A black police van was drawn up beside the hall and half a dozen men in navy blue boiler suits moved back and forth between the van and Dennison's caravan.

'Forensic experts,' Langham said. 'Going over the murder scene with the proverbial toothcomb.'

Ambler stopped and peered through a mullioned window. 'Hello . . . I wonder what's going on in there?'

Langham peered into the library and made out three figures.

Detective Inspector MacTaggart was pacing back and forth, gesticulating from time to time. His deputy, Ferrars, was propped on one elbow against the mantelpiece. The third figure, seated in an armchair and facing the window with his head in his hands, was Desmond Haggerston.

'Looks as if they're giving him a right old third degree,' Ambler said.

Langham led the way into the hall. 'I'll go and find Maria.'

He checked their room first, to no avail, and was coming down the stairs when he passed Evans the butler on the way up. 'I don't suppose you've seen Miss Dupré on your travels?'

'As a matter of fact, sir, I have. She was out by the lake five minutes ago with Miss Cartier.'

'Good man.'

He continued down the staircase and was passing through the hallway when Edward Marling wheeled himself from the drawing room. 'Donald, cook has made a Sunday roast, serving at one.'

'Excellent. Excuse me while I round up Maria, won't you?'

He moved along the corridor towards the rear of the house. He found the postern door leading into a kitchen garden and, beyond, the rolling greensward dotted with oak and elm.

He made out two tiny figures in the distance, strolling towards the house. Seen from a hundred yards away, they might have been sisters – both of them tall and striking, with cowls of dark hair and Mediterranean good looks. Only when they drew closer did the differences become apparent, and Maria's beauty pointed up the fact that the older woman was well past the first flush of youth; beside Maria, Varla Cartier appeared careworn and haggard.

'Maria was telling me the story of how she landed such a dashing husband-to-be,' Varla said.

Maria pulled an odd face, as if her recollection of their conversation bore no relation to Varla's.

'And there I was,' Langham said, 'thinking it was me who'd bagged the top prize. Hey-ho.'

'Excuse me while I go in search of a drink,' Varla said, and strode off.

'I was taking a stroll,' Maria told him, linking arms, 'when Varla pounced and starting chatting.'

'About?' he asked as they strolled towards the house.

'Various things, but I told her nothing about my "dashing hubby-to-be".'

Langham laughed. 'I think she was being ironic with that line. I get the impression she doesn't like men that much.'

They entered the house and made their way through the labyrinthine corridors.

'Well, she seems to think that Douglas Dennison shot Suzie,' Maria said.

'She does?'

'And she also told me something very interesting about Cynthia Marling.'

'Did she, indeed?'

Maria was about to continue when a door opened suddenly and three figures stepped from the library: MacTaggart and Ferrars escorted a shuffling Desmond Haggerston along the corridor. The latter avoided their eyes, even going so far as to avert his face. He looked like a man being led to the gallows.

At Langham's enquiring glance, MacTaggart paused, and murmured, 'We're taking Mr Haggerston in for further questioning, but we'll be back in the morning. Sergeant Briscoe will be on duty overnight.'

Langham watched the trio retreat along the passage.

'We should tell them that they are wasting their time,' Maria said. 'Mr Haggerston has a snoring alibi. He kept me awake from three until six last night.'

'You were telling me about what Varla said,' Langham reminded her.

'I'll tell you later,' Maria said as Terrence Ambler and Edward Marling appeared around a corner.

'Joining us for a spot of lunch?' Ambler said, and led the way to the dining hall, where Chuck Banning and Sir Humphrey were already seated at the table.

'Cynthia won't be dining,' Edward said as he manoeuvred his wheelchair into position at the head of the table. 'She has one of her "heads". And Varla excused herself on account of having to watch her figure. We'll be deprived of Douglas's company, too – he rarely "does" lunch, as he says.'

Chuck Banning laughed. 'Varla needs to eat more, not less.'

'Never say no to a good square meal,' Sir Humphrey declared. 'Keeps body and soul together, what?'

Evans and the maid served a traditional Sunday lunch of roast beef, Yorkshire pudding, mashed potatoes and vegetables, followed by spotted dick – 'But how can you call a dessert "spotted dick"!' Maria laughed – washed down with a couple of bottles of red wine.

Later, as they were taking coffee, Edward leaned forward and arranged his place mat so that it was parallel with the edge of the table. It was another example of the man's obsessive exactitude Langham had noticed at dinner last night.

'Before the war,' Edward said, 'we'd take the car across to Reston and dine at the Swan. These days, however, we hardly get out. I take the train down to London once in a blue moon, but it's all a bit of a palaver.'

'It must be hard,' Ambler said. 'Does Cynthia drive?'

'That's just the point, she doesn't. I've heard one can get specially adapted cars these days, but to be honest the expense would be prohibitive. The hall's a wonderful place, but its upkeep drains the bally funds. It cost me an arm and a leg to get a lift installed just after the war, so I could get around the place.'

Sir Humphrey said, 'Next time you're down in the Smoke, Edward, we must meet up. Tell you what, why don't I take you to Twickers? You're a rugby man, aren't you?'

Edward smiled. 'I played rugger at Oxford, and kept it up before the war. Ran, too. Five thousand metres and the occasional marathon. Hell, I miss being active . . .'

He replaced his cup on the dead centre of the mat and smiled around the group. 'You know, even after I underwent my fifth operation, back in 'forty-six, I thought that one day they might have me walking again.'

'But that was ten years ago,' Ambler said. 'Haven't you thought of getting a specialist to examine you again? They can perform wonders with new techniques these days, you know.'

'Every year, Terrence, every year since the war I've had a consultant from Harley Street look me over. You see, the injury was so close to my spinal cord that they couldn't remove the bullet for fear of doing even more damage. My lower vertebrae were done for, but a few strands of cord were still intact, so that I don't embarrass myself in the bathroom. Every year they take a gander, shake their heads and say, "No can do, old boy. Grin and bear it." Until last year, that is.'

Maria leaned forward. 'Last year? What happened?'

'My consultant knew a specialist chappie who'd pioneered a new operative technique. Upshot: he thought he could remove the bullet and possibly – he stressed, *possibly* – restore some mobility to my legs.'

Maria made a sympathetic face.

'You can't imagine the difference that made, even the slightest chance that I might be able to walk again. For a few months I was in seventh heaven. Cyn – ever the pessimist – warned me again and again not to get my hopes up, but did I listen? So I went into the operation full of hope and misplaced optimism.'

He paused, sipped his coffee, then reached into the pocket of his blazer and pulled something out.

He threw it up into the air and caught it in his palm; a small golden object glinting in the sunlight slanting through the window.

'They succeeded in removing the bullet – I keep it as a memento – but they could do nothing to get me walking again. I must admit I hit rock bottom. I was bedridden in hospital for a month, and wondered how I'd end it all when I got back to the hall. Shoot

myself or take a rope and . . . I know, I know, I was in no worse
a situation than I'd been in before the operation. I really shouldn't
have banked on a successful outcome. Cyn was right, blast her. I
endured a month or two of black moods . . .'

'And then?' Maria murmured.

'And then,' Edward said, 'I came through the other side. I woke
up one morning and the sun was shining and I heard the birdsong,
and it came to me that I really had had one hell of an adventurous
war, and if I couldn't regain what I had, then perhaps I could
relive those times by writing my memoirs. And for the past
year that's what I've been doing. And,' he finished, 'it's certainly
helped.'

'I'll drink to that!' Sir Humphrey said, hoisting his glass.

Langham was helping himself to a second cup of coffee a few
minutes later when the doors at the far end of the room burst open
and Douglas Dennison stood on the threshold, staring at the diners
with a face like thunder.

A silence descended over the gathering as everyone stared at the
director. Edward, with his back to the door, manhandled his wheelchair around in order to face the door.

Dennison had something clutched in his right fist – a rectangular
card, Langham, saw. His gaze raked everyone around the table and
came to rest on Chuck Banning.

'You low down little shit,' Dennison growled.

Banning's square jaw dropped and he coloured. 'I'm sorry . . .?'
he stammered, nonplussed.

Dennison advanced into the room, heading for the young man.
'How the hell could you?' the director yelled. He waved the card.
'What did Suzie ever do to you, hey?'

Banning pushed his chair from the table, as if preparing to run.
'I – I don't know what you're talking about . . .'

'This!' Dennison said, holding up what Langham saw now was
a postcard. 'So Suzie tells you where to get off, and you get her
back like this? And you didn't even have the guts to sign it!'

Banning looked around the table, desperately, and then back at
the director. 'Like I said, Doug, I don't know what the hell . . .'

Edward Marling said, 'Just what is all this about, Douglas?'

Dennison swung towards Edward, his face red with rage. He
waved the card again. 'I was in Suzie's room, going through her
things. I found this, screwed up in the corner.'

Chuck Banning half rose from his seat. 'But—' he began.

As if triggered by the word, Dennison turned and launched himself at the young man. He swung his right fist, dropping the postcard and missing Banning's jaw by an inch. Banning ducked back like a practised prizefighter and Dennison came at him again, this time aiming a roundhouse at the actor's midriff. He connected and Banning went sprawling.

Langham leaped to his feet and rounded the table.

Dennison stood over Banning, breathing hard and staring at the young man in unabated rage. 'Get up so I can hit you again, you little—'

Terrence Ambler jumped to his feet and called out, 'It wasn't Chuck!'

His words had the effect of stopping everyone in the act of moving: Langham came to a halt, staring at the scriptwriter; Banning lay on the floor, a protective hand raised before his face; Dennison looked up, scowling at Ambler. 'What the hell did you say?'

Ambler faced the director, having picked up the offending post-card; he held it aloft. 'I said it wasn't Chuck who sent Suzie the card. It was me.'

'Why, you little—!'

Before Langham could move to intervene, Dennison took two strides towards Ambler. The blow was lightning fast: Ambler's head jerked back and he cried out, blood spurting from his nose. Dennison would have pressed his advantage, but Langham dived at the director, grabbed a handful of shirt front, and pushed Dennison away from the table and up against the panelling.

'Calm it!'

'I'll beat the little shit halfway to—' Dennison snarled.

'I said calm it.'

The director struggled, his face empurpled. Langham fought to keep him pinned against the wall. He was reminded of an incident in his youth when a pit bull terrier had attacked a friend: he'd wrestled with the savage animal and pressed it to the ground until a couple of adults had intervened. Dennison had the same snarling, unreasoning desire to do violence as had the dog.

Langham pressed his forearm into the director's neck. 'Hitting Terry will do absolutely no good, Dennison. Do you really want to be hauled off to the cells for assault?'

'Nothing'd gimme greater pleasure, Langham!' Dennison snapped, but Langham felt the anger drain from the man, little by little.

Sir Humphrey had moved across to Ambler and was helping him up from the floor, pressing a napkin to the man's bloody nose. As Langham watched, he led Ambler from the dining hall.

Dennison seemed to deflate, and Langham removed his forearm from the director's throat.

Dennison looked across at Chuck Banning and nodded. 'I guess I owe you an apology, Chuck. No hard feelings, huh?'

Before Banning had time to reply, the door at the far end of the dining hall opened; Cynthia hurried over to the table, wringing her hands. She looked from her husband to Langham and the others, her face ashen.

'Just a little misunderstanding, Cynthia—' Edward Marling began.

She interrupted the explanation. 'Detective Inspector MacTaggart has just telephoned.' She paused and swallowed, as if to steady her voice, then went on, 'Desmond Haggerston has confessed to killing poor Suzie Reynard. His fingerprints were found on the murder weapon.'

A stunned silence greeted her words.

Langham looked across at Maria, who was shaking her head. 'But surely that's not possible?' she said.

Dinner that evening was taken in almost total silence.

The cook had prepared a cold chicken salad, but Langham ate without enthusiasm or appetite. Cynthia had absented herself from the meal – taking a sandwich in her room, Edward reported – and Douglas Dennison was absent, too. Varla Cartier hardly touched her food but compensated by drinking almost a whole bottle of wine. Chuck Banning tried to initiate conversation once or twice; his attempts were greeted with silence and he grinned uneasily and applied himself to the meal.

Terrence Ambler crept into the dining hall five minutes after the meal had begun, took his place in abject silence and ate without a word.

Sir Humphrey, half-cut even before he sloshed a generous measure of red wine into his glass, seemed oblivious to the funereal atmosphere at the table.

'Well, who would have thought it, eh? Old Haggers! Y'live and learn . . . But what gets me is why the hell shoot such a pretty young thing as Suzie?'

Varla Cartier stared at the old man. 'You sound as if it'd be perfectly acceptable for him to have shot someone who was old and raddled?'

'But Suzie, with all her life ahead of her . . .?'

Varla said, with an effective imitation of Sir Humphrey's upper-class tone, 'Put a sock in it, old man. There's a good chap.'

No one said another word for the rest of the meal.

Edward, Langham and Maria retired to the library at eight; despite the heat of the day, the big room was chilly. Edward insisted that he get Evans to light the fire, and a little later they were joined by Ambler.

The scriptwriter regarded the others and mumbled, 'I think I owe you an explanation.'

'Well,' Edward said, 'I was wondering what you wrote on that postcard.'

Ambler coloured. 'It was out of order and I should never have done it,' he muttered. 'It was a heat of the moment thing. I – I wasn't thinking straight.'

Maria leaned forward, and murmured, 'What happened, Terry?'

Ambler sighed. 'It was a few days ago. Wednesday or Thursday. I'd just had a long day with Dennison, going over some changes in the script. Later, after dinner, Suzie buttonholed me in my room. She *still* wasn't happy with her lines and demanded changes.' He fell silent, his face twisted at the recollection.

'And?' Langham prompted.

'And she threatened me.'

Edward stared at him. 'Threatened?'

'She said that if I didn't agree to the changes she wanted, then she'd get "Dougy" to sack me. And I could see that she was serious. So . . . so I made the bloody changes.'

'And then sent Suzie an abusive card,' Langham said.

Ambler gave a long sigh. 'I . . . I called her an "unconscionable little shit" and . . .'

'Go on.'

'And said,' he went on, looking up and staring at each of them in turn, 'that I hoped she died an unpleasant death. As I said, it was a heat of the moment thing, written without thinking. As soon as I'd slipped the thing beneath her door, I began to regret it.'

He rose to his feet with as much dignity as he was able to muster and said goodnight; as he was about to leave the room, he turned. 'Of course, I'll inform MacTaggart about the card at the first opportunity.'

He hurried from the room and closed the door behind him.

Edward broke the following silence. 'Well, I applaud the fellow for coming clean, as it were. I wonder what the police will make of it?'

Maria said, 'Probably very little, coming so soon after Mr Haggerston's confession.'

Edward looked at her. 'On which topic . . . I hope you don't mind my asking, but at lunch, when Cynthia informed us about Desmond's confession, you said something about it "not being possible".'

Maria nodded. 'The thing is, you see, Mr Haggerston's snoring kept me awake from around three o'clock until six.' She looked across at Langham. 'And when was Suzie killed, Donald?'

'At some point between three thirty when Dennison left the caravan, and six, when he got back and sat outside for forty minutes. If you take his statement as gospel,' he added.

'So you see,' Maria said, 'Mr Haggerston was snoring all the time between three and six. He was so loud that I had to get up and do a little work.'

Edward said, 'But what if Haggerston woke just before six, went out and shot Miss Reynard before Douglas returned to the caravan? Are you sure he was snoring right up until six o'clock?'

Maria worried her lower lip. 'Well . . . I cannot recall looking at my clock *before* six, and thinking, *Oh, the snoring has stopped.* I just recall that it was six when I went back to bed.'

'I'm playing the Devil's advocate here,' Edward said, 'but can you be one hundred per cent sure that you didn't drop off for a little while between three thirty and six? I know from experience that when I think I've spent a bad night and not slept a wink, in fact I've dropped off from time to time. Even in separate rooms, Cynthia has heard my snoring.'

Maria shook her head. 'I am certain. I did not sleep. Haggerston kept me awake all the time and I didn't drop off, even for five minutes. Even before I got up and read the manuscript I was working on, I was wide awake.'

Edward looked across at Langham. 'Did you hear Desmond's snoring?'

Langham nodded. 'He sounded like a chainsaw, though I must admit I was dead to the world and slept through most of it. I did get up around four, though, and spoke to Maria while she was reading.'

'So,' Maria said, 'if Mr Haggerston did wake up just before six, he would have had to hurry downstairs very quickly if he were to reach the caravan, shoot Suzie, and get away before Mr Dennison got back from his walk. And have you seen how slowly Mr Haggerston walks? He is like a tortoise.'

'Then how was it that his fingerprints were found on the murder weapon?' Edward asked. 'And why on earth would he confess to a crime he didn't commit?'

'That, I must admit,' Langham said, 'is one heck of a stumper.'

'And on that note,' Edward said, 'I think I'll turn in.' He bade them good night and propelled himself from the room.

Alone in the room, Langham refilled his glass and told Maria why he thought that Dennison had been the killer's target all along, and that Suzie Reynard's death had been incidental.

Maria heard him out. 'I see . . . But what if Suzie *was* the intended victim? What if Inspector MacTaggart is right, and the killer saw Dennison leave the caravan and took the opportunity to kill her?'

Langham frowned. 'It's possible, of course. But it just seems too convenient. I agree with you about Haggerston, though. I can't see him killing Suzie, even though his prints were all over the revolver.'

He stared at his drink, lost in thought. 'Oh. I've just remembered – you were going to tell me earlier something Varla told you about Cynthia.'

'And so I was.'

'Proceed.'

'Well, Varla mentioned that years ago, back in the mid-thirties, Cynthia had an affair with Douglas Dennison.'

Langham whistled. 'No kidding? That certainly puts an interesting complexion on things. Did she spill the sordid details?'

'She told me that Cynthia met Dennison while he was in London – Cynthia was a nurse, back then.'

'Just a tic. The mid-thirties? This was before she was married to Edward?'

Maria nodded. 'When I was chatting with Cynthia the other day, she mentioned that she had met Edward in 'thirty-nine and married him a couple of years later.'

'So Cynthia's fling with Dennison happened a few years before she met Edward? And . . . was it a fling, or something more serious? Did Varla know?'

'She said it was, in her own words, a "full-on, no-holds-barred, morning-noon-and-night affair".'

'I find that hard to believe of Cynthia . . . But obviously nothing came of it.'

'After six months Dennison went back to his wife in the States, some starlet he'd wed quickly and lived to regret, Varla said.'

He looked at Maria, contemplating Varla Cartier's gossip. 'I wonder if this has anything to do with Suzie's death? I can't see how they might be linked, if the killer did intend to shoot Dennison.'

'No? What if it was Cynthia, angry at what she saw as his betrayal, his desertion?'

He looked at her dubiously. 'Twenty years after the event?'

She shrugged. 'Stranger things have happened.'

He stretched and yawned. 'By crikey, I'm bushed.'

'Me too. But one thing is certain, tonight.'

'What's that?'

'I will not be kept awake by Mr Haggerston's *terr-ible* snoring.'

FIFTEEN

The following morning after breakfast, Langham made three telephone calls. The first was to a psychiatric asylum in Hunstanton, where he spoke to the chief registrar. He gave his name, mentioned that he was working on a murder investigation and asked if he might make an appointment to meet Mr Nicholas Haggerston.

The second phone call was to Ralph Ryland's home number; he spoke to his wife, Annie, and learned that Ryland had set off for Norfolk at first light.

The third call was to Detective Inspector MacTaggart at Norwich police station. He informed a desk sergeant that he had information concerning the Suzie Reynard murder case, and was told that Inspector MacTaggart was not available but would be calling at Marling Hall later that afternoon. Langham thanked the sergeant and hung up.

Maria had planned to return to London that morning – 'But there is no way I am leaving you all alone with a killer on the prowl,' she said.

When Langham tried to protest that he was hardly 'all alone', she waved this aside and said she'd ring Charles and ask for leave until Wednesday at least.

'What are you doing now?' he asked.

'I think I'll read a little more of the manuscript, Donald. You?'

'I might go and have a word with Dennison.'

Yesterday the forensic team had completed their investigations and secured the door of the caravan with a padlock, and Dennison had moved to the bedroom originally allocated to him in the hall. Langham found Evans polishing silver in the dining hall, and asked him which bedroom Dennison was occupying.

Two minutes later he stood before Dennison's door, waiting for the director to answer his knock.

He was about to leave and look for Dennison elsewhere, when the door was snatched open. 'Oh,' Dennison said, 'it's you.'

The director was unshaven and his shirt was open to reveal a mat of grey chest hair. The way he peered at Langham through slitted eyes suggested he was suffering a hangover.

Behind him the room was in disarray, littered with suitcases and piles of clothing.

'I'd like a word, if you're free.'

'Take a seat, if you can find one. Shift the stuff from the chair.'

Langham moved a pile of books and folders, placed them on the carpet beside the chair, and sat down.

Dennison paced up and down before the window overlooking the driveway. 'If you came here demanding an apology, Langham, think again. I might have gone off the deep end last night, but I was provoked.'

'It's always wise to make sure who you're accusing, before you wade in.'

'I still wish I'd landed another one on Ambler. You should've read what he wrote.'

'Terry mentioned it last night. He apologized. He's going to tell MacTaggart, today, just to make things clear. No doubt he'll apologize to you, too – but promise me not to hit him.'

Dennison grunted. 'I'll try to restrain myself.'

The telephone bell rang, sounding muffled. The director rummaged under a pile of clothing until he dislodged the receiver and snatched it up. 'Yes? No, not now. Look, I'm tied up at the moment. I'll call you back later, OK?'

He hung up, and said to Langham, 'I've been on the damned thing all morning, talking to the backers in London and a casting agency.'

'And?'

'The show goes on, Langham. I found someone to take Suzie's part. New England girl just finished a run in the West End. Negotiated a fee over the phone. She's coming up for a read through on Thursday.'

'That's good news.'

'Yeah. The not so good news is that the press is on the case.'

'I thought it wouldn't take them long.'

'They've got wind of Suzie's death and plastered it all over the front pages. Edward was just saying that he's already turned away a dozen reporters. Thing is, I don't want to pay for security. I'm on a tight budget as it is. Things like shelling out for security skims off the cream.'

Langham nodded. He wondered if Dennison's *the-show-must-go-on* bluster, his talk of finances so soon after the death of his lover, was his way of coping.

'When we spoke on Saturday,' Langham said, 'and I mentioned I was a friend of Suzie's . . .'

The director stopped his pacing and looked at Langham, his head cocked. 'Yeah?'

'I was being sparing with the truth.'

'That's what I like about you Brits, you don't use one word when ten will do. You mean you lied?'

Langham sat back and smiled. 'I wouldn't go so far as to phrase it in quite that way.'

'There you go again! A dozen words to say what you really meant, which was *no* . . . So, out with it, Langham, using short sentences. If you weren't Suzie's buddy, then what the hell are you?'

'I'm a private investigator whom Suzie hired on Friday.'

'There, that wasn't so painful, was it? So . . . what did Suzie tell you?'

'Just that she was worried about you. She said you were under some kind of threat.'

Dennison turned and stared through the window, muttering under his breath, '*Jesus Christ.*'

'She was right, wasn't she?'

Dennison sat down on the bed. 'Yeah,' he said. 'Yeah, the kid was right.' He looked up. 'So the killer came into the trailer for me, and it was Suzie's bad luck that I couldn't sleep and went for a hike.'

Langham nodded. 'That's the way it looks to me.'

'But what I don't get, Langham, is that the cops arrested Desmond last night, and he went and confessed. But Desmond wasn't the kind of guy who would've tried to kill me – and he wouldn't have done that to Suzie. So, what gives? They lay into him and beat a confession out of the old bastard?'

'I don't think so. But I haven't worked out, yet, why he did confess.'

Dennison looked at Langham with bleary eyes. 'So, if he didn't do it, who did?'

'I was hoping you'd be able to shed some light on that.'

The director dropped his gaze to the carpet.

'Who's threatening you?' Langham asked.

'I honestly don't have a clue.'

'But someone *is* threatening you?'

'Yeah.'

'Can you be more specific? What kind of threats have you had? Letters, telephone calls? Was the hare the first—?'

'No,' Dennison snapped, sarcastically, 'it happens all the time. I get all kinds of wildlife nailed to my property.' He shook his head and sighed. 'Look, I'm sorry. This is eating me up.'

'I understand,' Langham said. 'But if you can tell me anything about the threats, just what they were and when they came . . .'

Dennison stood up and walked around the bed. He opened a leather suitcase and pulled out a thick manila envelope.

He crossed to Langham and dropped it in his lap, a tic agitating his right eye.

Langham opened the envelope, withdrew its contents, and spread them across his lap.

He grimaced. 'Not nice.'

'You're a master of the understatement, Langham.'

The half dozen six by six black-and-white photographs showed a variety of dead animals. They were not, in Langham's opinion, stock footage, but taken impromptu by the photographer: several were roadkill, rabbits and pheasants plastered on tarmac, while one showed a fallow deer by the roadside, its entrails spilled across the grass verge.

Langham shuffled through the pictures, examining the animals and the backgrounds. He checked the postmark on the envelope, but it was smudged and all he could discern was that it was British. The address was typewritten, to Douglas Dennison, c/o Marling Hall, Norfolk.

'Did they all come at once?' Langham asked.

'No. One by one. The first two while I was in LA.'

'Do you still have the original envelopes of those two?'

'No, they're with a PI I hired in Hollywood.'

'Did you notice the postmarks of those two?'

Dennison nodded. 'British, from London.'

'How long ago did the first picture arrive?'

'Just over a couple of months ago.'

'And after the first one, how regularly did they arrive?'

'Roughly every week.'

Langham stared down at the photographs. 'So, you had two delivered to you in Hollywood, and two here? What about the others?'

'Two were sent to the hotel I was staying at in London.'

'So whoever sent them knew your itinerary pretty well.'

Tight-lipped, Dennison nodded.

Langham thought back to his original meeting with Suzie Reynard. 'Suzie mentioned that soon after you arrived at the hall, you had a phone call after which you seemed . . . troubled.'

Dennison was pacing the room again. 'That had nothing to do with it, Langham. I was talking to one of the backers in London. I wanted an extension to the shoot, but he said the budget wouldn't allow for that. I wasn't happy.'

'So the only direct threats you've received are the photographs, and the hare on the caravan door. Anything else?'

'No. That's all.'

'And you've no idea, no inkling at all, what all this is about?'

Dennison turned and faced Langham. With his shoulders hunched and his fists clenched, he looked like a compact, muscle-bound middleweight up against the ropes. 'I've no idea at all, Langham.'

'I take it you've shown the photographs to the police?'

Dennison's silence, as he turned and stared through the window, was answer enough.

Langham sighed. 'How on earth, if you don't mind my asking, do you expect the police to get to the bottom of what happened if you insist on withholding vital evidence?'

The director sighed. 'When they interviewed me, just after Suzie was killed . . . I wasn't in my right mind. I didn't think to show them the pictures.'

'But you will?'

'Sure, just as soon as I next see MacTaggart.'

'It's important, Douglas.' He hesitated. 'Are you armed?'

The director crossed the room and plucked his flying jacket from a peg on the back of the door. From an inside pocket he pulled a small black revolver. 'Another memento from the war. Colt 1903, US standard issue.'

'Ammunition?'

Dennison indicated a chest of drawers across the room. 'In there. I empty the shooter every night.'

'Perhaps,' Langham ventured, 'it might be wise to keep it loaded, and on your person, at all times.'

'Sure, I'll do that.'

Langham heard a car engine, rose from his chair and moved to the window. Ralph Ryland's clapped-out Morris Minor chugged up the driveway and pulled in beneath the elms.

Langham turned. 'One more thing before I go. And please don't think I'm prying. This is part of the investigation.' He hesitated. 'I understand that when you were in England back in the mid-thirties, you and Cynthia Marling – though this was before she was married – conducted an affair.'

'I like the way you phrase it. "Conducted an affair".' Dennison nodded. 'Yeah, that's right, we did. That's pretty impressive detective work, Langham. What of it?'

'And when you were back here, during the war?'

'What about it?'

'Did you resume your liaison with her?'

Dennison smiled again. 'No. No I didn't. I hardly saw Cynthia. She was working in London most of the time, and anyway she was married by then. And not only that, but Edward and I were friends.'

Langham stared across the room at the director. 'Isn't that something of a coincidence? That the war should throw you together with the husband of the woman you knew back in the thirties?'

'If you must know,' Dennison said, 'I saw Cynthia briefly when I came over here in 'forty-two. Just as friends, mind you. She told me she was married, and she introduced me to Edward. I liked the guy, really liked him. It was Edward, or his influence, who later got me out of the squadron and into Special Operations.' He shrugged. 'During the entire course of the war, I can't have seen Cynthia on more than three or four occasions.'

'And now?'

'What do you mean, "now"?'

'How is your relationship with Cynthia Marling now?'

Dennison snorted. 'If you haven't noticed, Langham, Cynthia is more interested in young Banning than with a third-rate, washed-up movie director like me.'

Langham glanced through the window. Ryland was standing in the driveway before the hall, staring up at the façade. The detective moved towards the entrance and disappeared from view.

'Do you think Edward is aware of what's going on between his wife and Banning?' Langham asked.

'Edward's no fool. He has eyes in his head. But if you ask me, he's past caring. He and Cynthia, if you haven't noticed, are not on the best of terms.'

Langham hesitated before taking his leave. '"He's no fool",' he repeated. 'Do you think he knows about your affair with Cynthia, then? I take it you haven't told him?'

Dennison shook his head. 'I . . . I didn't see the point, back in the war – or now. All that happened a long time ago. Water under the bridge. So, no, I don't think Edward knows about Cynthia and me.'

Langham moved to the door. 'Thanks for your time.'

Dennison waved him away, then said. 'Oh – there is one thing.'

'Yes?'

'Suzie hired you, but now that she's . . .' He shrugged. 'How much was she paying you, Langham?'

'Five guineas an hour.'

'That all? Look, buddy, I'll make it ten – but make sure you catch the bastard, OK?'

'I'll do that,' Langham said. He opened the door. 'Inspector MacTaggart is coming over this afternoon. I'd show him those photographs, if I were you.'

Dennison saluted. 'Will do.'

Langham heard raised voices before he came to the turn in the staircase and saw Evans remonstrating with Ryland.

'I'm sorry, sir, but I must ask you to leave the premises immediately.'

'Not on your nelly, mate!' Ryland expostulated.

Langham hurried down the stairs. 'What seems to be the problem?'

Ryland looked relieved to see him. 'This here little Hitler wants to kick me out.'

'I'm sorry, sir,' the butler said, 'but my express instructions, from Mr Marling, are that the press aren't allowed—'

'But like I said earlier,' Ryland cried, 'I ain't no bleedin' reporter!'

'I can vouch for Mr Ryland,' Langham said. 'He's a friend of mine, not a reporter.'

Evans eyed Ryland dubiously. 'A friend, sir?'

'That's right. I assure you that Mr Ryland isn't a reporter.'

'In that case, my apologies,' Evans said stiffly, and retreated.

Ryland nodded, running a finger around the inside of his collar and shooting his cuffs in the manner of the justifiably aggrieved.

Langham led the way along the corridor.

'I've come across those types before,' Ryland said. 'They've been in service so long they've adopted the airs and graces of the gentry.'

'Forget about him,' Langham said, ushering Ryland into the library where they sat down. 'How was the drive up?'

'Once I got out of London, plain sailing. I stopped at Ely, bought a paper, had a gasper and read about the case.' He pulled the *Daily*

Mirror from the pocket of his frayed suit jacket and showed Langham the front page.

Movie Star Slain in Country House, ran the headline above a publicity shot of Suzie Reynard smiling out at the world.

'Poor kid,' Ryland said. 'What a bleedin' waste. What I'd like to know, though, is how much of this—' he waved the paper – 'is sensation mongering. I mean, it says here she was shot ten times and her terrified screams woke the household. Ten times? So the killer reloaded when the ammo ran out?'

'Of course not. She was shot with a British army service revolver bearing a silencer, two or three times. And she probably didn't have time to scream. My guess is that she died pretty much instantly. The killer shot her in the head.'

'Says here she was found by her lover, the movie director Douglas Dennison.'

'They got that right. And Dennison came straight in to the house and got me.'

'So you saw . . .?'

Langham nodded. 'The odd thing is, the killer dropped the gun before he fled, and according to MacTaggart, the inspector from Norwich, it's covered in the fingerprints of Desmond Haggerston.' He told Ryland about the old man.

Ryland nodded. 'I heard a report on the radio before I set off that said the police had taken a suspect in for questioning.'

Langham explained about Haggerston's confession, and the fact that he'd kept Maria up half the night with his snoring.

'So, why'd the old geezer confess to the killing?'

'That's what I can't work out.'

'So this director,' Ryland said, 'claims he left the caravan at three thirty and came back at six, sat outside for a while, then went in and found the body?'

'That's right.'

'And you buy that?' Ryland asked. 'Because,' he went on, 'from an outsider's point of view it looks bloody suspicious. I mean, he ups and takes a walk at three thirty in the morning, leaving his bird in bed and the caravan unlocked?'

Langham shrugged. 'On the face of it, it does look odd, I suppose. But apparently he's an insomniac and often goes on night-time hikes. And then there's the state he was in when he hammered on my bedroom door. He convinced me.'

He told Ryland about his meeting with Dennison just now, and that the director had hired him to find the killer.

'Also, he'd been threatened,' Langham said, and explained about the photographs.

'Could always have sent them to himself,' Ryland said. 'Or had them sent.'

'Very well, but why would Dennison have wanted Suzie Reynard dead? It can't have been a heat of the moment thing, provoked by an argument – if he sent himself the photos, it was set up beforehand. Also, surely he would have had a weapon ready to use, not stolen one from Edward Marling's gun room.' Langham shook his head. 'I don't think Dennison did it. In fact, I suspect the intended target was Dennison himself.' He went over his reasoning to his partner.

'Very well. So, who are the suspects?' Ryland rustled through the paper until he found the continuation of the front-page story. 'Here we are. The press got hold of a few names, but you and Maria aren't among them.'

He showed Langham the page. The paper had dug snapshots of the actors from the files. Sir Humphrey Lyle, Varla Cartier and Chuck Banning smiled out, their faces reduced to little more than grainy black-and-white smudges. The headline ran: *Movie Stars in Country House Murder Mystery: Whodunit?*

Ryland said, 'The report also mentions Edward and Cynthia Marling.'

Langham went through the names one by one, giving Ryland brief descriptions of the people and adding one that the paper had missed: Terry Ambler, the scriptwriter.

Ryland sat back in his chair, listening attentively. 'Right-o, Don. What I think I'll do is have a poke around this afternoon and natter to a few people.'

'I'll have Maria introduce you,' Langham said.

'Then I'll get back to London and do some digging. Seems to me we need to know a bit more about these folk. Anyone I should concentrate on specifically?'

'It'd be nice to know a little more about all of them. One thing, Ralph – back in the thirties, Dennison and Cynthia Marling had a fling. If you could follow that up. I'd like to know how close they were during the war, when Dennison was over here. According to Dennison, they only met a few times then. Cynthia worked in St Bart's as a nurse before and during the war.'

'I'll look into it and get back to you,' Ryland said. 'What are you doing this afternoon?'

He told Ryland what he'd learned at Haggerston House yesterday about the death of Victoria Haggerston. 'Her son, Nicholas, was charged with the killing, but the death sentence was commuted to life imprisonment. I'd like to talk to Nicholas about his father. I'm driving up to an asylum near Hunstanton to talk to him at three.'

He climbed to his feet. 'Right, we'll find Maria, shall we, and I'll leave you in her capable hands?'

SIXTEEN

It occurred to Maria that if you wished to examine the cultural and social divisions prevalent in English society in the mid-twentieth century, then you could do worse than to invite a working-class cockney to lunch with the landed gentry at an Elizabethan manor house.

Ryland was clearly ill at ease in the environs of the vast dining hall, the censorious expressions of the portraits of the Marling lineage matched only by those of Edward and Cynthia as the detective ate with his elbows on the table.

Opposite Ryland sat Sir Humphrey, ploughing through his ox tongue salad and quaffing vast quantities of claret. He'd exchanged a few words with Ryland, decided they had little in common, and proceeded to ignore the detective despite Ryland's admiration of his role in an Ealing comedy. Varla Cartier and Chuck Banning ate quietly; the class structure of English society was nothing more than a quaint anachronism to most Americans, and the actors were oblivious both to Ryland's unease and the Marlings' disdain.

'And what do you do?' Cynthia asked at one point.

'What *haven't* I done, more like?' Ryland chuckled, and deflected the question with a resume of his curriculum vitae. 'I followed me dad into the printing trade when I left school at fourteen, but could I stick that? So I worked in a tannery for a few months, then got a job as a porter in an abattoir – nice bit of tongue, this, by the way – and after that I was a door-to-door salesman. Encyclopaedias. I couldn't even spell the word! Then the war came along and I never looked back. That's where I met Don, see, both of us working-class lads. We hit it off from the start, saw the world and did our bit.'

'And what do you do now, Mr Ryland?' Edward asked, dabbing his lips with a napkin.

'Now I work in space,' Ryland quipped.

'In space?' Cynthia furrowed her brow in mystification.

'That's right,' Ryland said. 'I travel in vacuums.'

'I'm sorry . . .?'

Ryland sighed. 'Vacuums – Hoovers. Geddit? I sell Hoovers, door-to-door.' He waved. 'Never mind.'

Maria smiled to herself but Cynthia remained po-faced at the detective's joke.

They ate in silence for a time, before Ryland finished the salad, pushed his plate away, and said, 'That was tip-top, by the way. Much appreciated.'

Sir Humphrey asked, 'And what are you doing here, old boy? Sorry if you've been through all that. Bit deaf, y'know?'

'I was passing,' Ryland explained, 'and I knew Don and Maria were staying here so I thought I'd pop in and say hello. Also,' he went on, smiling across at Varla Cartier, 'I wanted to meet some film stars. Me wife's a big admirer of yours. *Unreasonable Doubt* is one of her favourite films. Loves it, she does.'

'Why, that's very kind of you, Mr Ryland.'

'Call me Ralph. Annie'll be pleased as punch when I tell her I've been hobnobbing with the stars. I don't suppose I could blag an autographed picture of you?'

Varla smiled. 'I'm afraid I no longer keep any publicity shots, Ralph. But I'll scribble something suitable for Annie after lunch, OK?'

'Much obliged,' Ryland said, plucking a strand of cress from his moustache. 'And I'll certainly look out for your films, Chuck.'

'You'll have to look hard, Mr Ryland. I've only been in three, and I had tiny parts.'

'But you're the lead in this one, so Don told me?'

'Sure. Can you believe that? There I was, happy enough to get walk-ons in B movies, then Douglas comes along and casts me in this. I'm one lucky guy, I'll tell you that.'

'Not lucky,' Cynthia corrected. 'Talented. Dennison wouldn't have cast you if he didn't think you'd bring something significant to the part.'

Chuck Banning murmured, 'That's kind of you to say so, Cynthia.'

Varla poured herself a third glass of claret. 'I just hope the damned film gets made.'

'You think they'll pull the plug?' Ryland asked.

'It's hard to say how the backers will react,' she said.

'But who'd gain if the film wasn't made?' Ryland looked around the table.

Varla sat back in her chair. 'No one. It'd be a disaster for all of us. Me and Sir Humphrey are making our comebacks, aren't we, old boy? Chuck here is on the verge of stardom. And this is Dennison's pet project, a film he's wanted to make for years.'

'Talking of Mr Dennison,' Ryland said, 'I wouldn't mind meeting him.'

Cynthia said, 'Douglas is not partial to lunch, Mr Ryland, and since . . . since what happened, he's rather retreated into the background.'

Ryland nodded. 'I can understand that. Must've been one hell of a shock, finding his girlfriend like that.' He looked around the table. 'Shock for all of you as well.'

Cynthia smiled bitterly. 'Shock, Mr Ryland, is something of an understatement.'

Ryland indicated the folded newspaper which he'd tossed down at the far end of the table. 'And the things that rag's reporting . . .'

Edward said, 'And what might that be? I only ever read *The Times*.'

'You know how they like to rake up all the scandal? Lies, most of it. Or speculation.'

'Speculation?' Varla said. 'Let me guess. They're pointing the finger at one of us?'

Ryland shrugged, his weaselly gaze shifting around the table. 'That's what the rag claims,' he said. 'Inside job, they says. But I wouldn't listen to any of it. Rubbish, half of what they write.'

Cynthia threw down her napkin. 'It's disgraceful, what the papers get away with these days. The poor girl isn't yet buried, and the things they're writing about her . . .'

The meal finished, Edward Marling made his excuses and wheeled himself from the room, followed by Sir Humphrey and Cynthia.

Maria led Ryland along the passage to the conservatory, then out to the kitchen garden.

'Must admit I'm glad to be out of there,' the detective said. 'I felt like a canary in a cattery.'

'I thought you handled it very well.'

'I certainly got them gabbing, didn't I?' He laughed. 'Now, who's next?'

'The only people you haven't met are Terrence Ambler, Donald's film-writer friend, and Douglas Dennison.'

'I'm not too concerned about Ambler,' Ryland said. 'Don seems to think he's a diamond geezer.'

She looked at the detective. 'Did Donald tell you about what happened last night, between Dennison and Ambler?'

'No. Go on.'

She described the altercation in the dining hall, and Ambler's admission that it was he who had sent Suzie Reynard an abusive postcard. 'Despite all that, he is pleasant, in a odd kind of way.'

Ryland laughed. 'Don has a habit of befriending waifs and strays.'

They walked from the kitchen garden. 'I've noticed that Dennison's been spending time by the lake,' Maria said. 'We'll wander down and see if he's there.'

'Lead the way.'

They crossed the greensward and Ryland lit a cigarette as they strolled.

'All ready for the big day?' he asked.

'I think so. Everything is arranged, but for the minor details. And my father is hosting the reception at the French embassy.'

'He is? Lordy. Some slap-up nosh, then?' He laughed at himself. 'I mean, haute cuisine.'

The way he pronounced it, *'ort kwizeen*, made her smile.

'And the finest French wines,' she said.

Ryland looked worried. 'And a barrel or two of Fullers, I hope?'

'Don't worry, there'll be beer, too, for you and Donald.' She glanced at him. 'Have you prepared your best man's speech?'

He pulled a face. 'Don said it'd be fine if I just said a few words. He's like me, doesn't care for public speaking.'

'That's very strange.'

'Is it?'

'Donald was telling me that you cornered an East End racketeer single-handedly last week, kicked a gun from his hand and gave him a bloody nose. And yet you fear standing up and speaking in front of a few people?'

Ryland shrugged. 'Different, ain't it? I mean, what I did then, I was fighting for me life. I acted on instinct. Didn't feel any fear until later. But the thought of standing up in front of a hundred folk and spouting . . .' He shook his head. 'I can't do it.'

'Don't worry. Just a few words and a toast will be fine.'

Ryland scanned the lake ahead of them. 'Don't see any sign of this director johnny.'

Maria pointed to a weatherboard boathouse. 'If he's down here, he'll be over there.' They walked along the shore of the lake.

Maria glanced at the little detective. 'What is it like,' she asked, 'working with Don again, after so long?'

'Like old times. We were a good team, just after the war. And I'm sure we'll be just as successful now. Don has the brains, see, and I have the brawn.'

She smiled. Ryland had the physique of an undernourished jockey and smoked forty Woodbines a day, non-stop. 'Don't laugh,' he said. 'I mean it. I might not look like Charles Atlas, but I can handle meself.'

'I'm sure you can, Ralph,' she said. 'What do you make of this case?'

'Tricky one. I'm not used to country house murder mysteries – give me a simple case of burglary any day. Difficulty here is establishing a motive. I mean, this Dennison chappie seems to have more enemies than friends. I'll feel more confident when I've looked into these people's backgrounds. Once we can work out a motive, we'll have our man. Or woman.'

Maria pointed to the boathouse. 'Ah-ha, we are in luck.'

The director was sitting on a verandah at the side of the boat-house, staring down at something in his hands. As they came closer, she saw that the object was a revolver and that Dennison was spinning it on one finger like a Wild West gunslinger.

He looked up as they approached and quickly pocketed the weapon.

'I hope we're not intruding,' Maria said.

'Not at all. Take a pew.' Dennison gestured to the rough timber bench he was sitting on. Maria sat down, but Ryland elected to remain standing; he leaned against the rail of the boathouse and lit another cigarette.

'I thought you might like to meet Mr Ryland,' Maria went on, 'Donald's partner.'

'Sure. Good to meet you, pal.' They shook hands.

'I just want to reassure you, Mr Dennison, that Don and me are doing all we can to get to the bottom of this business.'

Dennison squinted up at the detective. 'At a fee of ten guineas an hour, buddy, I'd hope you are.'

Maria glanced at the director and wondered what had attracted shoals of women to him over the years; it certainly could not be his gruff, abrasive personality, nor his looks. Dennison resembled a boxer who'd gone too many rounds with a champion: he had the bullish, beat-up appearance of someone always on the lookout for a scrap. Perhaps it was this, his latent male aggression, that attracted some women: that, she thought, or the fact that in Hollywood he was a 'player', rich, powerful, and influential.

Ryland asked the director about his relations with members of the household and cast – learning no more, Maria suspected, than what Donald had already told him. Dennison was guarded, taciturn in his replies, saying that he got along fine with his cast, and with Edward and Cynthia.

'I don't know if Don's mentioned this,' Ryland said in closing, 'but it might be wise if you made yourself scarce for a while.'

'You realize I have a movie to make here?'

Ryland stared at him. 'What's more important, Mr Dennison, the film or your life?'

Dennison patted his pocket. 'Why do you think I'm packing a shooter? I'll be fine. If the bastard shows himself . . .'

'Which is all very well, Mr Dennison,' Ryland said. 'But what if the killer *doesn't* show himself?'

Dennison muttered something inaudible and stared across the lake.

Ryland pushed himself away from the rail and looked at his watch. 'Time I was getting along,' he said. 'People to talk to in the Smoke.' He nodded to the director. 'Pleasure meeting you, Mr Dennison.'

'Pleasure's mine, Ryland. And good luck.'

Maria smiled at the director as she stood and followed Ryland from the boathouse.

When they were out of earshot, Ryland said, 'Must admit, he wasn't what I was expecting.'

'And what was that?'

'I saw his photo in the paper and he seemed . . . slick and handsome, and somehow much bigger. In real life he looks like what he is . . . an average Joe grieving his loss.'

Maria glanced at the detective, chastising herself for being surprised at Ryland's sensitivity and insight.

'And maybe fearing for the future, too?' she added.

Ryland sighed. 'Poor bastard. I wouldn't like to be in his shoes for all the money in Tinseltown. Right, I must remember to pick up Varla Cartier's autograph before I shoot off.'

They made their way back to the hall.

SEVENTEEN

Palgrave House stood on the coast three miles north of Hunstanton. From its isolated, headland location it commanded an uninterrupted view over the sea. Langham had expected the institute to be a dour, Victorian asylum, more like a prison than a country house, but he was pleasantly surprised when a gatekeeper admitted him into grounds resembling a municipal park. The house itself was a low, rambling red-brick affair built in the twenties, with a number of similar outbuildings housing residential units, recreational facilities, and even a swimming pool.

He was met on the stroke of three by the institute's director, Mrs Havers, a tall tweed-clad woman in her fifties.

'I understand from my secretary that the murder case has been reopened?' Mrs Havers said. 'Isn't that a little odd, twenty-five years after the fact?'

'You've been misinformed,' Langham said as she led him along a bright, carpeted corridor towards the rear of the house. 'It's not the Haggerston inquiry I'm working on, but the incident at Marling Hall.'

'Oh, the actress . . . But what, if I might ask, is Nicholas's involvement in that affair?'

'His father was a guest at the house when the murder was committed,' Langham said.

'And just what do you want to know from Nicholas?'

Langham hesitated. 'Principally, I'd like to ask him about his relationship with his father.'

'I hope you understand that I must insist on being present during your interview with Nicholas.'

Langham nodded. 'That's fine.'

'You see, I wouldn't want Nicholas to be disturbed in any way.'

They passed through a conservatory where a dozen men and women sat around reading books and newspapers. Langham was reminded of a rather genteel residential hotel he'd once visited in Scarborough.

Mrs Havers led the way out into extensive gardens and a sloping lawn overlooking the sea. Patients strolled around in the sunlight or sat in the shade under trees.

Langham took in the scene, smiling to himself.

'I must admit, this isn't quite what I was expecting.'

'That is the reaction of quite a number of people when they visit for the first time,' Mrs Havers said. 'We try to do things differently here, Mr Langham. We deplore the more invasive practices of psychiatry such as electric shock therapy or surgery, and concentrate on behavioural therapy and, increasingly, the implementation of psychotropic drugs. We try to treat our patients as guests.'

'That's a commendable attitude.'

'Of course, our stratagem doesn't work with everyone, and I admit that we must be selective in whom we elect to treat. Also – another admission – Palgrave House is a private institution and as such can only administer to paying guests.'

He looked at Mrs Havers. 'And I take it that Nicholas Haggerston's care here is paid for by his father?'

'That is correct, Mr Langham.'

He looked out over the idyllic grounds, considering the dilapidation of Haggerston House he'd witnessed yesterday. He wondered at the annual cost of keeping Nicholas Haggerston at Palgrave House.

'Does Nicholas have many visitors?'

'His sister, Mary, comes to see him once a fortnight.'

'And his father?'

Mrs Havers shook her head. 'Mr Haggerston has never once, in the twenty-odd years that Nicholas has been here, visited his son.'

Langham nodded. 'I see.'

Mrs Havers gave a tight smile. 'Perhaps he sees the payment of his son's treatment as sufficient generosity,' she said. 'But who am I to speculate? Now—' she indicated the steps leading to the sloping lawn – 'as it's such a fine day, Nicholas will be out here, indulging one of his two obsessions.'

'Which is?'

'I suppose you could call it ship-spotting, Mr Langham. Nicholas has an encyclopaedic knowledge of all the shipping that passes along the coast.'

'And his other obsession?'

'The law, Mr Langham. When the weather does not permit his being outside, he spends time in his room, buried up to his ears in his collection of legal tomes.'

They passed from the shadow of the house and strolled across the lawn.

On first learning about Nicholas Haggerston from his sister, Mary, Langham had assumed him to be profoundly mentally disabled.

What he'd heard so far from Mrs Havers contradicted this impression, as did the reality when she led him over to a bench and a short, dumpy grey-haired man in his mid-fifties. He wore beige flannel trousers and a green-and-yellow-striped blazer. Equipped with a pair of binoculars and a notebook, he looked like a town clerk indulging his weekend passion for ornithology.

'Nicholas,' Mrs Havers said in a soft, comforting tone, 'I've brought someone who would like to speak to you. This is Mr Langham.'

Nicholas Haggerston leaped to his feet and stuck out his hand. His movements had the stiff, rehearsed formality of gestures learned by rote. 'Pleased to meet you, Mr Langham. Won't you take a seat?'

He had the doughy, formless features of a child, as if the experiences of life had failed to inform the lineaments of his face; a pair of round, rimless glasses heightened the impression of innocence.

Langham sat down beside him. Mrs Havers strolled off and stared out to sea, still within earshot.

Nicholas pointed out to the shipping lanes, indicating a dark fleck on the horizon. 'One of the Ostend line, Mr Langham. Hull to Hamburg every week.'

He had his notebook open on his lap, and Langham saw a list of names and columns divided into weeks. Nicholas had ticked off various names on the list.

'And there!' Nicholas said. 'A ferry of the Blue Star line, Hull to Rotterdam twice a week.' He bent over his notebook and ticked off the ferry with a stubby pencil.

'Mrs Havers mentioned that you're also interested in the law, Nicholas.'

'The law and shipping, Mr Langham.'

'I'm interested in the law, Nicholas.'

'You are? I say, what a coincidence. Are you interested in shipping too?'

'I'm more interested in the law.'

'Are you a policeman, Mr Langham?'

'A kind of policeman. I'm a private investigator.'

Nicholas blinked at him through his round glasses. 'If you have come to ask me about what happened to my mother, Mr Langham,' he said agitatedly, 'then I must tell you that I have no recollection at all of the incident.'

Langham smiled. 'That's fine,' he said soothingly. 'I wasn't going to ask you about that.'

Nicholas raised his binoculars and pressed them to his glasses for a minute. Then he lowered them, and said, 'I loved my father, Mr Langham.'

'Did you?'

'He was a good man. He did his best, but the house was too big for just four people, and it was always falling down. I really didn't like all the mess. I like order, Mr Langham. Order and routine.'

'Order and routine are good, Nicholas.'

'But the house was falling down.' He said this sadly, shaking his head. 'And there was nothing my father could do to stop it. Do you know what I called him, Mr Langham?'

'No. What did you call him?'

'King Canute, because he couldn't stop the house from falling down.' He entered another tick in his notebook and turned to Langham. 'I loved my father, but I didn't love my mother.'

Langham glanced at Mrs Havers. She was standing a few yards away with her back to the bench, arms folded, seemingly intent on the sea.

'Why was that?'

'Because she was like the house.'

'Like the house? In what way?'

'She was . . . she was always falling down. My father tried, but he could never do anything to make things better.'

'Better?' Langham asked. 'Better in what way?'

'Just . . . *better*. He couldn't make things better. She was always falling down.'

'You mean . . . she was falling down the stairs?'

Nicholas shook his head. 'No. No, she was like the house . . .'

'And you didn't like her?'

Nicholas screwed up his eyes, as if trying to remember that far back. 'My mother was sometimes at the house, and sometimes away. Sometimes there at mealtimes, and sometimes not. Sometimes there at bedtime, sometimes not.'

'And you didn't like this?'

Nicholas shook his head. 'But my father was always there. He would come home from work, and we would repair the house together, and then we would have dinner, and then he would say goodnight to me at bedtime.'

'Routine,' Langham said. 'You liked the routine.'

'Routine,' Nicholas repeated softly. 'Black and white. Good and bad. The ships . . .' he went on, gesturing to the sea. 'They run to a timetable. The timetable is like the law.'

'And you like the law?'

Nicholas turned his innocent moon face to Langham and smiled. 'The law is for colder days, inside. Winter days, not summer. Black and white. Good and bad. I like to study the law. You see . . . it tells you what to do. Good and bad.'

They sat in silence for a time, and then Langham said, 'You see your sister, Mary, from time to time?'

'Every fourteen days,' Nicholas said. 'Every Wednesday at ten o'clock in the morning.'

'And what do you talk about?'

'I tell Mary about the ships.'

'And about the law?'

'No, Mary doesn't like to hear about the law, Mr Langham. I think the law frightens her.'

'Frightens her? Why's that?'

'Because of what it did.'

Langham leaned forward. 'And what did it do, Nicholas? Did it put you in here?'

Nicholas blinked, as if trying to make sense of what Langham had said. 'No, Mr Langham. The law killed my father.'

'Killed him . . .?'

'The law hanged my father by the neck until he was dead,' he said. 'That's why he never comes to see me.'

Langham stared at the man, nodding slowly.

Mrs Havers turned and smiled at Langham. 'I think it might be time to call it a day,' she said.

Langham touched Nicholas on the forearm. 'It's been nice talking to you, Nicholas.'

'And it's been nice talking to you too, Mr Langham,' Nicholas said, jumping up again and thrusting out his hand as Langham got to his feet.

They shook hands and Langham joined Mrs Havers.

As they strolled away from the bench, Langham looked back at Nicholas. He sat down, looked at his notebook, then raised his binoculars and focused on the horizon. 'P&O line from Newcastle to Le Havre,' Langham heard him say.

They left the lawn and moved through the house, Langham taking in the patients who were reading or playing snooker or taking afternoon tea. He tried to discern, in the faces of these people, the trauma of their past lives which had brought them here – but the ministrations of Mrs Havers and her staff made that impossible.

She saw him to the entrance and shook his hand. 'I hope your visit hasn't been a complete waste of time, Mr Langham.'

'Far from it,' he said, and thanked her. 'I've learned far more than I thought I would.'

EIGHTEEN

Inspector MacTaggart's Humber was parked beneath the elms when Langham returned. As he pulled in beside the police car and crossed to the hall, Maria emerged to greet him.

'The inspector and his deputy are in the library,' she reported.

'Have you said anything about Haggerston?'

'I thought I'd better wait until you returned,' she said, hurrying up the steps after him.

'How long have they been here?'

'About ten minutes, but he says he's impatient to get back to Norwich.'

They crossed the hallway and turned right.

'There you are,' MacTaggart said when Langham and Maria entered the library. 'Now, why did you need to see me?'

Langham replied with a question of his own. 'What's the situation regarding Desmond Haggerston?'

He sat on the sofa with Maria, while MacTaggart dropped into an armchair and Ferrars adopted his favoured position against the mantelpiece like an extra on a film set.

'Haggerston has confessed to the shooting of Suzie Reynard,' MacTaggart said. 'His dabs are all over the murder weapon, and I'm about to get back to Norwich and charge him with the woman's premeditated murder.'

'His motive?'

'Motive be blasted, for the time being. I'll have time enough to get that out of him over the course of the next few days.'

Maria leaned forward. 'But I think you are making a mistake, Inspector. You see, I doubt that Mr Haggerston could have killed Suzie Reynard.'

MacTaggart exchanged a superior look with his deputy. 'You doubt it, do you? And why is that, Miss Dupré?'

'Because the only time that Mr Haggerston could have killed Suzie Reynard was in the few minutes around six o'clock – and I don't think, being as infirm as he is, that he could have left the hall fast enough—'

MacTaggart interrupted. 'And why can't he have killed Suzie Reynard *before* six o'clock?'

'Because before six on Sunday morning, Desmond Haggerston was fast asleep in bed.'

MacTaggart tried to keep an expression of amusement from his face. 'And you can testify to that, can you?'

'Yes, as a matter of fact she can,' Langham said, riled by the inspector's assumed superiority.

'This should be interesting,' Ferrars said from his position at the mantelpiece.

Maria looked contemptuously from Ferrars to MacTaggart. 'I was kept awake, from around three o'clock until six, by Mr Haggerston's snoring. He *cannot* have left his bedroom much before six, and as I was about to say, I doubt he could have moved swiftly enough to have reached the caravan and shot Suzie Reynard before Mr Dennison's return.'

'And are you sure that you didn't fall asleep at any point during that time,' MacTaggart asked, 'even for a few minutes?'

'I am absolutely sure, Inspector. I was awake all the time. I got up and took the opportunity to do some work.'

'And are you certain that it was Haggerston's snoring that kept you awake? What about the person in the room on the other side?'

Langham said, 'That bedroom is vacant, Inspector.'

MacTaggart steepled his fingers and pressed them to his lips in contemplation. 'The fact that the murder weapon is covered in Mr Haggerston's fingerprints, together with his confession, leads me to believe that you are mistaken, Miss Dupré. He *must* have got down to the caravan before six o'clock. I am of a mind to stick to my original decision and charge him with murder.'

'I don't think Haggerston's guilty, Inspector,' Langham said.

'But dammit, man. His prints are on the blessed weapon! How do you account for that, if he didn't commit the act?'

'What if he made his way down to the caravan – to buttonhole Dennison about the film – while the director was making his way up to my room to raise the alarm around six forty—?'

'But surely Dennison would have seen him!'

'Not,' Langham said, 'if Haggerston used the lift.'

'Very well,' MacTaggart said, 'for the sake of argument we'll say that he did use the lift, made his way to the caravan, saw the body and then the revolver, and for some reason known only to himself picked it up. Then he dropped it, covered with his fingerprints, and drove from Marling Hall while Dennison was knocking on your door.'

Langham nodded. 'He drove to Haggerston House, made his way to the knot garden where twenty-five years ago his wife was murdered and proceeded to drink himself almost senseless so that he could confess.'

'To a crime he didn't commit?' MacTaggart finished incredulously. 'But, Langham, in all reasonableness . . . why would he do that?'

'Because he was guilty.'

'Guilty? But you just said—'

'Guilty – but not of the killing of Suzie Reynard.'

'Then of who—?' Ferrars began.

'Of his wife, Victoria, whom he shot dead in the knot garden of Haggerston House twenty-five years ago.'

A silence met his words. Maria stared at him, her wide-eyed expression almost comical.

MacTaggart was the first to find his voice. 'But – but Nicholas Haggerston was found guilty of shooting his mother.'

'I think mistakenly, Inspector. Nicholas Haggerston was found in the woods beyond the house, in possession of a rifle. Apparently, during the trial, he said nothing either to incriminate himself or to deny the charge. He was deemed mentally subnormal by the doctor who examined him at the time, according to his sister, and was on record as disliking his mother. But it was Desmond Haggerston who hated Victoria, hated her for refusing to sell the house and for making him work to keep it up – and for all I know for a hundred and one other reasons. My guess is that he snapped one morning, shot his wife and dropped the rifle in shock at what he'd done. Nicholas either saw him do it and picked up the weapon, taking it into the woods where he was found later, or he stumbled over the body of his mother and the weapon. My supposition is the former. He might be considered "subnormal", whatever that means, but he loved – and still loves – his father. It would have been well within his reasoning at the time to have accepted the guilt in order to save his father.'

'And Desmond Haggerston,' MacTaggart said, 'knowing full well that his son might face the death penalty for his supposed crime, allowed him to take the blame?'

Langham shrugged. 'I think that Desmond Haggerston knew that his son would be found to be of "diminished responsibility". But it was a terrible decision he had to make – and one which preyed on his mind over the years. The guilt he felt must have been appalling, both at the crime of commission, the killing of his wife, and the crime of omission, not owning up to the killing and allowing his son to take the blame. It came to a head on Sunday morning when, already beside himself at the thought that a film based on the incident was going to be made, he found the body of Suzie Reynard and realized how he might atone for the crime he did commit by confessing to one that he didn't . . . He went to the scene of the original crime, got himself drunk, and thus fortified with Dutch courage, confessed to you later that day.'

MacTaggart sat with his fingers steepled, lost in thought. At last he said, 'This is all supposition, of course.'

'It is, I admit, but I think that if you question Desmond Haggerston, and his son, Nicholas – and look into the particulars of the original murder – you'll find that it's a supposition based on sound evidence. I think you'd be making a big mistake in charging an innocent man with the crime, quite apart from allowing the actual killer to go scot-free. All I'm asking is that you look at the evidence again, in light of what I've said, and review your decision to charge Haggerston with the killing.'

MacTaggart tapped his lips with his fingers. 'You make an interesting case, Langham. Very well, I'll use the information you've supplied when I interview Haggerston again.'

'That's all I ask, Inspector. Thank you.'

In due course, MacTaggart and Ferrars took their leave. In the following silence, emphasized by the ticking of the grandfather clock, Langham sat back wearily and closed his eyes.

Maria leaned over and kissed him. 'I'm proud of you, Donald.'

'I just hope they do take me seriously and get to the bottom of Haggerston's confession.'

'I am sure they will,' she said, and added with a note of irony, 'and I am sure British justice will be seen to be equal to the challenge.'

Langham grunted. 'On that score, I think it failed miserably twenty-five years ago.' He reached out for a glass and the brandy. 'I don't know about you, but I need a drink.'

At dinner that evening Chuck Banning said, 'I don't know . . . It doesn't seem right, us all here enjoying a fine meal after . . . after what happened to Suzie. But at least the cops have caught her killer.'

At the sudden silence, Banning said, 'What? Have I said something I shouldn't have?'

Langham said, 'I wouldn't be so sure about Haggerston's arrest. The police have had second thoughts about charging him.' He looked around the table to judge how this was received.

Varla Cartier drained her glass and, with the acid wit of the incurably sardonic, announced, 'So . . . once again suspicion falls on present company. Someone should make a film of it.'

'I'm sure someone will,' Terrence Ambler said, dabbing his full lips with a napkin. 'It has all the makings of a big hit, especially if the killer turns out to be someone famous.'

Sir Humphrey smacked his lips around a mouthful of vintage Bordeaux. 'In all modesty, speaking as the most famous person present—' he raised his glass – 'I'd like to announce my innocence to one and all.'

Varla leaned forward; she attempted to rest an elbow on the table, but missed and almost spilled her refilled glass. 'You announce your innocence,' she said drunkenly, 'but can you *prove* it?' She looked around the table. 'For that matter, can *anyone* here prove they didn't kill Suzie Reynard?'

'That's enough, Varla,' Douglas Dennison drawled.

Varla ignored him. 'No, I'm serious. Deadly serious. Clearly one of us killed Suzie. We're all suspects and not one of us – *not one* – can prove conclusively that he or she didn't pull the trigger.'

'For God's sake . . .' Edward muttered, flinging down his napkin.

At the other end of the table, Cynthia Marling skewered Varla with a frosty glare. Surreptitiously, Dennison reached for Cynthia's hand beneath the edge of the table. Langham noticed the gesture – and noticed also that she snatched her hand away with a quick, irritable gesture.

'I think we should go round the table,' Varla went on regardless, 'one by one, every one of us, and state why – why we hated Suzie Reynard. Because I'm pretty damned sure that no one loved the little—'

'Varla!' Dennison thundered.

'Stop this!' Cynthia commanded. She stared around at the guests. 'Please stop this at once! I've had quite enough. I'm telling you, I'm at my wits' end with all of you. We throw our home open to you, and – and what happens? If the killing of an innocent young woman isn't terrible enough, then your subsequent behaviour and appalling manners are!'

'Hear, hear!' Sir Humphrey said.

Maria rolled her eyes in a gesture to Langham that they should escape. He nodded.

Varla rose to her feet and swayed. 'No, no! I *demand* my say—'

'That's quite enough from you for one night, m'dear,' Sir Humphrey said, taking the actress around the waist and propelling her from the room.

Terrence Ambler drained his glass. 'And so to bed.'

NINETEEN

Langham was finishing his breakfast the following morning when Evans approached, and murmured, 'A telephone call, sir. Inspector MacTaggart.'

He excused himself and took it in the drawing room. 'Langham here.'

'I thought I'd better call to keep you abreast of the situation.'

'I appreciate that.'

'I think any appreciation should be on my side, Langham. I might have sounded grudging last night, but as far as I was concerned we had the bird in the bag. Always a bit of a blow to have your certainties overturned like that.'

'What happened?'

'I hauled Haggerston over the coals when I got back yesterday. He retracted his confession to the killing of Suzie Reynard.'

'Did you broach the issue of his wife's murder?'

'I did. He broke down, but I couldn't get a thing out of him. He was in a hell of a state, and to be honest I was worried about him. I had the police doctor check him over. He was given a sedative and spent a quiet night.'

'Is he still in custody?'

'No,' MacTaggart said. 'I had him driven back to Haggerston House first thing. His daughter's taking care of him.'

'How will you proceed with the old murder investigation?'

'The case will have to be reopened, of course. I went through the files last night, into the early hours. There were no witnesses, and to be honest the forensic report was rudimentary – but then this was back in the early thirties, remember. All we'll have to go on is what Desmond Haggerston is willing to tell us, and Nicholas's testimony, too.'

'I would have thought, given Desmond Haggerston's desire to atone for the killing of his wife, you wouldn't find it hard to extract a confession.'

'We'll see. I'll make a report and get it to my chief superinten-
dent. It'll be his responsibility then.'

'And if he was to be brought to trial?'

A thoughtful silence greeted his question. 'The irony is that
Desmond Haggerston was receiving psychiatric counselling at the
time of his wife's murder,' MacTaggart said. 'I suspect he'd get
away with manslaughter due to diminished responsibility – the same
verdict as was handed down to his son.'

'I might motor over to Haggerston House and have a word with
him,' Langham said. 'Did you question him about what he might
have seen on the morning of Suzie Reynard's murder?'

'If I'm honest, he was in such a state last night that I decided to
postpone the interrogation. I'll pop over later this afternoon, once
I've returned to Marling Hall. On that matter,' the inspector went
on, 'I wonder if you'll do me a favour and have everyone assemble
at the hall at one o'clock today?'

'I'll do that, Inspector.'

MacTaggart thanked him and rang off.

Langham left the drawing room and returned to the dining hall.
Everyone was present at the breakfast table with the exception of
Varla Cartier, who was no doubt sleeping off her hangover. The
newspapers had been delivered and were piled on a low table beside
the bain marie; Langham saw that reports of the murder had been
pushed off the front pages by news of Khrushchev's state visit.

The atmosphere around the table was subdued, the occasional
comment or request to pass the salt serving only to point up the
oppressive silence.

'That was Inspector MacTaggart,' Langham said. 'Desmond
Haggerston was released from police custody last night. The
inspector asked me to say that he'd be here at one o'clock for a
further round of interviews.'

Cynthia looked up from her untouched plate of eggs and bacon.
'Again? But didn't he learn everything the first time?'

'Formality, dear,' Edward said. 'They've got to go through the
motions, be seen to be doing the right thing.'

'We've got nothing to fear,' Sir Humphrey chipped in, 'if we
didn't do the deed, what?'

Chuck Banning paused long enough between hearty mouthfuls
of kidney to comment, 'At least they aren't hauling us down to the
station for the third degree.'

'The situation,' Langham said, 'has changed somewhat. Desmond
retracted his confession yesterday. However, as he was on the scene

of the crime on Sunday morning, it's quite conceivable that he might have noticed something relevant to the investigation.'

He looked around the staring faces as he said this, but not one of the diners betrayed themselves.

He drank the last of his Earl Grey, waited for Maria to finish her coffee, then left the room with her. They strolled along to the entrance hall and paused in the sunlight that poured in through the open front doors.

'What are you doing now, Donald?'

'I thought I'd drive over to Haggerston House and have a word with Desmond. If he's in any fit state to talk, that is. He was pretty distraught last night, according to the inspector.' He hesitated. 'Why not come along?'

'I would, but I really must finish off reading the manuscript.' She rolled her eyes towards the dining hall. 'I'll lock myself away in our room. I'm not sure I can stand much more of their company.'

'Because one of them might have . . .?'

She shook her head. 'No, not that. I just find the atmosphere unbearable.' She gave a theatrical shiver. 'There's no love lost between them at the best of times, and add to that the terrible atmosphere of suspicion . . . I'll be glad when we can leave here, Donald.'

'Tell you what, when I get back and the interview with the inspector is over, let's escape down to the Seven Sleepers for a quiet drink, just you and me.'

She kissed him. 'Yes, let's do that, Donald.'

Langham left his car in the drive before Haggerston House, pushed through the creaking front door, and strode along the cobweb-festooned corridor to the west wing, calling out to announce himself as he went.

Haggerston was not in the living room where he and Ambler had looked for the old man yesterday. He made his way outside and followed the overgrown pathways through the jungle of shrubbery towards the knot garden where, he suspected, he might find Desmond Haggerston.

He paused beside the oak tree and stared into the garden.

The old man was slumped on a bench, staring across the hexagonal garden with unseeing eyes. He looked mentally and physically drained, and Langham wondered what agonies were passing through his mind.

As Langham looked on, Haggerston patted his tweed jacket

absently, as if looking for a packet of cigarettes. Langham smiled and touched the hip flask in his pocket.

He pushed himself away from the oak and joined Haggerston on the bench.

'Oh, it's you. Mr . . . Mr . . .?'

'Langham. Donald Langham.' He withdrew the flask from his pocket. 'Were you looking for this, Desmond?'

'My word. Yes, I was. I wondered where on earth I'd left it. Back at the hall, eh?'

Langham refrained from correcting him. 'I refilled it from Edward's stock of brandy in the library,' he said.

'You did? Why, that's jolly decent of you, Langham. Good man.' With shaking fingers, Haggerston unscrewed the cap and took a long swallow. The brandy seemed to revive him somewhat. 'Care for a shot?'

'Not for me, but thank you.' Langham hesitated, then withdrew his private investigator accreditation from his inside pocket and showed it to Haggerston. 'I was economical with the truth the other day when I introduced myself as Suzie's friend. I came to Marling Hall because I was hired . . . and now I'm working on the murder investigation.'

Haggerston waved away the card. 'Thought there was something fishy about you from the off, old boy. All those questions . . . And then last night, MacTaggart confirmed it. He said you'd seen through my confession.'

Langham shrugged. 'I want to get to the bottom of who really did murder Suzie Reynard.'

Haggerston took another shot of brandy and stared blindly ahead.

At length, he said, 'Do you know what it's like to live for years and years with the burden of a terrible guilt?'

Langham stared down at the crazy paving between his brogues. His shooting of the Vichy French soldier in Madagascar had been legitimized by the fact of war – and yet still he woke occasionally in the early hours, riven by guilt. What torture must Desmond Haggerston have suffered over the years at the guilt of having killed his own wife, and then seen his son incarcerated for the crime?

He shook his head. 'No,' he said quietly.

'I don't quite know what overcame me, twenty-five years ago on this very spot, Langham. I was going through hell . . . though I do not claim that as any excuse at all. My marriage was a shambles; our hatred was mutual – and I'm not blaming Victoria, you understand?

It takes two people to fail so miserably at a relationship. But . . . but that morning over breakfast Victoria said something . . .'

Haggerston fell silent, staring off into the past.

Langham sat quietly, not wishing to rush the old man's fraught recollection of the fateful day.

'She said . . .' Haggerston's voice caught on a sob. Langham glanced at him, attempting to make his attention unnoticed. 'She said that . . . that I was weak and ineffectual, and that all I'd even given her was heartache and . . . and an *imbecile* son.'

He leaned forward, held his head in his hands, and wept.

Haggerston had placed the hip flask on the bench between them. Langham picked it up, unscrewed the cap, and proffered it to the old man.

Haggerston sniffed, smiled at Langham, took the flask and drank.

'There . . . that's better. That's what I needed, old boy. Where was I? Ah, yes. Nicholas.' He shook his head. 'Victoria was wrong, Langham. Nicholas wasn't an imbecile. He was . . . different – simple, perhaps. But . . . but I loved him, Langham. I loved him, and yet . . . yet look what I did to him.'

He took another hit of brandy and pursed his lips.

'What happened?' Langham asked quietly.

'I saw red. Isn't that the term? Well, literally, it was as if a sheet of blood fell before my eyes. I was enraged. I went to where I kept my guns . . . Selected one. Followed Victoria out into the garden. This garden. Her favourite place . . . Frosty morning. Bitter cold. I confronted her. I said, retract those foul words, take them back!' He shook his head. 'She laughed at me, Langham. *Laughed.* Called me as simple-minded as my imbecile son and – and God help me, I raised the rifle and shot her dead, shot my wife dead . . .' He gazed ahead, his eyes wide and his mouth hanging open aghast, as if seeing the consequences of his deed for the first time in years.

'I sat down here, on this very bench, and stared at what I'd done, at Victoria's body with the bloody wound in the centre of her chest. I . . . I don't know how long Nicholas had been there, Langham – I don't even know if he saw me shoot Victoria. But, do you know, a very strange thing happened. Nicholas very calmly came up to me, and hugged me, and took the rifle and walked from the garden.' He shook his head. 'I don't recall anything for a number of hours. Apparently the man we had in twice a week to help with the garden . . . he found her, and then the police located Nicholas in the woods. They arrested him, and I said nothing. Nothing, Langham. I look back and wonder. I wonder if a part of me, then, did hate

Nicholas for . . . for being born. Perhaps, without him, things between Victoria and me might have been better. Maybe I resented Nicholas, and wanted to selfishly save myself, which was why I said nothing.'

He fell silent and took another long draught of brandy.

'My lawyer assured me that Nicholas would get off with manslaughter . . . and so it was. But that did nothing to assuage my guilt over the years. If it wasn't bad enough that I had Victoria's blood on my hands . . . Nicholas was imprisoned in some appalling mental asylum.'

'And you never visited him?' Langham said.

Haggerston stared down at the flask clutched in his gnarled hands. 'Could never bring myself to. What a terrible coward I am, Langham, but the thought of Nicholas languishing in some madhouse, because of my action, or rather inaction . . .'

'I visited Nicholas yesterday,' Langham said. 'He assumes that you hanged for the crime of killing your wife, which is why you don't visit him. But I think he should know the truth. You should go and see him, perhaps.' He paused. 'Palgrave House isn't what you'd think of as a "madhouse". Far from it. You'd be surprised. It's run by a far-sighted woman and dedicated staff, and do you know something? It struck me that your son is very happy there.'

Haggerston turned and stared at Langham, suspicion in his watery eyes. 'He is? You aren't just saying that?'

'See for yourself. Visit Nicholas. I know there's nothing you can do to atone for – for what you did. But at least you can make Nicholas happy. I think he'd like to see you.'

The old man was silent for a time, then nodded. 'I might do that, you know, for the first and last time, before . . . before I finally pay for the crime I committed.'

The sun came out from behind a cloud, warming the men; the scent of clematis and brandy fumes filled the air, and bees bounced from bloom to bloom. Langham thought of Maria and looked forward to having a quiet drink with her later that afternoon.

'I hope you don't mind,' he said, 'but I'd like to ask you about Sunday morning, and what happened in Dennison's caravan . . .'

'Sunday morning . . . Dennison's caravan.' Haggerston smiled bleakly. 'Did you know that during the war Dennison was billeted here briefly? He knew the story of Victoria's killing – and then earlier this year I heard he was making a film of the affair. I wasn't having it, you know. As if I wasn't suffering enough . . . I pleaded with him not to make the blessed film, but he wouldn't listen to me. Claimed that the finished thing would in no way resemble what really happened. As if he could even guess at what had *really* happened! But I wanted none of it.'

'And on Sunday morning you woke early and went out to the caravan?'

'I was still a little sozzled. Might even have had a nip or two before I decided to take the bull by the horns and have it out with Dennison.'

'What time was this?'

'Bit before six, I think.'

'So you entered the caravan, saw the revolver and picked it up?'

'No. Oh, no, no, no . . . Wasn't like that at all.'

Langham blinked. 'It wasn't?'

'I didn't find the revolver in the caravan, Langham.'

He stared at the old man. 'Then where . . .?'

'I left the hall, walked around the corner and went smack bang into someone. Knocked me off my feet, dazed me, I can tell you. When I recovered myself, picked myself up, I was quite alone. Then I saw the revolver on the ground at my feet. So, as y'do, without thinking, I picked it up.'

Langham leaned forward and touched the old man's tweed-clad elbow. 'Just a sec. You bumped into someone – presumably the killer, fleeing the caravan with the revolver?'

'That's correct.'

'But who was it, Desmond? You must have seen who it was?'

Haggerston shook his head. 'But that's the ruddy thing, old boy. I didn't. It was a hell of a shock. I came round the corner, eager to beard the lion in his den, as it were – and he must've been going at a fair lick, too. And bang! Over I go, dazed. By the time I picked myself up, the fellow had skedaddled.'

'So it was definitely a man? Can you describe him?'

Haggerston compressed his lips. 'I'm sorry, Langham. It was over so quickly, y'see.'

'Very well, look at it this way. Could you say who it *couldn't* have been?'

Haggerston thought about this, and said at last, 'Well, the fellow was tallish, I think, so I don't think it was little Terrence Ambler, or Dennison for that matter.'

'Tall? Fair or dark, can you recall?'

He shook his head. 'Sorry, Langham. Happened so fast. And you must remember that I'd had a nip or two and might've been a little the worse for wear.'

'Tallish, male . . .' Langham said to himself. 'Chuck Banning, Evans, myself?' he finished, smiling.

'Sorry, old boy.'

Langham nodded. He watched a magpie hop and jump across the crazy paving, pecking at the ground.

'And when you reached the caravan, gun in hand . . .?'

Haggerston gave a grim laugh. 'Didn't intend to shoot Dennison dead, if that's what you're thinking! I entered the caravan and called his name. It was light in there, with the sun streaming in through a little window, and I saw poor Suzie lying there, dead . . . Then I looked down at the revolver in my hand.' He smiled, almost beatific- ally. 'And do you know something, Langham? The idea came to me in a sudden, beautiful instant, almost an epiphany. I knew what I should do . . . I placed the revolver on the carpet, then left the caravan, came here and got meself even more sozzled. Then I drove back to the hall and confessed to the law. What a fool I was, Langham, then and earlier! What a damned fool . . .'

Langham laid a hand on his arm. He felt an inexpressible pity for Haggerston then, as the old man looked back on a life marred by the terrible consequences of a split-second decision – and perhaps, even worse, dreamed of how it might have been so much different.

Haggerston took another swallow of brandy and slipped further down on the bench.

Langham murmured about having to get back, then stood and moved off.

He paused a few feet away and turned to look back at Haggerston. 'And take my advice, Desmond. Visit Nicholas. It will do you, and him, the world of good.'

Haggerston smiled abstractedly and raised the flask in a drunken salute.

'Will do, Langham. Will do!'

TWENTY

As Langham turned off the lane and approached the gates of Marling Hall, a posse of reporters and photographers pounced, despite the best efforts of a lone police constable to clear the way. Langham found a camera thrust into his face through the open window, and voices called out, 'What's happening at the hall, sir?' and, 'Is it true there's been an arrest?'

Langham ignored the questions and eased his way through the melee. The constable opened the gates and saluted him as if he were a dignitary.

He parked under the elms – Inspector MacTaggart had yet to arrive, even though it was just after one o'clock – and was climbing from the car when someone approached, and said, 'I think I owe you an apology, Mr Langham.'

Varla Cartier was hugging herself as if she were freezing, despite the warmth of the day. A newly lighted cigarette drooped from her scarlet lips and a swathe of black hair fell down over her right eye like a raven's wing. 'I've done the rounds and apologized to everyone. You're the last person on my list. I was out of order and shouldn't have said what I said.'

He locked the car and pocketed the keys. 'That's OK. We've all said things . . .' he trailed off.

'I was about to take a turn around the grounds before the inspector calls,' she said. 'Care to accompany me?'

'Why not?'

They made their way along the side of the hall opposite the caravan and the maze, passed the kitchen garden, and strolled across the rolling greensward towards the lake.

'I think it was the situation last night,' Cartier went on. 'The idea that Haggerston might not have been the killer, after all . . .'

Langham glanced at her. 'And wondering, if he didn't kill Suzie, then who did? You seemed rather adamant that we should each of us state why we hated Miss Reynard.'

She winced. 'Was I? To be honest, I can't recall that much.'

'I think,' he said tentatively, 'that you were eager for us all to know why *you* hated her. Perhaps you'd care to tell me?'

'Fancy yourself as a psychologist?'

'Strictly amateur,' he said.

She gave him a one-eyed glance through the rising smoke of her cigarette. 'Why do *you* think I hated her, Mr Freud?'

He kicked at a dandelion head in passing. 'Oh . . . all the usual reasons.'

'Which are?'

'Do you really want to know? Promise you won't hate me for being candid?'

'I'm a big girl, Mr Langham. I can take the brickbats.'

'Very well. A superficial analysis would be that you resent her youth, beauty and success.'

Her red lips described a contemplative lasso around the filter of her cigarette. 'And a less superficial analysis?'

'That, as well as all the above, you were more than a trifle put out by the fact that Suzie was . . . was seeing Dennison, with whom you'd had an affair.'

She laughed. 'You're so wrong! Me, jealous of Suzie bedding Dennison?' She paused, then asked, 'And anyway, how come you know that me and him . . .?'

'The proverbial little birdy.'

'Suzie, right?'

'Wrong.'

'Dennison hasn't been bragging, has he?'

'No, it wasn't Dennison.'

'Only, it was never in the papers back home. We managed to keep it quiet. And boy, was I glad about that when it all blew up in my face.'

'What happened?' He raised both hands. 'And of course you don't have to say a word if you'd rather keep schtum.'

She smiled at his use of the Americanism. 'No, it helps to talk, and you have a good bedside manner, Doctor Langham. What happened? Dennison beat me up is what happened. Things in the sack turned from rough – playful but acceptable – to downright nasty.' She tapped her head. 'Dennison might be famous, and fêted, but let me tell you that he's one hell of a screwed-up son of a bitch. Ego problems, I'd say. He craves power, and doesn't like it when someone in his thrall becomes empowered themselves.'

She took a last draw on her cigarette, flung it to the ground and screwed it out with the toe of her shoe. 'This was way back, just after the war, when I was still box-office. I'd starred in one of his films and it'd done OK, and he wanted me for the next one, only I had a much better offer from Metro. So off I went. And of course Dougy boy didn't like that one bit and took it out on me big time.'

'So . . . you dislike Dennison as well as Suzie?' he said.

'Say, you must have me down as some kind of sociopath! My grievance with Dougy is genuine.'

'And with Suzie? Which, if I recall, is where this conversation started.'

She sighed. 'As I think I told you, me and Suzie go way back.

We were friends, once, before I realized what a low-down, lying little bitch she really was.'

'Care to elucidate?'

'I was up for a big part, back in 'forty-seven, and Suzie started a whispering campaign. The woman in charge of casting was high-powered and influential, and Suzie put it about that I was having an affair with her husband. I mean, do I look stupid enough to bed the hubby of a powerful player like that?' She shrugged. 'Anyway, the shit stuck and not only did I not get the part, but the casting director put the word around and I didn't get any decent parts ever again. Period.'

Langham grimaced. 'I see now why you two were at daggers drawn.'

'And what made it worse is that the little bitch denied, to the day she died, she had anything to do with the lies. She effectively ruined my career, Langham, and had the gall to play the innocent.'

'I'm sorry.'

'Don't be. I'm a tough cookie. I survive.' She gave a bitter laugh, and said under her breath, 'which is more than can be said for little Miss Butter-Wouldn't-Melt . . .'

They turned and made their slow way back, and a minute later Langham pointed to MacTaggart's Humber as it drew up under the elms. 'Here's the inspector.'

As they strode more purposefully towards the hall, Varla lighted a cigarette and said, 'So, who do you think was responsible for the murder? Looking at it objectively, Langham, wouldn't you say that I'm pretty much the prime suspect? I have the motive, after all.'

Langham wondered if she knew full well that Douglas Dennison had very likely been the intended target, and that Suzie Reynard had been in the wrong place at the wrong time.

'I wouldn't rule anyone out at this stage,' he said noncommittally.

As they walked, Langham glanced at the actress.

She was tall, and dark, and broad across the shoulders. Might Desmond Haggerston have mistaken Varla Cartier for a man, if he'd collided with her on the morning of the murder?

Langham left Varla smoking in the driveway and entered the hall. He found Inspector MacTaggart pacing the library like an impatient stork, his hands clasped behind his back and his long, thin head thrust forward. Ferrars was at the mantelpiece.

'I'd like a quick word before you begin the interviews,' Langham said, closing the door behind him. 'It's about Haggerston.'

'You saw him this morning?'

Langham recounted his interview with the old man, telling MacTaggart how Haggerston had come to pick up the revolver on Sunday morning.

'And you say Haggerston's quite sure he didn't recognize the person he collided with?' MacTaggart said.

'He couldn't say who it was.'

'Tall and male . . .' MacTaggart mused.

'That's what he said, but whether it was a man or not, I wouldn't be so sure. Haggerston had been drinking, and he was caught totally by surprise.'

'But that's all we have to go on, Langham. And there's not many people who fit the bill.'

From the mantelpiece, Ferrars observed laconically, 'Off the top of my head, I'd say just three. Evans the butler, Banning, and you, Langham.'

'That's right,' Langham said. 'That's why I said I'd take Haggerston's testimony with a pinch of salt. He might have collided with anyone that morning.'

MacTaggart continued his pacing. 'Do you know something, Langham? I'm more than a little inclined to suspect that Dennison has more to do with this than I first thought.'

'I suppose we can't rule him out,' Langham said. 'Though what would he be doing coming around the side of the house just after committing the murder?'

Ferrars said, 'What if he intended to plant the revolver in the hall, to incriminate someone else?'

'It's possible, I suppose,' Langham said. 'But what about motive?'

MacTaggart waved this aside. 'Lover's tiff, an argument of some kind . . . I'm sure we'll find a motive if we dig deep enough.'

'Against the lover's tiff theory,' Langham said, 'remember that the killer broke into the cabinet in the gun room and stole the weapon, which rules out a spur-of-the-moment action. This killing was premeditated. I still suspect that Dennison himself was the intended target.'

'I'll keep an open mind, I assure you.' MacTaggart looked at his watch. 'Very well, let's get the show rolling. Could you tell young Ambler to toddle along quick-sharp, Langham?'

*   *   *

One hour later, the interviews concluded, Langham and Maria left the hall. They took the car and accelerated through the gates and along the lane to the Seven Sleepers before the reporters could follow.

'How did it go?' he asked.

Maria stuck out her lower lip. 'Oh, the same as before. The same questions, the same answers. Was I sure I remained awake from three o'clock until six? Did I leave the room? Did *you*, Donald, leave the room?'

He parked the Austin around the back of the Seven Sleepers in case the press should attempt to track them down. The last thing he wanted now was a reporter interrupting their lunch.

'I don't know about you,' he said as they climbed from the car, 'but I'm famished. I could even eat a stale cheese sandwich.'

'Do you think they know what a G&T is, Donald?'

'That might be pushing it a bit.'

They sat outside, hidden from the lane by a trellis laden with honeysuckle.

Langham entered the pub and ordered two rounds of ham-and-mustard sandwiches and a pint of bitter, and was surprised to find that the barmaid was au fait with the exoticism of gin and tonic.

While he was waiting for his bitter to settle before being topped up, he glanced through a door to the snuggery. Another guest at the hall had decided to escape its claustrophobic confines after his grilling. Seated on a padded bench, reading a newspaper, was Chuck Banning. Evidently he'd just arrived, as a full glass of lemonade stood on the table before him.

Langham carried the drinks outside.

'Mmm . . . but that is very good, Donald,' Maria said, sipping her drink. 'And they even have ice.'

He told her about his visit to Haggerston House and his meeting with the old man. 'He described in detail what happened back in 'thirty-one, the shooting.'

She stared at him. 'He admitted to killing his wife?'

'Do you know something? I think it was a relief, a weight off his conscience. He'd been living with the guilt for so long.'

Maria sat back and contemplated her drink. 'Strange . . .' she mused.

'What is?'

'I never thought I would feel sorry for someone who had shot his wife dead.' She shrugged. 'But I do.' She frowned. 'Do you understand that, Donald?'

'Of course. You can feel empathy with someone without condoning their actions. I feel the same, to be frank. Sitting with him in the knot garden, as he drank himself senseless, I felt something of the tragedy he'd made of his life.'

She shivered. 'Sometimes, Donald, I cannot believe my luck.'

He laughed and squeezed her hand.

The barmaid came out with their sandwiches, great hunks of white bread and generous slabs of ham. Langham bit into his and nodded. 'Mmm,' he said. 'This is very good.'

Maria smiled. 'For a country pub in the middle of nowhere, Donald, it is acceptable.'

'The Maria Dupré seal of approval: "The cuisine at the Seven Sleepers is acceptable."'

A car drew up in the lane and Langham recognized the Marlings' black Rover with Evans at the wheel. As he watched, Cynthia Marling climbed out and walked around the car.

Maria murmured, 'We have company, Donald.'

'Not us,' he whispered.

Cynthia crossed the lane, smiled unsurely at Langham and Maria as she passed, and hurried into the pub. The Rover pulled away.

'That is strange. I didn't think Cynthia the type to frequent public houses,' Maria said. 'And what did you mean by "not us"?'

He thumbed over his shoulder. 'Young Chuck is in the snug,' he said.

'Ah . . .' Maria said. 'Do you think Edward knows about them?'

'To be honest, I think he wouldn't be much bothered if he did. Or maybe his pride would be dented.' He sat back and enjoyed the warmth of the sun on his face as he watched Maria bite into her doorstep.

'Do you know what I would like?' she said. 'And I am being serious.'

'I'm intrigued. Go on.'

'When we are married, I would like a little house in the country.'

He paused with his glass frozen before his mouth. 'And live there?'

'No, Donald, I would stable horses in it. Of course we would live there.'

'A house? In the country? Well, I'd never considered . . .' The thought was novel, almost bizarre, but the notion of living anywhere with Maria Dupré, of embarking upon any venture, filled him with excitement. 'And leave London, you mean?'

'Well, yes. As so much of my job is spent reading manuscripts and speaking to people on the phone, I could easily do all that from home. If we lived in the country, I would go into London perhaps two or three days a week, and spend the rest of the time with you.'

'It's certainly an idea.' He looked at her. 'How long have you been contemplating this?'

She shrugged. 'A month or so. I don't dislike London, but the traffic and the noise . . . You wouldn't miss the city, would you?'

He frowned. 'I'm not sure. No . . .' he mused, 'perhaps not. I can write anywhere, and as I only do two days a week at Ralph's . . . Would we rent somewhere?'

She reached out and tapped his knee. 'We could actually buy a three-bedroom cottage for around £800 or a thousand.'

He pulled a face. 'But steep, isn't it? Though if you do take over the running of the agency . . .'

'And if you have a few bestsellers,' she added.

'In my dreams,' he laughed.

Maria smiled. 'Oh, you never know. Something might come along . . . And with three bedrooms,' she went on, 'it would be big enough for a study for each of us, with plenty of room for all your books.'

'Well . . .'

'There are places in Suffolk, not far from where Charles lives, which are only a short drive from a train station on the line to London. We could be in the city in an hour and a half. I'll show you the *Bury St Edmunds Gazette* when we get back home, Donald.'

He laughed.

'What?' she asked.

'A year ago, Maria, there I was, living the life of a bachelor and not even dreaming that you'd look twice at me.'

'When all along, every time you came into the office, I was hoping you'd pluck up the courage to ask me out for a meal.'

He drained his glass. 'How about another?'

'Perhaps a lemonade for me, Donald.'

He returned to the bar and ordered a pint of bitter and a lemonade with ice. Glancing through at the snug, he saw Cynthia and Chuck seated at a corner table. They were leaning forward, speaking intently and oblivious of his attention.

'I don't know . . .' he said as he rejoined Maria.

Her face clouded. 'About living in the country?'

'What? Oh, sorry. No, I meant, I don't know about . . .' He indicated the snuggery. 'Cynthia and Chuck in there.'

She smiled at him with that mischievous twist to her lips that told him she was agog at what he had to say, but that she thought it was probably erroneous. 'Go on.'

'Their relationship. It seems a bit odd . . .'

She frowned. 'Because she is in her fifties, and he is twenty, yes?'

'Well, maybe,' he said. 'I don't know, it just seems . . . strange.'

'Would it strike you as strange if it were the other way around? If Chuck were fifty-odd and Cynthia twenty?'

He shook his head. 'I honestly don't know,' he admitted. 'Perhaps it's because a relationship like this is so uncommon – you usually see older men chasing younger women.' He shrugged. 'Or . . . perhaps it's because in every other aspect of her life, Cynthia seems so straight-laced and . . .'

'Catholic?'

He smiled. 'You said it. I wonder how she squares what she's doing with her faith?'

'Shhh!' Maria said, looking past him to the entrance of the public house.

Chuck Banning hurried out, pointedly ignoring Langham and Maria, and turned left along the lane. Maria raised her eyebrows as she watched him go.

Two minutes later the Rover drew up in the lane, and in due course Cynthia Marling stepped from the pub. As she passed Langham and Maria, she hesitated and gave a uncertain smile.

'I hope you don't think . . .' she began nervously. 'What I mean to say is, this isn't what you think it is.'

Langham opened his mouth, but found a suitable reply beyond him. Maria stared into her drink.

Cynthia paused, as if considering whether to say something else, then shook her head and hurried away. She climbed into the car and it drove off.

Maria stared after her. 'I wonder what she meant by that, Donald?'

'What else can "it" be but a frustrated, rather plain middle-aged woman wildly recapitulating the wanton excess of her long-lost youth?'

Maria clutched his hand. 'You have such a way with words,' she mocked. 'You have me reaching for my red pen.'

They finished their drinks and drove back to the hall.

TWENTY-ONE

Maria retired to their room to lie down and Langham was in the library, a little later, when Edward Marling appeared in the doorway.

'Ah, there you are,' he said. 'The other day I invited you to my study . . . Care to pop up now?'

Langham lay aside the copy of *Country Life* he'd been leafing through and followed Edward from the room. He was about to climb the stairs, but Edward said, 'This way, Donald. You might as well take a ride in my little toy.'

He thumbed a control set flush with the oak wall panel and a section of the wall slid back to reveal a small lift. Edward rolled himself inside and Langham followed. The door slid shut and they rode up to the gallery.

'Life was a bit more difficult before I had the lift installed,' Edward said. 'It makes things much easier.'

The door sighed open opposite Langham's bedroom and, thinking of Maria lying on the bed beyond the door, he turned left and followed Edward along the passage to the room at the far end.

Edward's study was stocked with what Langham considered to be real books, as opposed to the morocco-bound volumes that served a purely decorative function in the so-called library they'd just left.

'Modern firsts on that wall,' Edward said, indicating the floor-to-ceiling shelving, 'and on that wall, my crime collection. I must admit I'm an aficionado of the American hard-boiled school.'

Langham strode around the room, admiring the books and making appreciative noises.

Edward said, 'I've found, ever since the war, that fiction acts as a great . . . I was about to say escape, but that isn't quite right. It's almost a surrogate life, a way of appreciating a reality not your own.'

Langham smiled. 'I sometimes wonder if that's why I write – to escape the exigencies of reality.'

'Humans can't bear very much of it, after all,' Edward said. 'Now, who said that?'

'I think it might have been Eliot.'

Langham paused before a long shelf given over to an orderly line of military figures.

'A throwback to my boyhood,' Edward said. 'I started to collect these after the war.'

Each figurine represented soldiers from various armies down the ages; there were perhaps fifty of them, each one positioned at exactly the same distance from its neighbour.

In the centre of the room stood a big desk laid out with several pens, a stapler, a rocking-horse blotter and a ream of typing paper. Like the military figures, these items were arranged with Edward's regimental precision. Next to a Remington upright typewriter sat a pile of manuscript pages.

'Ah, the work in progress,' Langham said.

'I've just finished the chapter detailing my very last mission. And what a fiasco that was . . .'

'What happened exactly, if you don't mind my asking?'

Edward stared at the manuscript, as if reliving the events. 'It should have been a relatively simple operation to blow up a marshalling yard at Narbonne. It was a strategic position on the Germans' railway network – lots of bauxite passing through. The plan was to blow up a signal box and an electrical substation, which would have taken the Germans a couple of weeks to repair. That was the hope, anyway. Eight of us set out that night. I knew and trusted all of them, which made what happened later all the more difficult to take.'

He paused, his gaze distant. 'We approached the station at three in the morning. Pitch black, moonless night. Two groups of four, one heading for the signal box, the other for the substation. Plan was to plant charges without being seen and skedaddle. Piece of cake. I was with Douglas and two experienced Resistance fighters, a man and a woman I'd known for years. We were to take the substation. When we reached the marshalling yard, all hell broke loose. The bastards were lying in wait and opened up with everything they had. I thought I'd managed to get away, then something hit me in the back. *One-two-three*, one after the other, very fast – like hammer blows. I went down, thinking I was dead. I passed out, and the next I knew I was in the back of a German truck, being taken to hospital. I was patched up, then handed over to the Gestapo . . . and I've described what I went through at their hands.'

'And then the Resistance rescued you . . .'

'I was lucky. The fact was that I knew a hell of a lot of names, and if I'd blabbed . . .' he shrugged, 'many people would have died.

I held out, and then the Resistance raided the headquarters and got me out – though if I'd died in the raid it would've been all the same to them. They concealed me in a truck going over the Pyrenees and got me out that way. Only later, when I got home, did I find out what'd happened to Douglas and the others. The four-man team attacking the signal box were killed at the scene. Of my team, the man was injured in the ambush and though he managed to get away, he died a few days later. The woman . . .' He compressed his lips bitterly. 'She slipped away before the firing started and made it back to where we had holed up. She was questioned by fellow members of the Resistance found to have informed the Germans of the operation, and was dealt with . . . As they say, all's fair in love and war. Douglas got away, but as his cover was more than likely compromised it was thought best to get him out of the country. A sub took him from a fishing boat off Marseilles a few nights later.' Edward smiled grimly. 'As I said, a fiasco.'

Langham indicated the manuscript. 'How do you find having to relive the experiences?'

'Cathartic, in a word. But it's taking much longer than I anticipated when I began the thing. I find that I can only dictate for an hour or so at a stretch.'

'You dictate it?'

Edward laughed. 'I sense the disapproval of a real writer, Donald.'

'Whatever works for you.'

'Cynthia and I come up here at three every afternoon and I dictate the next instalment for an hour.'

'Cynthia?' Langham tried not to sound surprised.

Edward smiled at Langham. 'You find it odd that she should be my amanuensis? But it's perfectly understandable, from her perspective. You see, she does it because she wants to control this aspect of my life, just as she controls every other. I began pecking out the memoir myself, but she insisted she help me. Hell,' he said in a bitter undertone, 'it's the only thing we do do together.'

Discomfited by Edward's candour, Langham moved from the desk to the far end of the room and stood before the window overlooking Dennison's caravan and the maze beyond. This wall was the only one not fitted with bookshelves; instead it was hung with a dozen crossbows, some of them, judging from the worn, polished wood, of considerable age.

Edward said, 'They belonged to Cynthia's father. She was something of a crack shot in her youth. I keep expecting her to use one of the things on me.'

Langham stood with his back to the invalid, staring through the window at the padlocked caravan.

Edward said, 'Please, I don't want you to pity me.'

Langham turned. 'I beg your pardon?'

When Edward spoke next, Langham had the impression that he was fighting some intense emotion. 'I know what Cynthia's doing, Donald. She tried to keep it a secret, but Evans acts as my eyes and ears. I know all about Cynthia and Mr Banning.'

'I'm sorry,' Langham said instinctively. 'I mean . . .'

Edward went on, 'It's not so much the fact of their – their affair that hurts so much, Donald. Our relationship died many years ago. What really riles me is Cynthia's hypocrisy. Her piety when it comes to her regard of the actions of others, her censure of those she thinks immoral . . . while all the while – all the while she's committing a sin herself.'

'Have you considered divorce?'

Edward looked broken, and despite the man's earlier plea that he did not want to be pitied, Langham felt an abiding sympathy for Edward Marling.

'Cynthia wouldn't grant me a divorce,' Edward said quietly. 'And even if she were to, then I would find myself in an impossible situation.'

He did not elucidate, and thinking back on it later, Langham assumed that the 'impossible situation' referred to the public shame that Edward would suffer as a cuckolded husband.

'But enough of all that,' Edward said, wheeling himself across to a bookshelf. 'Take a look at this. I've recently acquired a nice first edition of Chandler's *The Long Goodbye*.'

They talked of books for the next half hour, and then Langham excused himself. As he made his way from the study, he experienced a profound – but at the same time obscurely shameful – sense of relief at having escaped.

TWENTY-TWO

After breakfast the following morning, Langham received a phone call from Ralph Ryland.

'Sorry I wasn't in touch yesterday, Don. Spent all day nipping from one end of London to the other.'

'Learn much?'

'Quite a bit. I talked to people who knew Sir Humph before he became a sir, and I tracked down a woman who was a friend of Cynthia Marling's in the thirties.'

'What did she have to say?'

'Not much, over the phone. She was an old-fashioned type who wouldn't speak to strangers on the blower. So I've made an appointment to interview her after lunch today. Thought you'd like to come along. She's retired to a village halfway between Marling Hall and Norwich, a place called Little Gamling. Now according to my Norfolk gazetteer, the village has a half decent pub. I thought we might meet there around half eleven, talk over what I've found out, then have a natter with this Edna Mayhew at one.'

'Excellent, let's do that. I'll see if Maria would care to come along.'

'Oh, one other thing,' Ryland said. 'Do you think there'd be room for me at Marling Hall tonight?'

'Plenty of room. The place is like a half-empty hotel. Don't you fancy the drive back to London?'

'It's not that, Don. After finding out about the people at the hall yesterday, I'd like the chance to hobnob. Get to know 'em a bit better, like.'

'Good idea. And after dinner we can talk through the case over a brandy.'

'That sounds civilized. Right, I'll meet you at the Red Lion,' Ryland said, and rang off.

Langham found Maria in their room, lying on the bed and reading her manuscript.

'I'm popping over to interview an old friend of Cynthia's.' He told her about Ryland's call. 'Fancy a spin?'

She sighed. 'I'm so far behind on this thing,' she said, rolling her eyes, 'that I'd better buckle down and try to get it finished.'

'Rather you than me, from the sound of it.'

They parted with a kiss, and Langham found Cynthia and arranged for Ryland to stay the night. Five minutes later he left Marling Hall and drove east into the heart of Norfolk.

The day was sweltering, and after driving for ten minutes he pulled into the side of the lane to take off his jacket, roll up his shirtsleeves, and wind down the window. He could have downed a couple of pints now, never mind having to wait until eleven thirty.

As he drove through the rolling green farmland of Norfolk, he found himself thinking about the imminent wedding and the guests they'd invited, many of whom they hadn't seen for years. Maria had invited half a dozen girls from the private school she'd attended at the start of the war, as well as her London friends. The few remaining members of Langham's family were coming down from Nottingham, along with a couple of old school friends and some colleagues in publishing. It would be a lavish do in St Michael's in Highgate – paid for by Maria's father, at his insistence – and a far cry from the meagre registry office affair of his wedding to Jane in 'thirty-seven.

Langham turned his thoughts away from that big mistake, and his subsequent unhappy marriage, and soon found himself contemplating the affair at Marling Hall. He had studied the suspects over the course of the past couple of days, looking for telltale signs of remorse. But the killer, whoever it might be, had been practised enough, or sufficiently cold-hearted, not to exhibit that remorse in the slightest.

His musings on the identity of the killer were not helped by the fact that he liked many of the people in question. He was enjoying the renewal of his friendship with the self-deprecating, melancholic Terry Ambler, and he found Chuck Banning's youthful naivety somewhat endearing. Varla Cartier's sardonic black humour and pessimism might have been tiring in anyone else, but it was leavened in her case by a wit often directed at herself. Edward Marling was personable, and Langham felt a good deal of sympathy for the man. He even found himself feeling sorry for Cynthia Marling, caught as she was on the horns of a dilemma, torn between doing the right thing by her disabled husband, and her feelings for the youthful Chuck Banning. The only person Langham didn't take a shine to was the lascivious Sir Humphrey Lyle.

He found the village of Little Gamling down a warren of winding lanes between fields of corn. The term village, he thought as he pulled up beside the green, was something of a misnomer: it was more a hamlet, consisting of a dozen houses, many of them thatched, a small Norman church and a half-timbered public house.

Ralph Ryland's Morris Minor was pulled up outside the Red Lion, and Langham found the detective at the bar, chatting to the publican.

'And here he is,' Ryland said. 'The man himself, looking as if he could down a pint for England. What're you having, Don? Mine host recommends the Harvest Light . . .' He took a sip from his glass. 'And I agree, it's bloody marvellous.'

'That'll do me, Ralph. What about food?'

The publican informed them that they didn't do meals, but sold pork pies and pickled eggs. They ordered a couple of pies apiece and an egg each. 'And throw in a packet of pork scratchings for good measure,' Ryland added.

They carried their pints and food out to a back garden and sat at a table under a timber sunshade like a lychgate. Langham raised his glass. 'Here's to getting this affair wrapped up sooner rather than later.'

'I'll second that,' Ryland said, wiping foam from his clipped ginger moustache with the back of his hand.

For the next ten minutes Langham recounted his meeting with Desmond Haggerston the previous day, and the old man's confession to the murder of his wife. He went on to detail Haggerston's movements on the morning of the murder.

When he finished, Ryland said, 'So he actually bumped into the killer . . . Tall, and probably male?'

'But as I said to MacTaggart, I'd take that with a pinch of the proverbial. Haggerston was drunk at the time.' He bit into his pie and washed it down with a mouthful of ale. 'Anyway, what have you got?'

Ryland pulled a battered notebook from the inside pocket of his jacket, opened it to the relevant page, and screwed his eyes up as if having difficulty reading his own tiny handwriting.

'I'll go through 'em in alphabetical order, Don. First up we have your old mate Terry Ambler. Well, drew a bit of a blank on this geezer. Never been in trouble with the law. He was married briefly in the early fifties, but divorced soon after, and his ex-wife emigrated to Canada in 'fifty-three. He lives in Camden and has a few mates down the local boozer who vouch for him. But you probably knew most of this anyway.'

Langham nodded. 'He strikes me as one of the least likely of our suspects.'

'Next up,' Ryland said, flipping a page in his notebook, 'is Chuck Banning. I have a mate in Los Angeles, Irish chap who was in this game before the war. I got on well with him, for a Paddy. He married a Yank and set up shop as a private eye in California. Anyway, I rang him the other night and asked him to look up the folk on my list, and he got back to me yesterday. Not a lot on Banning, other than the fact that he was born in England in 'thirty-five and left for the States with his folks when he was one.'

Langham took a draught of ale. 'He mentioned that.'

'He took US citizenship a couple of years ago, when he was eighteen. He worked as a carpenter in the MGM studios until "discovered" by some director, on account of his good looks. No police record, played bit parts in three or four films. This is his first big break.' He turned the page, took a mouthful of beer, and smacked his lips. 'Now, this is where it gets juicy. Varla Cartier.'

'I suspect she's led an interesting life?'

'Interesting? Not half, Don. When I said her name to Mick, he laughed and reeled off everything he knew about her before he even started digging.'

'And?'

'First, she has a record as long as your arm. She was in trouble with the law when she was fourteen, shoplifting and petty theft. When she was twenty she was involved with an older man, a rich estate agent, and was prosecuted for attacking him with a kitchen knife. She only got off with a suspended sentence because she pleaded self-defence. She got into films in her mid-twenties – this was in the early thirties, but she dragged her troubled past with her. A few counts of possession of illegal drugs, cocaine and cannabis, prosecuted in 'thirty-nine for trashing the house of an ex-lover, destroying lots of valuable paintings. Was quite a star until after the war, when she found parts harder to come by. Oh, and she plays the cello with sticky fingers.'

Langham lowered his pint and stared at his friend. 'I beg your pardon?'

'She prefers women to men, but not exclusively,' Ryland explained.

'That's a new one on me.'

'Well, you live and learn, Don.'

'That might explain the looks she keeps giving Maria,' Langham said, biting into his pork pie.

Ryland continued, 'Word in Hollywood is that she and Suzie Reynard were close until some spat about a casting director. Mick didn't know the details. Also, there was a rumour going around LA that she and Dennison had had a stormy affair just after the war.'

Langham nodded. 'I knew about that,' he said, 'and the spat with Suzie Reynard. Varla gave me her side of the story.' He recounted the details to Ryland.

The detective consulted his notes. 'Sir Humphrey. Turns out he's quite a bird. Married five times and a serial philanderer – in the words of his best friend, the actor Cyril Eastbourne. Been an actor all his natural, knighted ten years ago for services to the stage. Not so much as a parking ticket – but he's bedded every actress in London. People are divided, some hate him, others think he's God's gift.' He shrugged. 'But no links at all to Reynard or Dennison, other than the fact that the latter hired him for this film.'

'The Marlings?' Langham asked.

'Edward, commissioned as an officer with the Royal Gloucester-shires when he graduated from Oxford back in 'thirty-one. Exemplary war record, ending when he was shot by the Jerries in 'forty-four. Inherited Marling Hall just before the war when his father died, but the death duties were crippling – more of that in a sec. Married Cynthia Forster in 'forty-one. That's about as much as I've got on him.'

'And Cynthia?'

'Much more on her, Don.' He squinted at his notes. 'I talked to an old doctor at St Bart's who remembered Cynthia and gave me the name of a friend of hers, a nurse now working at the Maudesley. I tracked her down and had a chinwag with her between shifts. She was big buddies with Cynthia from the late thirties to the end of the war, and she was around when Cynthia met Edward Marling, fell in love and tied the knot. Only . . . and this is the interesting bit . . . it's Cynthia who has all the money.'

'The money?'

'Oodles of the stuff, according to her nurse friend. See, her father was Reginald Forster, the furniture manufacturer, and when he shuffled off, Cynthia inherited the lot. Worth a million, apparently. This was in 'thirty-eight, and three years later she married Edward.'

Langham whistled. 'He certainly fell on his feet,' he said, and then, recollecting his conversation with Edward yesterday, decided otherwise.

'It doesn't end there, Don. When Cynthia and Edward got hitched, part of the deal was that she'd pay all the death duties and other expenses accrued by the estate, but that the hall and all its land should be ceded to her. Edward was in no position to refuse the offer: the alternative was to sell the hall in order to pay off the death duties. It isn't widely known – and I can understand why Edward wants to keep it quiet – but Marling Hall is owned lock, stock and barrel by Cynthia.'

'Ah, I begin to see . . .' Langham gestured with his half-eaten pork pie. 'Edward said something to me yesterday. He was talking about the state of his marriage – he knows Cynthia is carrying on with Chuck Banning – and I asked him why he didn't divorce her. He said he'd find himself in an "impossible situation" – and now I understand what he meant. If he divorced her he'd be out on his ear, without a roof over his head or a penny to his name. No wonder he resents Cynthia.'

Ryland regarded his pint. 'But does this have any bearing on the murder, or on the threats to Dennison?'

Langham finished his second pork pie and dusted his hands. 'Can't see that it does, Ralph, but it does go some way to explain the Marlings' mutual antagonism.'

'Anyway, this nurse I was talking to at the Maud, she tells me something else about Cynthia. A few years before they met, Cynthia was involved in some kind of scandal.'

'Scandal? What about?'

'She didn't know what it was. But it threatened her post at St Bart's, apparently. This here nurse is still in contact with the woman who was Cynthia's best friend at the time, a certain Edna Mayhew, and she gave me Mayhew's address here in the village. I'm hoping Miss Mayhew might know more about the scandal.'

Langham drained his pint. 'What about Dennison? Did your contact in LA have much to say about him?'

Ryland referred to his notebook. 'Dennison's one of the bad boys of Hollywood. A brawling bully, according to Mick. There are some people, producers and executives, who refuse to work with him. He's made more enemies than films, which is no mean feat as he's made over fifty movies since the late twenties.'

'Did Mick know anything about his relationship with Suzie Reynard?'

'Nothing, other than it was the latest in a long line of affairs with young starlets – each one lasting a few months.' He finished his beer and looked at his watch. 'I could kill for another pint, but it's five to one and we don't want to turn up kaylied at Miss Mayhew's.'

They returned their empties to the bar and left the Red Lion.

TWENTY-THREE

The Primroses was a tiny thatched cottage a short walk down a winding lane from the pub. Its limewashed walls were divided into squares by cross-hatched timber beams, and the wire-netted thatch sloped to within five feet of the ground, back and front. Surrounded by a bountiful cottage garden, it struck Langham as impossibly pretty – and probably was, though its quaint exterior probably concealed a multitude of defects. He'd known a writer chap before the war who'd rented a seventeenth-century thatched cottage one winter as the 'perfect writing retreat', only to it find it impossible to keep warm, incessantly draughty, and infested by every type of rodent known to humanity.

If Maria was serious about moving to the country, he would have to warn her off thatched cottages.

A sprightly grey-haired women in her fifties was on her knees in the front garden, tugging groundsel from a border with a vigour that verged on the ferocious. Ryland opened the gate and Langham followed him up the cinder path. The woman looked up and smiled, climbing to her feet.

'And you'll be Mr Ryland, no doubt?' she said.

'And this is my colleague, Donald Langham,' Ryland said.

'I'd invite you into the house, but as it's such a beautiful day perhaps we should take tea out here?' She indicated table and chairs in a stone-flagged area in the shade of a flowering cherry tree. 'How do you take it, gentlemen?'

'Black without for Don,' Ryland said, 'and white with three for me.'

Minutes later Miss Mayhew returned carrying a tray and set it on the table before them.

'I've read all about the awful incident at Marling Hall, of course. It must be terrible for poor Cynthia, what with all the publicity.'

'How long did you know her for, back in the thirties?' Ryland asked, blowing on his tea.

'I met Cynthia at St Bart's in 'thirty-four,' she said, 'and we hit it off from the start. Cynthia liked a good time, and in that she and I were of one accord. She also liked the occasional drink, I don't mind telling you, though up to that point I'd never touched a drop. My father, you see. Strict Lancastrian Methodist. He would have turned in his grave if he'd seen Cynthia and myself, out on the town.' She beamed at the recollection. 'But we were young, Mr Ryland, young and fancy free with all our lives ahead of us.'

'That doesn't sound like the Cynthia I know now,' Langham commented.

'Ah, well, you see . . . that was before she got religion.'

'She wasn't Catholic back then?' Ryland asked.

'Certainly not! I don't know what she was, as we never discussed religion. We were too busy enjoying ourselves to worry about things like that.'

'Do you know when she converted?' Langham asked.

'That would be at some point in the late thirties, 'thirty-eight, perhaps, though by that point we weren't seeing eye to eye.'

'You weren't?' Langham said. 'Do you mind my asking why?'

Miss Mayhew raised a bone china cup to her thin lips and sipped, her expression distant. 'We had a disagreement, a difference of opinion, and we fell out. I've often looked back and regretted . . .'

Ryland replaced his cup on its saucer and leaned forward. 'I've heard that Cynthia was involved in some kind of scandal in the mid-thirties.'

'That's right, Mr Ryland. That was it.'

'Would you care to explain what happened?' Langham coaxed.

Miss Mayhew nodded, but abstractedly, as if still troubled by the events of all those years ago. 'Cynthia had an affair, Mr Langham. Oh, we had young men friends aplenty back then, but this was different. Cynthia was smitten. And it's strange how it happened, because you see it was I who first took a fancy to the fellow. We were on an admissions ward at St Bart's and this young man was brought in, bruised and bloody from a beating he'd received. I took a shine to him straight away – well, he was handsome and had a way with words, and it helped that he was American.'

Langham exchanged a glance with Ryland.

Miss Mayhew went on, 'He was a film director, over here on some business or other. He'd got into an altercation in a bar in Chelsea and received a nasty cut to the forehead. We were getting on like a house on fire while I patched him up, and then Cynthia walked in and it was as if I'd ceased to exist. He was all over Cynthia like a rash and it was amazing to watch. It was as if they were made for each other. Well, she was a great beauty, back then, tall and glamorous.'

'And you and Cynthia fell out over him?' Langham said.

'Oh, it wasn't that that spoiled our friendship, Mr Langham. We were closer than that. We wouldn't fall out over some young man.'

'So . . . what happened?' Ryland asked.

'Cynthia and Dugs – that was her pet name for him – were inseparable for the next few months. I hardly saw her, though we did go out when I had a young man to make up a foursome. But Dugs – Douglas Dennison – there was something about him I didn't take to, and I soon thanked my lucky stars that it wasn't me he'd decided to go for. He was aggressive, and more than a little arrogant. He thought he was God's gift, and the way he treated people . . .'

'And the disagreement with Cynthia . . .?' Ryland prompted.

Miss Mayhew sighed. 'Cynthia became pregnant. She was dead set against an abortion; wouldn't countenance the idea. She was head over heels with Dennison and wanted to keep the child and go back to America. But Dennison, of course, had other ideas. He finished with her . . . and the state she was in! It took her years to get over the awful man. I heard, much later – this was during the war – I heard from a friend that Dennison was back in England, and apparently he regretted how he'd treated her and wanted her to give him another chance. Can you believe that! To her eternal credit, Cynthia wasn't having any of it. According to my friend, Dennison took it badly. He wasn't accustomed to having women say no to him, you see. But Cynthia told him what was what. She told Dennison that she'd never forgiven him for deserting her and her son.'

Langham stared at the woman. 'Her son?'

'Yes, her child was a little boy, Mr Langham. She christened him Charles. But, you see, this was why she and I fell out. It was over her beautiful little boy. I could never forgive her for putting him up for adoption. It seemed such a crime to me.'

She shook her head, tears in her eyes. 'You see, I was unable to have children, myself, and what she did seemed so unforgivable – even though little Charles was adopted by a very loving couple, who emigrated to the States not long after. I often wonder if Cynthia misses her son, Mr Langham, and wishes she could see him again, one day. That *would* be nice, wouldn't it?

'Now, would you care for more tea, gentlemen?'

'What I want to know,' Ryland said ten minutes later as they left the cottage and made their way back to the village green, 'is whether the fact that Chuck Banning is Cynthia's son has any bearing on the killing of Suzie Reynard or the threats to Dennison.'

Langham told Ryland what he and Maria had overheard between Cynthia and Banning in the maze on Saturday night. 'He asked her if she'd "told him", and when she replied in the negative, Chuck insisted that she must.'

'Tell "him"?' Ryland said. 'Do you think he meant his father, Dennison, or Edward Marling?'

Langham shook his head. 'I don't know. Either, I suppose. Dennison knows he has a son to Cynthia, but there's no evidence that he knows it's Chuck Banning.'

They came to the green and walked towards their cars.

'Isn't it a bit of a coincidence,' Ryland said, 'that Dennison should cast his son in a film to be shot in a country pile owned by Banning's mother?'

'It certainly is. We need to ask Cynthia about that, amongst other things. Also,' Langham on, 'what Miss Mayhew said about Dennison wanting to renew his affair with Cynthia during the war – it doesn't accord with what the director told me. He said he'd hardly seen Cynthia then.'

Ryland stopped beside his car, and said, 'Would Chuck Banning have had any reason for wanting his father dead? Maybe as revenge for how Dennison treated Cynthia, way back?'

Langham frowned. 'It seems a bit unlikely to me, Ralph.' He unlocked the door of his car. 'See you back at the hall.'

TWENTY-FOUR

Langham lost Ryland on the open road somewhere between Dereham and Swaffham, and arrived back at Marling Hall before his partner.

He remained in the car in the shade of the elms, staring across the drive at the house. Douglas Dennison was sitting in his canvas chair under a beech tree beyond the caravan, speaking on the telephone extension.

Ryland pulled up a few minutes later. Langham joined him and glanced at his watch. 'A couple of minutes to four. Cynthia will almost be finished taking dictation from Edward. Shall we . . .?'

They entered the hall and climbed the stairs to the gallery. Langham led the way to Edward's study and rapped on the door. The clatter of typewriter keys ceased, and seconds later Cynthia appeared, her expression one of surprise at seeing Langham and Ryland.

'Cynthia, I wonder if we might have a word?' Langham said.

'Of course. Come in.' She stood aside as they entered.

Edward Marling propelled himself across the room from the open window. 'Excellent timing, gentlemen. We've just finished for the day.' He turned to Cynthia. 'I need a drink. I think I'll go downstairs and see if Humphrey will join me.'

'He'll need no encouragement,' Cynthia said. 'He was already sozzled at lunch. Little did I know, before he arrived, that the pair of you would drink the cellar dry.'

'That's a bit of an exaggeration, Cyn.'

She smiled thinly. 'Exaggeration often proves a point.'

Edward was on the verge of replying, but thought better of it. He nodded to Langham and Ryland. 'I'll see you at dinner, gentlemen.'

He pushed himself from the room and Langham eased the door shut behind him.

He moved to the open window and stared out. Birdsong and the scent of honeysuckle wafted into the room. Down below, under the beech tree, Dennison was taking a pen to what looked like a script and scoring through it with determination.

When Langham turned, Ryland was standing before the tall figure of Cynthia Marling, and she was staring at the card he'd just shown her.

'A private detective?' She sounded bemused.

'And Donald is my assistant,' Ryland said.

She looked at Langham, her grey eyes censorious at his deception. 'But I thought . . .' she began. 'That is, I was given to understand that you were a friend of Suzie Reynard's?'

'Miss Reynard hired me to investigate certain matters,' Langham said, and left it at that.

'The poor girl was obviously frightened for her life,' Cynthia said, sinking onto the upright chair before the desk and fingering the string of pearls at her neck. 'How can I help you, gentlemen?'

Ryland pulled up a chair and positioned it before the woman. Langham remained on his feet, pacing back and forth. He stopped beside the desk and glanced at the arrangement of meticulously ordered objects.

Ryland said, 'We'd like to know how Douglas Dennison came to choose Marling Hall as the location for the film.'

Her high brow furrowed in thought. 'Well, we heard that he was interested in coming to England—'

'You mean, you were in contact with him?' Ryland interrupted.

'Not me, personally; Edward. They remained in contact after the war, you see.'

'So, when Dennison said he wanted to make a film about the events at Haggerston House . . .'

'Edward mentioned that it might be possible to shoot the film here,' Cynthia said.

'And what did you think of this?'

'I was in full agreement. We would be remunerated by the production company, and I don't mind admitting that the fees received are most welcome.'

Langham crossed the room to a low shelf on which a row of photographs was arranged with Edward's characteristic precision. They showed a young Edward Marling in the thirties, smart in a grey flannel suit, posed with friends beside a sports car and on the deck of a yacht. There were no photographs of Cynthia.

He turned. 'When exactly did Edward contact Dennison about using Marling Hall?'

'That would be about a year ago, not long after his last operation. He took himself off to some hotel in Bournemouth to get over the disappointment. He was . . . Well, to say that he was depressed at its unsuccessful outcome would be an understatement. He even refused to see me during that time. He rang me and told me that Dennison wanted to make the film, and Edward suggested that we approach him about renting the hall.' She smiled from Langham to Ryland. 'The operation had been performed by a top Harley Street surgeon, and his services didn't come cheap. The money we would receive from the production company would be a way of allaying the crippling cost of the procedure.' Belatedly, she realized her awful pun, and winced. She hurried on, 'It took that long, almost a year, once Dennison had accepted our offer, for him to arrange things with the production company and everyone else. The making of a film, I am told, is a complex business.'

Ryland asked, 'And do you know who was responsible for casting the film?'

Cynthia blinked. 'Why . . .' Her hand left her pearls and gestured vaguely. 'I presume they had a casting director for that side of things.'

'Would Dennison have had any say in which actors were selected?' Ryland asked.

'I . . . yes, I presume so. Suzie Reynard had already been chosen for the female lead role, after all.'

Ryland glanced across at Langham, and nodded minimally.

Langham leaned against the wall, and said, 'The actor we were thinking of was Chuck Banning.'

Cynthia caught her breath. She gathered herself and, smiling with dissimulation, said, 'What about him, Mr Langham?'

'Who was responsible for his selection?'

'Why, the casting director, I presume.'

'With no outside influence?'

She tried not to appear flustered, but failed. 'Whatever do you mean?'

Langham said, 'Did you ask Douglas Dennison to cast your son, Chuck Banning?'

She reddened to the roots of her grey hair, and for a second Langham thought she was about to deny the suggestion. Her gaze dropped to the carpet and she murmured, 'How do you know that Chuck . . .?'

'That doesn't matter,' Ryland said. 'We're trying to get a full picture of what's happening here. We need you to be open with us about your relationship with Banning and Dennison.'

Cynthia took a long breath, then nodded. 'Yes, I asked Dennison to cast Chuck,' she said. 'To be perfectly honest, I paid him to do so.'

Langham pushed himself away from the wall, crossed the room and sat on the corner of the desk. 'You paid Dennison? Let's get one thing straight: does Dennison know that Banning is his son?'

Cynthia shook her head. 'No, he was never interested. Back in 'thirty-four, when – when I told him I was having his child, he dropped me and ran off. Left the country just as soon as he could. I wanted to keep Charles, but it was impossible. You see, I dared not tell my father about the child, and I couldn't have survived on my nurse's wages at the time. I *had* to put my son up for adoption. My only consolation was that he was taken by a wonderful, loving couple. It was a private arrangement, you see, done through my solicitor, with the agreement that they would inform me of Charles's progress from time to time, but that they would not tell him about me until he reached the age of twenty-one, which they did.'

'This year?' Langham said.

'In January.'

Ryland said, 'So, when you contacted Dennison and said you'd pay him if he cast Chuck in the film, what excuse did you use?'

'I contacted him last summer. I knew that Charles had started working in Hollywood – I went down to London and saw him in a film. Can you imagine that, gentlemen? I lived from year to year, waiting for the annual letter from his adoptive parents with news of my son, and then I discovered that he had a small part in a film which was due to be released over here.' She reached into a pocket of her skirt, withdrew a lace handkerchief, and dabbed at her eyes. 'Excuse me. I'm sorry . . .' She smiled from Ryland to Langham. 'Last year I saw him on the screen in the dingy cinema in Leicester Square. There he was, larger than life, so tall and handsome . . . my son. The scene lasted only a couple of minutes. I wanted to stop the film, rewind it and watch it over and over!' She smiled. 'And then Edward mentioned the idea of having Dennison shoot one of his films here, and I saw the opportunity . . .'

'But what excuse . . .?' Ryland began.

'I'm sorry, that was your original question, wasn't it? I wrote to Dennison and said that Charles was the son of great friends of mine, that he was a talented actor with some small film credits to his name already, and that I would be willing to pay Dennison personally if he were to cast Charles.'

'And Dennison wasn't at all suspicious?' Langham asked.

She shrugged. 'Not to my knowledge. He wrote back a month later to say that not only had he agreed to my offer, but that he'd given Charles a screen test and was casting him in the *lead* role.'

'That must have been . . . gratifying,' Langham commented.

'But even more so, Mr Langham, was the thought that after more than twenty years I would be seeing my son once again . . .' She smiled at them. 'The day he arrived, just last week . . . the sight of him climbing from the car and standing there, looking up at the hall . . . A few weeks earlier I'd received the most endearingly naive letter from Charles, saying how wonderful it would be to meet me after all these years, and marvelling at the coincidence of being cast in a film being shot at the hall.'

'He never suspected that you were behind his being cast?' Langham asked.

'One thing I have learned about my son, gentlemen, is that he is still in many ways a child, naive to the ways of the world. I don't want to disappoint him by admitting that I secured him the part. He is talented enough, according to Dennison, to get by in the jungle of Hollywood without any influence on my part.'

Langham said, 'This explains what you said when you saw Maria and me at the public house yesterday.'

She smiled. 'This isn't what it seems,' she repeated.

'On Saturday evening you met Chuck in the maze. Maria and I happened to be passing, and we overheard you speaking.'

Cynthia coloured again. 'My word, you must have thought it a midnight tryst.'

'We were puzzled by what we heard, Cynthia. Chuck was exhorting you to "tell him". I presume, in light of what we've just learned, that he was referring to the fact that he was your son. But whom did he want telling? Edward, or Dennison?'

She nodded. 'The former. He, and this is a measure of my son's nature, gentlemen, but he doesn't like the idea that we are keeping our relationship from Edward. As Chuck sees it, Edward has a right to know.'

'But you disagree?'

Cynthia looked tortured. 'You might have realized by now that my marriage to Edward is far from . . . harmonious, let us say.' She paused, then went on, 'But I fully intend to tell him about my son, when the time is right.'

'And when might that be?' Langham asked. 'You do realize that Edward thinks that you and Chuck are conducting an affair?'

She looked at him, surprised. 'He does? He told you that?'

'He did,' Langham said. He thought about his next words, then went on, 'I think it would be the decent thing to tell him the truth about you and Chuck.'

'It would come as something of a shock, Mr Langham. He has no idea that Douglas and I . . .'

'But it will also be a relief, perhaps,' Langham interrupted, 'given that he's convinced that you're having an affair behind his back.'

'Yes. Yes, you're right.'

Ryland asked, 'Does Chuck Banning know who his father is? Has he asked you?'

'He asked me a few days ago, and I was loath to tell him. However, he insisted . . . and I relented. He was surprised, to say the least. He wanted to speak to Dennison about the fact that he was the director's son, but I prevailed upon him to hold his tongue, at least until the filming is over and everyone has moved from the hall.'

Langham said, 'And Chuck didn't cotton on to the fact that you were behind his being cast?'

Cynthia smiled. 'As I said, in many ways my son is naive . . .'

Ryland rose from his chair and crossed to the shelf of military figures. He examined them for a while, then turned and asked, 'How would you describe your relationship with Douglas Dennison now?'

'Whatever do you mean by that?'

'Just what I say. How do you get on with him? Are you friends, or do you still hate him for walking out on you, all those years ago?'

'Whatever negative feelings I had for Douglas dissipated long ago, Mr Ryland. I find that hate is a corrosive emotion, which does more harm to the person who feels it than the person to whom it is directed.'

'Are you speaking from personal experience?' Langham enquired.

'I hated Douglas with every shred of my being, back in 'thirty-four when he deserted me. It took me a long time to get over the hurt, gentlemen; I admit I was trusting and inexperienced. It was a good number of years before I reached an emotional equilibrium.'

'And then during the war,' Ryland said, 'when Dennison contacted you again?'

Her eyes widened, perhaps in surprise that he should have this information. She collected her thoughts, and said, 'What is the question, Mr Ryland?'

'Did you resent Dennison during the war, when he tried to renew the . . . affair?'

'I'll give you this, Mr Ryland: you certainly know how to ferret out a lot of personal information. I hope you will be as successful at discovering who perpetrated this terrible murder.'

'We'll do out best,' he assured her. 'Now, about you and Dennison during the war . . .'

She shook her head. 'I was past hatred, I assure you. I had found my religion by then. When he came to London in 'forty-two and contacted me, I agreed to see him again – not out of any desire to renew our affair, but from curiosity. I'd thought quite a bit about him over the years, trying to work out certain aspects of his personality. When I met him again, my suspicions were confirmed.'

'Suspicions?' Langham echoed.

'That he was an emotionally insecure man who used his fame and domineering personality to browbeat and coerce young, impressionable women. He thought I was still the meek and ineffectual girl he'd seduced in the thirties. He told me he was still in love with me – and there was a part of me, a tiny part, which did wonder if perhaps he was telling the truth. Fortunately, common sense prevailed. I saw him attempt to manipulate one of my friends – perhaps he was doing it to make me feel jealous – and I realized that he was still the same old predatory charlatan as ever.'

Ryland asked, 'How do you feel about him now?'

'I – I feel nothing but sympathy for the man. Douglas is so imprisoned in the cage of his defective personality that he can see no way out – indeed, he is probably unaware of the bars surrounding him. He has the supreme advantage of the egoist in that he is blithely unaware of his own failings. Perhaps that's a blessing, for if he could discern his defects – see how others perceive him – then it would destroy the image he has constructed of himself as the successful, self-made man.' She shook her head and smiled from Langham to Ryland. 'No, gentlemen, I no longer hate Douglas Dennison. I pity him.'

She looked from Langham to Ryland, and said, 'I seem to find most men in my life, these days, pitiable.'

Langham looked at her. 'Your husband?'

'Especially Edward,' she said. 'Though he wouldn't admit it, the war took a great psychological toll on him. You can't fail to have noticed his obsessive behaviour.'

Langham looked around the room. 'He does seems to crave order and exactitude.'

She smiled. 'It is his way of controlling his drastically circumscribed existence, gentlemen. He was severely traumatized by what happened to him in France.'

Ryland looked across at Langham. 'Anything else you'd care to ask, Don?'

'No, I think that just about covers everything.'

They were leaving the room together, and Cynthia was closing the door, when the telephone bell sounded from within. 'Excuse me for one moment, would you, while I answer this?'

She returned into the study.

Ryland said, 'I'll just pop down to the car and fetch my case.'

'I'll show you to your room,' Langham said, 'then we'll find Maria and have a drink before dinner.'

He kicked his heels on the gallery for a minute, admiring a series of oil paintings depicting the local landscape. The surrounding countryside seemed to have changed little in almost four hundred years.

Cynthia stepped from the study, smiling her apology. 'The secretary of the WI,' she said, 'ringing about the Spring Fair. Now, I think I'll go and lie down before dinner.'

'I'm sorry if our questioning has exhausted you.'

She smiled wanly. 'Thinking over the past like that, and dwelling on the mistakes one inevitably makes . . .' She paused. 'Still, had I not made that mistake, Mr Langham, I would not be blessed with my wonderful son, would I?'

Langham agreed, and found himself admiring the woman.

He looked down from the gallery and saw Ralph Ryland step onto chequered tiling, his slight stature diminished even more by the hallway's huge proportions. He advanced two squares, like a pawn, and stared up at Langham.

Aware that something was wrong, Langham said, 'Ralph?'

'It's Dennison,' Ryland said. 'He's been shot.'

Beside him, Cynthia gave a gasp and reached for the mahogany rail.

Langham raced along the gallery and down the stairs. He followed Ryland outside and around the building, thinking back to Sunday morning when he'd followed Dennison from the hall to the caravan and Suzie Reynard's body.

When they turned the corner, Langham stopped in his tracks. Twenty yards away, towards the back of the house, the director lay on his back.

They raced across to him and Langham knelt. The man was still alive – his breath coming in ragged spasms – despite three huge holes ripped through the front of his shirt. Blood pumped from the chest wounds and pooled on the ground around his torso.

Langham lowered his face to Dennison's mouth as the director tried to speak. The sound was barely a breath, and Langham wondered if he'd actually heard the words or merely the man's final exhalation.

Seconds later, Douglas Dennison was dead.

'What did he say?' Ryland asked.

Langham climbed to his feet. 'I don't know . . . but it might have been "No way".'

He wondered, as he hurried back into the hall to phone the police, whether he had indeed heard the director's last words and, if so, whether those words had been an egoist's incredulous response to the fact of his own demise.

TWENTY-FIVE

He found Maria in their room, lying on the bed and reading a manuscript. She looked up, wide-eyed, when he flung open the door and stared at her. He must have presented a startling sight, his face soaked in sweat, his hair dishevelled, and his right hand covered in blood.

'Donald! What—?'

'Dennison's dead,' he said. 'Shot, just now. I've phoned the police.'

He moved to the basin in the corner of the room and scrubbed off the blood. 'Will you come with me? We'll go round the house, try to find everyone, and have them gather in the dining hall until the police arrive.'

She hurried to him. 'What happened?'

'I've been with Ralph, questioning Cynthia in Edward's study,'

Langham said as they made their way downstairs. 'Ralph was fetching a bag from his car when he found Dennison.'

They located Edward Marling, Sir Humphrey and Chuck Banning in the library, enjoying a pre-prandial drink. Edward and Sir Humphrey were drinking sherry, Banning a glass of home-made lemonade.

The trio turned as one as Langham and Maria appeared on the threshold.

'I'm afraid Douglas Dennison is dead,' Langham said. 'The police are on their way.'

Edward opened his mouth to speak, but no words came. Banning blinked, incredulous; he looked shell-shocked at the news that his newly discovered father was dead. Sir Humphrey downed his sherry in one, and croaked, 'Dead? Good God, man . . . What happened?'

'He was shot,' Langham said, 'perhaps five minutes ago. Do you know where the others are? Terry, Varla, Evans and the maid?'

'Evans and the maid took the afternoon off,' Edward said. 'Terrence was in the dining hall, reading a paper. I don't know about Varla.'

'I think it'll be best if everyone gathers in the dining hall, as per last time, until MacTaggart gets here.'

'Certainly,' Edward said, pushing himself towards the door. 'Yes, that would make sense.'

Langham led the way from the library. He found Terrence Ambler at the far end of the dining hall, seated on a settle before the window and reading *The Times*. He looked up as they entered en masse. 'Bit early for dinner, isn't it?'

Langham was spared having to issue the news yet again when Edward explained the situation to Ambler. The scriptwriter had risen to his feet, but he sank back down, deflated, when he learned of the director's death.

'Do you know where Varla might be?' Langham asked him.

'We had a stroll around the grounds after lunch,' Ambler said. 'When we got back, she said she was going to rest before dinner. I'd try her room.'

Maria murmured, 'I'll stay here with everyone.'

'If you would,' Langham said. 'I'll find Varla and Cynthia, then get back to Ralph and wait till the police arrive.'

He left the dining hall and made his way upstairs.

Cynthia was leaving a room halfway along the gallery when he reached the top of the stairs. She was dabbing her eyes with her handkerchief, but straightened and attempted a smile when she caught sight of Langham. 'This is hellish,' she murmured. 'I don't know if I can stand much more.'

Langham found himself reaching out and taking her hand. 'The police are on their way. Everyone is in the dining room.'

'I'll join them. Paradoxically, given the circumstances, I'll feel safer in company.'

'Which room is Varla's?' he asked, and Cynthia indicated a room next to Edward's study.

He moved to the door and knocked.

Varla Cartier called, 'Come in.'

The actress was sitting in an armchair beside the window, gazing out at the rolling greensward behind the house. She had a cigarette in one hand and a glass of gin in the other.

She turned her hooded eyes towards him. 'What is it, Langham?'

'Douglas Dennison is dead. He was shot.'

He watched her reaction – or, rather, he looked for a reaction on the pale, oval face. There was very little. Her scarlet lips puckered in a quick *moue* of distaste, and she said, 'So someone's nailed him at last.'

'You don't sound surprised.'

'Should I be? Suzie's killer obviously intended to shoot Dennison, and he had more enemies than Genghis Khan. So, no, I'm not in the slightest bit surprised.'

'Everyone is in the dining hall. I'd be grateful if you'd join them until the police arrive.'

'And if I'd rather remain here?'

He shrugged. 'That's your choice. I'll summon you when the police get here.'

Varla muttered something with ill grace. 'No, I'll come down. I'll be interested to see how the others are taking it.' She drained her glass and stabbed out her cigarette in an ashtray. 'And there I was, thinking that this might be my comeback.'

Langham paused as he stepped from the room. 'Inconvenient, isn't it, when someone is murdered?'

'If you think I'm in the slightest bit concerned about you thinking me cynical, Langham, think again. It was only a matter of time before someone got even with Dennison, and you won't find me shedding any tears.'

They made their way downstairs. In the hallway Langham watched her move along the corridor until she reached the dining hall and passed inside, then he stepped out into the brilliant sunlight and joined Ryland at the back of the house.

The detective was pacing back and forth, smoking a Woodbine. Dennison's body appeared even shorter than usual as it lay supine on the gravel.

'That's everyone accounted for, Ralph. They're in the dining hall.'

'How're they taking it?'

'Shocked, for the most part. Only Varla Cartier didn't seem overly concerned. Said he had it coming.'

'She's a cold bitch, that one.'

'I'd probably feel the same about Dennison if he'd beaten me.'

'You don't suppose . . .?' Ryland began.

'That Varla shot him? I wouldn't put it past her.'

Langham stared at the body, at the messy holes in the chest, then looked up at Ryland. 'Did you actually see him being shot?'

The detective shook his head. 'I was walking back to the hall, and I saw Dennison get up and move to the rear of the building and pass from sight. Then I heard him cry out – a cry of pain or surprise.'

'You didn't hear the shots?'

'Nothing. The killer must've used a silencer.'

'I noticed other revolvers in the cabinet the other day,' Langham said. 'But Edward locked the door to the gun room when we left.'

'Do you know where he kept the key?'

'I presume on him.'

Ryland nipped out his cigarette and lodged it behind his right ear. 'Probably wouldn't have been that hard to get into the room, if you wanted to that badly.' He glanced down at the corpse. 'So much for Dennison being able to look after himself.'

They moved around the body and walked along the path that paralleled the rear of the house. Langham kept his gaze on the gravel, looking for any sign of disturbance, though the surface didn't take footprints as would soil or grass.

Ryland turned, sighted an imaginary gun towards Dennison's corpse, and fired off three shots. 'The killer appears at the corner – Dennison sees him and stands up, approaches him or her, then is hit by the bullets, cries out and falls flat on his back before he can draw his own shooter.'

He looked thoughtful for a moment. 'I've been wondering about what you heard him say, Don. "No way".'

Langham shrugged. 'The more I think about it the more I think I might *not* have heard him say that. It might have just been a breath.'

'Or how about this. What he said was Varla's original surname, Novy?'

'Novy . . .?' Langham squinted at the detective. 'I wonder.' He shook his head. 'I don't know. It might have been.'

They continued along the back of the house, around the conservatory, and strolled through the kitchen garden.

'The only way the killer could have got out at the back was through here—' Ryland indicated the kitchen door – 'or through the door a bit further along.'

'The tradesmen's entrance,' Langham said.

They retraced their steps along the back of the house and Langham indicated the series of ground-floor windows. 'Or they could have opened a window and climbed out.'

Ryland approached the nearest window, shielded his eyes with his hand and peered through. 'Looks like a laundry room.'

Langham moved on. 'And this one's a storeroom of some kind.'

Ryland moved to the next window. 'A drawing room or reception room.'

The last window before the corner was the gun room.

Ryland said, 'Bingo.'

'What?'

'Look,' the detective said, indicating a geranium in a pot on the ground beneath the window sill.

'I don't see . . .'

Ryland picked up the terracotta plant pot and pointed to a circular stain on the sill. 'Now, if it fits . . .'

He lowered the plant pot to the stain. 'There we are, Don. It's a guess, but how about this: the killer took a revolver from the cabinet, opened the window, shifted the plant to the ground so he didn't knock it over, then crept to the corner and hey presto.'

Langham nodded. 'You might have something there.'

They made their way back around the hall, Langham consciously looking away from the body as he stuffed his pipe and set it alight. Then they sat on a bench at the front of the hall, smoking, until the local bobbies arrived.

One hour later MacTaggart and Ferrars, accompanied by a couple of forensic specialists, rolled up the driveway.

Detective Inspector MacTaggart questioned Langham and Ryland for the next fifteen minutes, listening with a grave expression on his undertaker's face as Langham described the events surrounding the director's death, and Ryland then went on to detail his theory of the killer having exited through the gun room window.

'And we learned a bit more today about Cynthia Marling and Chuck Banning,' Ryland went on, and apprised the detective about their true relationship.

'And you say Cynthia told Banning that Dennison was his father?' MacTaggart asked.

Langham nodded. 'That's right.'

MacTaggart stared down at the corpse. A police photographer was moving around Dennison's body, taking shots with a bulky box camera. Two forensic scientists knelt beside the corpse, gathering samples of cloth from around the wounds with tweezers.

'Right, let's get inside and get the questioning over with.' MacTaggart looked from Langham to Ryland. 'How would you care to sit in on the interviews? I wouldn't mind hearing what you make of their stories – seeing as how you've been acquainted with these people for the past few days.'

TWENTY-SIX

MacTaggart lowered himself into an armchair before the empty hearth. Ferrars, as ever, leaned against the mantelpiece, while Ryland sat on a sofa. Langham occupied a small table before the window, his notebook open.

Opposite MacTaggart was a vacant armchair.

The door opened and Terrence Ambler ducked in, bobbing his head to Ryland and Langham as he did so. He moved his portly little frame self-consciously to the empty armchair and, at MacTaggart's curt gesture, sat down.

'You know the routine,' the detective said. 'Just a few questions to establish the facts.'

'I'll be a dab hand at writing police procedurals after this,' Ambler said nervously, and appeared cowed when his quip failed to raise a smile from either MacTaggart or Ferrars.

'Now, where were you this afternoon from four o'clock until around half past the hour?'

Ambler laced his fingers over his paunch. 'I was in the dining hall most of the afternoon. That is, from around three when I came back from a walk with Varla, until Donald and the others came in and told me about the ghastly business.'

'And why were you in the dining hall, Mr Ambler?'

The scriptwriter appeared nonplussed. 'Why? Well, I was catching up with the morning papers.'

'Isn't the dining hall an odd place to do this?'

Ambler gave a nervous half smile and shrugged. 'Not at all. It's comfortable enough, and the papers are placed there in the morning.'

'Were you aware of where Dennison was at four o'clock today?'

'I had no idea where he might have been.' He shrugged. 'I didn't really give him a thought.'

'And how did you regard the director, as someone to work with?'

Ambler hesitated, flicking a glance at Langham. 'To be quite frank, he could be a pain. He was demanding, and wanted umpteen rewrites – but that's par for the course in this business.'

Ferrars asked, 'What will become of the film, Mr Ambler, now that its director is dead?'

'I don't know, to be honest. I suppose the production company could get another director in, or promote the fellow who was slated as second director. But to be honest, what with Suzie's death and now Douglas's . . .' He shrugged. 'I wouldn't be surprised if they wrote it off against insurance. It was Douglas's pet project, after all.'

'And if that happened, Mr Ambler,' MacTaggart said, 'you'd be out of a job.'

Ambler shook his head. 'I've been paid already. My contract stated I was to be on hand for rewrites, and I was due to do some preliminary camera work for Douglas, but if the film was to be cancelled now I wouldn't lose out.'

MacTaggart nodded, scanned his notes, and then dismissed the scriptwriter. 'If you could send in Mr Banning.'

The detective looked up at Langham and Ryland once Ambler had left the room. 'Any thoughts?'

'For what it's worth,' Langham said, 'I can't see Terry killing anyone. I've known him for years, and he would have nothing at all to gain from Dennison's death.'

The door at the far end of the room opened and Chuck Banning strode in, his display of knuckle-cracking belying his anxiety. He flashed a quick smile from Ferrars to MacTaggart and dropped into the armchair.

Langham studied the young man, attempting to see in him any resemblance to his father; it appeared, rather, that he had inherited his mother's salient characteristics, her impressive height and rather square jaw.

'I don't know what to say,' he began nervously. 'Douglas was a fine director, one of the best. I don't know what the papers will make of all this . . .'

MacTaggart interrupted. 'And as well as being a fine director, Mr Banning, am I correct in saying that Douglas Dennison was also your father?'

Banning stared at the detective open-mouthed. 'Why . . . yes. Yes, that's right.'

'How long have you known?' MacTaggart asked.

'I . . . I found out just the other day. My . . . That is, Cynthia told me—'

'Your mother?'

Banning coloured. 'Yes, that's right.'

'It must have come as something of a shock, Mr Banning.'

'Yes. Yes, it did. Hell of a shock.'

MacTaggart eased himself back in his armchair and regarded the young man. 'And how much did Cynthia inform you of her relationship with Douglas Dennison?'

Banning shrugged, looking gauche. 'Nothing. Very little. Just that she'd had an affair with him back in the mid-thirties, and he'd left her to return to the States.'

'And when you learned of this, you didn't in any way feel . . . resentful towards Dennison, angry at his behaviour?'

Banning shrugged and looked around the room at the men regarding him. 'No, not at all. Why should I have felt angry? Cynthia said nothing to make me feel at all angry or resentful towards him.'

'Very well,' MacTaggart said, referring to his notes. 'Now, can you tell me where were you from four o'clock until half past this afternoon, Mr Banning?'

'I was in here, having a drink with Sir Humphrey and Edward. Sir Humph was telling us all about his early stage career.'

'And you didn't leave the room at any time during that period?'

'I *did* leave the room, briefly. I popped across the corridor to the rest room.'

MacTaggart looked up. 'And what time was this?'

Banning shook his head. 'I'm not sure – some time after four. I can't say, for sure.'

'And the others with you, Edward and Sir Humphrey?'

'They were there all the time, sir.'

'And when you say you popped out "briefly", Mr Banning – just how long is "briefly"?'

The young man shrugged. 'Say a minute or two.'

'Thank you, Mr Banning,' MacTaggart said, writing in his note-book. 'That will be all. If you could send in Varla Cartier.'

Banning pushed himself from the armchair with the fluid, easy movements of a gymnast dismounting from a piece of apparatus.

MacTaggart looked up when he'd left the room. 'Well?'

Ferrars said, 'He had time, while out of the room, to run along the back of the house and . . . *pop*.'

'Motive?'

'What if he did resent Dennison for running out on his mother?' Ferrars said.

Ryland grunted. 'That's no reason to go and stiff his old man.'

Varla Cartier entered the library with a preoccupied, insular air, her dark eyes directed at the carpet, and folded herself into the armchair without a word. She lit a cigarette with a noisy Zippo lighter, blew out a thick plume of smoke, and eyed MacTaggart with what might have been hostility. 'Fire away.'

'Very well, if you could tell me where you were between four and half past four this afternoon?'

'I was in my room, sleeping. I'd taken a hike with the scribbler, Ambler, and I was bushed. So I went to my room around three, slept for a little, then had a drink.'

'And can anyone corroborate this?'

'I doubt it. I was quite alone.'

'And you didn't leave the room at all during this time?'

'No.'

'How would you describe your relationship with Douglas Dennison?'

'Professionally, we rubbed along OK, I guess. We got the job done. I've worked with him before. He's a pro, and so am I.'

'And personally?'

She vented a veil of smoke. 'Personally, I hated the son of a bitch.'

MacTaggart referred to his notes. 'Ah . . . that's right. You two had a . . . history, if I might call it that.'

'Call it what you want, pal. I'd call it a one-sided, abusive rela-tionship.' She shrugged. 'But that's just my take on the affair.'

'How long were you together?'

'Six months, a little more.'

'So, would you say that you had reason for wishing Douglas Dennison dead?'

Varla Cartier smiled without the slightest hint of humour. 'Listen, if I wanted to kill the bastard, I would have done so back then, the first time he used me as a punching bag. But I didn't kill him, I just got the hell out.'

'And your hatred festered over the years, built to the point where it could no longer be contained, and burst out here, just over an hour and a half ago?'

She tilted back her head and laughed. 'You can think what you like, Inspector. For all I hated Dennison, I wasn't foolish enough to kill him.'

MacTaggart nodded. 'I think that will be all, for the time being. If you could ask Maria Dupré to join us.'

Ferrars whistled when the door closed on Varla Cartier. 'Hell of a performance.'

'She didn't hide the fact that there was no love lost between her and Dennison,' Ryland said.

MacTaggart said, 'She had the motive *and* the opportunity.'

'But in my opinion,' Langham said, 'not the temperament. She isn't the kind of woman to store away her resentment. She wears her emotions on her sleeve, and as she said, if she wanted to harm Dennison she would have done so years ago.'

The door opened, Maria entered, and the atmosphere in the room changed suddenly.

Langham had more than once, since dating Maria, noticed the effect that her presence had on a roomful of men – and she was having that hypnotic effect now. She moved to the armchair with a smile at Langham, eased herself into it with a silken languor and crossed her legs.

Ferrars had come to attention at the mantelpiece, his hand unconsciously straying to the knot of his tie, and MacTaggart sat up and allowed a smile to crease his lugubrious face for the first time in Langham's memory.

'Just a formality, Miss Dupré,' the detective said, and asked where she had been during the relevant times.

'I was in my room, alone, between two o'clock and around four twenty, when Donald told me what had happened to Mr Dennison.'

'And you didn't leave the room during that time, perhaps to visit the bathroom?'

She shook her head. 'Not once, no.'

My word, Langham thought, seeing her through the eyes of the other men in the room, *and I'm marrying Miss Dupré next month* . . .

'And did you hear anything during the relevant times, Miss Dupré? Your room overlooks the rear of the house, I understand?'

'That's correct. But no, I'm sorry, I didn't hear a thing.'

'And your personal dealings with the director?'

'I had no "personal dealing", as such, Inspector. I hardly exchanged a dozen words with him.'

MacTaggart smiled. 'I won't keep you any longer,' he said. 'If you could send in Sir Humphrey when you return to the dining hall.'

Maria smiled, thanked the detective, rose like a dream and padded from the room. All eyes were on her as she slipped through the door.

Ferrars grinned across at Langham. 'Christ, boy, you've found yourself a pearler there. How did an ugly northern git like you bag a peach like that?'

Langham winked. 'Natural charm, Ferrars. And I'm from Nottingham.'

The detective muttered, 'Well, that's north, isn't it?'

Ryland said, 'Midlands. Don gets touchy if you call him a northerner.'

'Very well, gentlemen,' MacTaggart said, 'can I safely say we can cross Miss Dupré from our list of suspects?'

'The only violence I've ever seen Maria commit,' Ryland said, 'is when I saw her kiss Don when she thought no one was looking.'

'Thanks for that, Ralph,' Langham said.

He was saved further embarrassment when the door opened and Sir Humphrey Lyle shambled in.

The old man dropped into the armchair and gazed around the room like a tortoise that had emerged, prematurely, from hibernation.

'And how,' he asked with the gravitas of the old ham he was, 'might I be of assistance, gentlemen?'

MacTaggart asked where Sir Humphrey had been between four and four thirty, and the actor blinked. 'Why, I was here, in this very room, enjoying an excellent sherry with mine host. Amontillado, I believe, the finest from Montilla.'

'And you didn't leave the room for any reason?'

'Not even to toddle off to the little boy's room, gentlemen.' He slapped the arm of the chair. 'I was here all the time, in this very chair, don't you know.'

'And the others, Edward and Chuck Banning?'

Sir Humphrey screwed up his eyes as if he'd been asked to recall an incident from many years ago. 'As far as I recall, yes, I *think* they were here all the while. I had 'em spellbound, y'see, with tales of me old acting days on the stage with Gielgud and Olivier.'

'Are you quite sure about that?'

'Of course – had 'em in the palm of me hand!'

MacTaggart sighed. 'No, I mean about neither of them leaving the room. Are you sure Mr Banning didn't pop over to the loo?'

Sir Humphrey rubbed his face. 'Now you come to mention it . . . perhaps he did, at that.'

MacTaggart jotted the fact in his notebook. 'Now . . . how did you get on with Douglas Dennison?'

'Like a house on fire, sir! Salt of the Earth! A fine director. Well . . .' he said, leaning forward and leering at the detective, 'he cast me, didn't he!' He laughed uproariously.

'I think that will be all, Sir Humphrey. If you'd care to ask Edward to join us, please.'

The old man shuffled from the room.

Ferrars muttered, 'I doubt the old sot could shoot straight from a yard away.'

A minute later Edward Marling wheeled himself into the library.

He positioned his wheelchair beside the vacant armchair and spent a fussy second or two aligning himself precisely so that he faced the detective square on. He reached forward and minutely adjusted an offending mat on the coffee table.

MacTaggart used the line about this being a mere formality, and asked Edward Marling where he had been between four and four thirty.

'I was in here, taking a drink with Sir Humphrey and young Banning.'

'And you didn't leave the room during that time?'

Edward blinked. 'But I did.'

MacTaggart leaned forward. 'You did?'

'I went to the kitchen to fetch a cloth. I happened to spill a little of my sherry on the carpet, you see.'

'And what time was this?'

Edward frowned. 'I'm really not that sure. Not that long before Donald arrived with the news about Douglas.'

'And how long were you out of the room?'

'No more than a couple of minutes. Two minutes, I should say.'

'And you didn't notice anyone around the hall at that time, anyone acting at all suspicious?'

'No. No one.'

MacTaggart made a note. 'And the other two, Sir Humphrey and young Banning?'

'I really can't say. They were here all the while that I was in the room, but they might have nipped out while I was in the kitchen.'

Langham wondered how long it might take a man in a wheelchair to propel himself out through the kitchen door, along the back of the building, shoot Dennison, return to the kitchen to pick up a cloth and make his way back to the library . . . Certainly more than two minutes.

'Now, your relationship with Douglas Dennison,' MacTaggart said, 'how might you describe it?'

Edward swallowed. 'We were friends. Good friends. We've known each other for a long time.'

'I understand you fought alongside Mr Dennison during the war?'

'That's correct. On one mission, yes.'

'And how did you meet Mr Dennison?'

'It was in London, in 'forty-two, I think. Cynthia introduced us.'

MacTaggart nodded, paused, then said, 'And were you aware that your wife and Douglas Dennison had been lovers, before you met Cynthia?'

Langham was watching Edward closely when the detective asked this, and he was convinced that the news came as a shock. 'No . . .' Edward shook his head. 'No, I knew nothing about . . . When was this?'

'In the mid-thirties.'

'No, I knew nothing. Of course, Cynthia never mentioned old lovers.'

'Don't you think it odd that neither Cynthia nor Dennison should have made a clean breast of the affair?'

Edward considered this for a time, before saying, 'No, I don't think it odd at all. Cynthia clearly felt nothing for Douglas by the time she introduced us, and as Douglas and I became friends soon after . . . No, she probably thought it wise not to mention their liaison.'

MacTaggart nodded. 'Very well, that will be all. Thank you. If you could ask your wife to come in, please.'

When Edward had propelled himself from the room, Ferrars said, 'Interesting.'

MacTaggart looked at his colleague. 'What if Marling was lying, and he knew that his wife and Dennison had had an affair? And what if he knew that Cynthia had had a son by Douglas Dennison? Don't you think that it might have given him reason to reassess his friendship with the director?'

'To the point where he decided to have a hit man kill Dennison?' Ryland said. 'I don't buy it. His beef would be with Cynthia, surely, for keeping it a secret all these years.'

'I agree,' Langham said. 'It'd be a flimsy reason for wanting

Dennison dead. And we've no reason to believe that he knows about Cynthia's son.'

The door opened and Cynthia Marling stepped into the room. She was subdued, and had evidently powdered her face; her eyes were red, her cheeks deathly pale. She sat down without a word, then smiled across at Langham as if grateful for there being a friendly face in the room.

MacTaggart began by asking her where she was between four o'clock and four thirty that afternoon.

'I was in my husband's study, with Edward until four, and then with Mr Langham and Mr Ryland.'

MacTaggart glanced at Langham. 'And you can confirm this?'

Langham nodded. 'That's right.'

'However,' Cynthia went on, 'there was a brief period, during that time, when I was alone.'

Langham was taken aback, for a second, until he recalled the telephone call.

Cynthia said, 'As we were leaving the room, the phone rang in Edward's study. I returned to answer the call, leaving Mr Langham on the gallery.'

'And what time was this?' the detective asked.

'Perhaps four fifteen.'

'Who was the call from?'

'A friend in the Women's Institute, wanting to chat about the forthcoming Spring Fair.'

'And how long were you on the phone?'

'A minute, perhaps a little more.'

MacTaggart flipped the pages of his notebook until he came to what Langham saw was a double-page hand-drawn diagram of Marling Hall's layout.

'I see that your husband's study overlooks the gravelled area where Mr Dennison's body was discovered.'

'That is correct, yes.'

'And—' the detective flipped back to his notes – 'Mr Dennison was shot at approximately four twenty.'

'So I am given to understand.'

'So . . . and I'm speculating here, Mrs Marling . . . it would have been possible, during the minute or so you were alone in the room, for you to have leaned from the window and shot Douglas Dennison.'

Cynthia kept her composure admirably. 'Entirely possible, Inspector. If I just happened to have had a weapon to hand, and had

I known that I would be called back to the room at that time precisely, and if I had known that Douglas would have been where he was. Of course I was talking to Margaret all the while, but I could have held the receiver in one hand while pulling the trigger with the other, and then explained that the report was nothing more than a car backfiring in the drive. And then we must consider a motive, Inspector . . . which, I am sorry to say, entirety eludes me at the moment.'

She smiled at the detective, and Langham resisted the urge to laugh. As a display of caustic sarcasm, Cynthia's little speech had been priceless.

MacTaggart nodded reasonably. 'Very well, as for motive . . . how about you resented the way Douglas Dennison walked out on you all those years ago, leaving you with a son?'

Cynthia sighed. 'As I explained to Mr Langham and Mr Ryland earlier, any resentment, even hatred, I once felt towards Dennison, I feel no more. The idea that I should allow twenty years to elapse before exacting some kind of revenge . . .' She waved the idea away as the farcical notion it so obviously was.

'And you have no idea, or suspicion, who might have wanted the director dead?'

'None whatsoever, Inspector.'

'Thank you, Mrs Marling. That will be all.'

Cynthia rose, nodded to each of the men in turn, and left the room with dignity.

MacTaggart inflated his cheeks and blew in exasperation. 'Any thoughts?'

Ryland said, 'The only person with any kind of motive, though it's slight, as well as the opportunity, is Varla Cartier.'

'I can't really see the Marlings as key suspects,' Ferrars said.

'Ambler? Banning? Sir Humphrey?' MacTaggart asked.

'Sir Humphrey has a cast-iron alibi,' Ryland said. 'He was in here with Banning. Banning himself? He's an outside possibility. As for Ambler?' He shrugged. 'We need to establish a motive, before we seriously consider him as a suspect.'

MacTaggart looked across at Langham. 'Anything to add?'

Langham shook his head. 'I'm afraid not. I'm as perplexed as the rest of you.'

MacTaggart slapped shut his notebook. 'I'll take a wander around, see how the forensic boys are faring. I think I'll leave a bobby here overnight, and we'll be around again tomorrow at some point.'

*   *   *

At dinner that evening Cynthia and Edward, Langham noticed, exchanged not a single word and barely glanced at each other. The meal was taken in almost total silence until, tinned peaches and Carnation milk consumed, the port made its way around the table and Sir Humphrey said suddenly, 'I was in one hell of a play, during the war. Ran for months. Audience lapped it up, and the critics were kind, too.'

Cynthia perked up, pleased that someone had broken the ice. 'Oh, and what play was that, Humphrey?'

'Christie's *And Then There Were None*,' Sir Humphrey said, knocking back his drink. 'I'm sure you know the tale? Ten people in a country house, murdered one by one . . . Good God,' he exclaimed, beaming around the table, 'what a coincidence! The original number of people gathered at Marling Hall was ten. Now . . .' he went on, 'I wonder who'll be next to be bumped off?'

Cynthia murmured, 'I think that highly inappropriate, Humphrey.'

'Oh, I don't know . . . Two down, eight to go.'

Terrence Ambler said, 'Except, Sir Humphrey, your counting is a little out: originally there were *eleven* people gathered here.'

Sir Humphrey waved. 'Ten? Eleven? The principle still holds . . .'

Maria caught Langham's glance and nodded that they should make their excuses and retire.

Varla said, 'You're not in the play now, Humph, old boy. My guess is, the rest of us are safe. Suzie's death was a god-awful mistake. Dennison was the intended victim all along.'

'He was?' Sir Humphrey exclaimed. 'Good God! Well, I think this calls for a drink!'

Langham announced that he thought an early night was in order and he and Maria left the room.

TWENTY-SEVEN

After breakfast the following morning Langham and Maria spent an hour in the library, catching up with the daily papers. The murder of Douglas Dennison was front-page news, the more sensationalist red tops wallowing in the double death and declaring a bloodbath at the stately home.

Over breakfast, Terrence Ambler had mentioned that someone from the production company was due at the hall that morning to discuss the situation vis-à-vis the possibility of continuing with the film. Duly, at eleven, two executives in pinstriped suits and bowler hats arrived in a chauffeur-driven Jaguar and summoned those involved in the making of the film into the drawing room.

Langham had limited himself to a strong coffee at breakfast, and by midday was feeling peckish. He was about to suggest to Maria that they should find Ralph and wander along to the Seven Sleepers, when Terry Ambler poked his head into the room. 'Ah, there you are.'

'And what did the bowler-hatted gents have to say?' Langham asked.

Ambler's pudding face became even more lugubrious. '*Finito.* The production bods are pulling the plug. Apparently the insurance company played silly buggers about shelling out over the increased costs of continuing the shoot – what with having to hire extra cast, and a second director – so the producers have decided to cut their losses and get out. Personally, I won't lose out, but Varla, Chuck and Sir Humph aren't happy about it. Meanwhile, we're stuck here, kicking our heels. Don't know about you, but I'm going stir crazy.'

'I was about to suggest we repair to the pub for a sandwich and a pint. Any takers?'

Maria said, 'I've been dreaming of ice cold G&Ts all morning.'

'You've twisted my arm,' Ambler said.

'Right-o,' Langham said. 'I'll fetch Ralph and we can be off.'

'Better not go through the main gates,' Ambler warned. 'Place is swarming with leeches from the press. Edward was telling me about a side entrance to the hall last night, through the woods.'

Langham found Ryland in the billiard room, absorbed in a game with Chuck Banning. Edward Marling sat to one side, watching the game. Langham said they were about to depart for the Seven Sleepers, and asked if there were any takers. Ryland said he'd come just as soon as he'd beaten Chuck.

Edward said, 'Not for me, thank you, Donald. But how about meeting in the library for a drink at four?'

Ryland duly beat the American by twenty points; as they were leaving the room, Edward challenged the actor to a game.

'Interesting youth,' Ryland said as they crossed the drive and passed along a dappled pathway through the woods, following Maria and Ambler. 'He was telling me all about Hollywood and the parties. Wait till I tell Annie I've been hobnobbing with the stars. Oh, and I learned something interesting.'

'Go on.'

'Banning has plans for the hall.'

Langham looked sideways at his friend. 'What on earth did he mean?'

'That's what I asked him. Seems to think he'll own the place, one day. He said, "When all this is mine, I'll run it as an exclusive hotel." So I asked him why he thought it'd be his one day.'

'What did he say?'

'Well, he coloured up and said he intended to buy it from the Marlings, when he'd made his fortune. Know what I think? I think Cynthia has been making promises to him.'

'About the ownership of the hall?'

Ryland nodded. 'It's hers, lock, stock and barrel, right? She probably said something along the lines of "when Edward shuffles off", she'll make sure Chuck inherits the place. Which has got the lad all excited.'

They came to the perimeter wall, slipped through a rusted gate and turned along the lane. Ten minutes later they were seated in the snug of the Seven Sleepers with three pints of bitter and a gin and tonic. An order of ham-and-mustard sandwiches was on the way.

Conversation soon turned to the murders.

'Question is,' Terry Ambler said, 'who stands to gain by Douglas Dennison's death?'

'Depends,' Ryland said, hoisting his pint, 'on how you define "gain". Gain money-wise, or simply gain the satisfaction of seeing someone you hated dead?'

'Very well,' Langham said, 'who stands to gain financially by the director's death? Who's the main beneficiary of his will?'

Ambler said, 'He had no relatives. We got drunk in London a while back and I remember him saying he was the last in a long, illustrious line of no-account losers.'

'Except,' Ryland said, 'he did have family – Chuck Banning.'

'What's that?' Ambler said, spilling ale down his shirt. 'Chuck is Dennison's son?'

'By Cynthia,' Ryland said.

'Bloody hell,' Ambler said.

Langham explained. 'Cynthia and Dennison had an affair back in the thirties, and the result was a son, Charles Banning.' He told Ambler about the boy's adoption and emigration to the States, and Dennison's shabby treatment of Cynthia.

'But,' he went on, 'I can't really believe that Banning would have killed his own father.'

'So . . .' Ryland asked, 'who *would* be happy to see Dennison dead?'

'He wasn't well liked,' Langham said. 'Cynthia, despite her holier-than-thou claims that she no longer hated the man . . . Well, there wasn't much love lost there. Varla detested him.'

'What about Edward Marling?' Ambler asked. 'He says he was the director's friend, but what if he knew about Cynthia's affair with Dennison? What if he'd found out that Chuck Banning was Cynthia's son by the director?'

Langham shook his head. 'No, I just can't see Edward being provoked by something like that.'

Their sandwiches arrived and conjecture was temporarily set aside as they ate.

'Thing is,' Ryland said ruefully, 'we took the case on the promise of five guineas an hour – and then when Suzie Reynard died, Dennison upped it to ten. Now he's gone and croaked, we're never going to get paid.'

'You win some, you lose some,' Ambler said.

Maria laid a hand on Ryland's arm in mock-consolation. 'I suppose you could always contact Dennison's lawyer, if you solve the case, and demand payment.'

Ryland muttered something to himself and took a long draft of bitter.

They ate in silence for a while, then Langham finished his sandwich, and said, 'I wonder what he would have thought of Chuck Banning being his son?'

Maria murmured, 'We will never know, now.'

Ryland drank up, asked who was for a second, and when he came back with a tray of drinks, said to Langham, 'And talking of kids, Don . . . Any plans in that department yourself?'

Maria smiled at Langham's disquiet. 'I think we will have two, a boy and a girl, and a cottage in the country, with a dog and two cats, and maybe chickens, and Donald will write bestsellers and keep me in the luxury I deserve.'

They raised their glasses. 'Here's to that,' Ambler said.

Maria steered the conversation away from both children and murder, and regaled them with a story of life in Paris in the early thirties. Langham sat back and watched her, wondering how things might have worked out had he met Maria ten years earlier when, after the war and back in Civvy Street, he'd led the lonely life of a bachelor in a London much changed from the city of the late thirties, drinking too much and turning out his early Sam Brooke thrillers.

My word, he thought, looking around at his friends and at the woman he loved, how things have changed.

Ambler insisted on buying a third round, and an hour later Langham remembered that he'd agreed to meet Edward Marling for drinks at four. At this rate, he thought, he'd be thoroughly inebriated by dinner time tonight.

They finished their drinks and wended their way back to the hall.

Langham and Maria stepped from the sunlight and entered the cool, shadowed hallway, pausing for a second to allow their eyes to adjust. Maria responded to a story he was telling about an old editor, her laughter filling the air; Langham was at that pleasant stage of inebriation where all was well with the world.

Edward Marling appeared, propelling himself along the corridor. 'There you are,' he said. 'I've just finished a session on the memoir, and I'm in need of that drink. See you in the library? I must just pop up to the bathroom.'

'I don't suppose there's coffee available?' Maria asked.

'I'll have cook brew a pot,' Edward said. 'And I'll ask MacTaggart and Ferrars if they'd care to join us. They were in the drawing room earlier.'

He turned his chair towards the lift, waited until the doors slid open and wheeled himself inside.

Langham wondered what was taking Ryland and Ambler so long. They'd lagged behind on the walk back, having discovered a mutual interest in the fortunes of Millwall football club. He was about to make his way to the library, a moment later, when a deafening report echoed through the building.

Ryland and Ambler ran into the hallway.

'Crikey!' Ryland yelled. 'What the hell was that?'

'Up there,' Langham said, already heading for the staircase. He took the steps two at a time and arrived on the gallery just as Edward was emerging from the lift.

'It came from along there,' Edward said, pointing towards the west wing and his study.

Langham set off, Ryland at his side. At the far end of the gallery, a door opened next to Edward's study and Varla Cartier appeared. 'What's going on? What was that?' Her hair was dishevelled and she appeared the worse for drink.

Langham paused before the study door, his heart hammering. He was aware of the others behind him, and Edward saying frantically, 'Go on, man . . .'

He turned the door handle and stepped into the room.

The first thing he saw was Cynthia Marling, seated in the upright chair before the desk; her head was tipped back and the upper right side of her skull was missing. The sight of her head was so bizarre, so at odds with how a head should appear, that the effect was less grotesque than surreal. What made Langham gag, however, was the quantity of blood that soaked her shoulder and upper torso and pooled on the rug around the chair legs. Her right hand hung loose, and on the floor, inches from her lifeless fingers, a small silver pistol lay in a lagoon of blood.

Varla Cartier screamed. Langham turned briefly to see a gallery of white faces at the door; Maria was clutching Edward's hand as he stared, unbelieving, at his wife's body.

'Ralph, go and find MacTaggart and Ferrars,' Langham said. 'I believe they're in the drawing room.'

Ryland nodded and moved off at speed.

Someone appeared, craning to see over the heads of those blocking the doorway. 'What gives?' Chuck Banning said.

In barely a whisper, Edward said, 'My wife . . .' and with fumbling fingers raised a hip flask to his lips and took a drink.

Langham turned to the desk and took in the piled manuscript and the sheet of paper in the typewriter. Avoiding the pooled blood, he moved to the desk and read what had been typed.

I'm sorry. But I had to accomplish what I set out to do. Dennison was blackmailing me, threatening to make our affair public. He asked for a thousand pounds to begin with.

I'm so very sorry about what happened to Suzie, so very sorry that I find it hard to go on.

Cynthia.

Edward Marling sagged in his wheelchair, his head in his hands.

Langham asked, 'When did you last see her?'

Edward had closed his eyes, as if by doing so he might banish from his memory the sight of his dead wife. He shook his head. 'Fifteen minutes ago, perhaps a little more. She . . . she said she wanted to correct what she'd typed . . .' He pressed his thumb and forefinger to his eyes and hunched over in his chair.

Langham nodded to Maria, and she gripped the handles of the wheelchair and pushed Edward from the room. Chuck Banning took a few trance-like steps forward, staring at the corpse. He read the note in the typewriter and shook his head in disbelief.

'No . . .' He sagged against the desk, making a strange gagging sound in his throat.

Ambler took his arm, and murmured, 'Best go and lie down, c'mon . . .'

Beyond their retreating figures, Langham made out MacTaggart, Ferrars and Ryland as they appeared at the top of the staircase and hurried along the gallery. They stepped into the room and Ferrars shut the door behind them.

'Christ Almighty . . .' MacTaggart said.

Ferrars stepped around the slick of blood and read the suicide note. He waited until MacTaggart had read it, then said, 'We never considered blackmail, sir.'

MacTaggart nodded. 'Ring Norwich and get the forensic team here quick smart. And get Sergeant Briscoe in to stand guard.'

Ferrars slipped from the room.

'Who found her?' MacTaggart asked.

'We heard the sound of the shot while we were in the hallway,' Langham said. 'Ralph, Terry, Maria and myself were first on the scene, perhaps half a minute later, maybe less, with Edward who'd just emerged from the lift. Oh, and Varla who was in the next bedroom.'

MacTaggart turned from the body. 'Who's with Edward now?'

'Maria took him away.'

MacTaggart read the note again. 'Bloody hell . . . I can't imagine what she must have been going through.'

Langham moved to the door. 'If you don't need me for the time being . . .' he said.

'I'd appreciate a word or two a bit later,' MacTaggart said, 'when the forensic team's had a chance to go over the scene.'

Langham nodded and left the study.

He found Maria in their room, sitting on the edge of the bed with her head in her hands. She looked up bleakly as he entered.

'Edward?' he asked.

'I took him down to the library. He's with Evans.'

Langham pointed to the open window; a cooling breeze was tempering the heat. 'Good idea,' he said.

'What?'

'The window. Good idea to open it.'

'I didn't.'

'Then the maid must have when she came to clean—'

'But that was this morning, while I was here, and she didn't open the window.'

'Then who . . .?'

'It doesn't matter, Donald. Come here and hold me, please.'

He moved around the bed, kicked off his shoes, lay down and pulled Maria to him. He kissed her forehead and held her until, minutes later, she was asleep.

The combination of warmth and alcohol must have worked to send him to sleep too, as he was awoken much later by a tapping on the door. He sat up and moved quietly across the room so as not to wake Maria.

It was Ferrars. 'If you'd care to join us, Donald.'

He glanced at his watch: six thirty. He'd slept for a couple of hours. He eased the door shut and followed the detective downstairs to the library.

MacTaggart was pacing the room, his chin sunk on his chest. Ryland had appropriated Ferrars's position at the mantelpiece, smoking a cigarette and looking grim.

MacTaggart looked up as they entered. 'We're taking Varla Cartier in for questioning,' he said. 'We don't believe for a minute that Cynthia Marling killed herself.'

Langham nodded, not in the least bit surprised. 'I did wonder,' he said. 'I don't believe she was the type of woman to succumb to blackmail. She would have called Dennison's bluff and faced the consequences.'

MacTaggart said, 'And practically, too, it wouldn't have worked. The only way she could have killed Dennison was when she returned to the study to answer the phone. But as she herself pointed out yesterday, she would have needed a weapon ready and somehow rigged the telephone to ring when it did. I've got someone checking that she did receive the call from her WI friend. Also,' he went on, 'the forensic bods say that from the initial examination of Cynthia's remains, the shot was fired from about two feet away.'

'So you think Varla Cartier killed all three—?' Langham began.

MacTaggart interrupted. 'Let's go over this again.'

He sat down and opened his notebook on the coffee table. Langham, Ryland, and Ferrars joined him, poring over the two E-shaped plans of the hall, ground floor and first floor.

'I've just finished questioning Edward Marling and the guests,' MacTaggart said, 'and this is where everyone was when Cynthia Marling was shot.' His long index finger indicated each person in turn, denoted by their initials.

'Yourself and Maria, Ambler and Ryland . . . You were all in the hallway or nearby at five past four when the shot was heard. You'd just spoken to Edward Marling, and he was emerging from the lift on the gallery, here, by the time you reached the top of the staircase

– so he was in the lift when the shot was fired. Evans and the maid were in the dining hall, over here. Sir Humphrey was in the library. Chuck Banning was in his room next to Varla's. Now he could have left his room, shot Cynthia, and returned, but he would have had to be damned quick about it.'

'And I don't think he'd have shot his own mother,' Ryland said.

'Now Varla Cartier was in her room, next door to the study, here, and as you, Langham, turned along the gallery she emerged from the room.' MacTaggart prodded her initials. 'She was the only person, other than Banning, close enough to have shot Cynthia Marling and arranged the pistol so that it appeared to have fallen from her hand. She must have typed the note at some point earlier in the day, when the study was unoccupied and she was sure Edward and Cynthia were elsewhere. She shot Cynthia, arranged the gun and placed the note in the typewriter, then hurried back to her room, emerging as you reached the top of the stairs.'

'The pistol?' Langham asked.

MacTaggart shook his head. 'We don't know where it came from. Edward's never seen it before, and he's certain it didn't belong to his wife.'

'Have you checked Varla and her clothing for bloodstains?' Langham asked. 'There must be a good chance that the killer was covered in the stuff.'

'Cartier says she went back to her room soon after the body was discovered,' MacTaggart said. 'If she were covered in Cynthia's blood, she would have had time to wash it off then. The chances are that she'd have left traces. The forensic team is going over her room with a fine-toothed comb as I speak, and they'll do the same with Banning's.'

'And Varla's motive in wanting Dennison dead was revenge?' Ryland asked.

MacTaggart nodded. 'She's made it clear from the outset that there was no love lost between them. As for Suzie Reynard's death . . . perhaps revenge was also the motive? I understand that Cartier felt that Reynard wrecked her career.'

Langham said, 'And she killed Cynthia in an attempt to close the case and get off scot-free?'

'That's the assumption I'm working on, yes.'

Langham sat back on the sofa. 'If she did kill Cynthia, wouldn't she have made herself scarce – not shown herself immediately after the sound of the gunshot?'

MacTaggart shrugged. 'Maybe she thought that that's exactly

what we'd think she would have done. Anyway, we should know more when we've hauled her over the coals.'

He looked up at his deputy. 'Right, let's go and get her.'

When the detectives had departed, Langham asked Ryland, 'What do you think?'

'Leaving aside what the forensic boys said about the shot being fired from two feet away,' Ryland said, 'I doubt that Cynthia topped herself. Not in her nature, if you ask me. And logistically she can't have shot Dennison.' He shrugged. 'Varla Cartier's the main suspect, as far as I can see, with Chuck Banning as an outsider. But I can see you're not convinced that it's Cartier.'

Langham stared through the window at the lawn and the distant trees. 'No, I'm not. She's been so forthright in her dislike of Dennison – and Suzie – all along, and unless she's playing a very clever double-bluff . . .' He shook his head. 'I think the guilty party is someone else entirely.'

'Banning?'

Langham frowned. 'As you said, I don't think he would have killed his own mother. Or his father.' He massaged his neck. 'I need to lie down and mull this over, Ralph. I might snatch a bit of supper later, but I couldn't eat a thing right now.' He moved to the door.

Ryland saluted. 'See you later, Cap'n.'

Langham returned to his room; Maria was still asleep, her breathing even. He crossed to the open window and stared out. Experimentally he shut the window and opened it again, but quietly so as not to wake Maria. It ran easily on its sash without a sound. Frowning, he moved to the bed and lay down.

TWENTY-EIGHT

It was three in the morning and Langham was unable to sleep.

At nine o'clock last night he and Maria had taken a supper of cheese on toast with Ryland and Ambler, sitting in the quiet dining hall and discussing the case. At eleven they returned to their room and Langham had tried to sleep, but more than just his late supper was keeping him awake.

Now he heard Maria stir. 'Donald?'

'Mmm?'

'What are you doing?'

'Sitting,' he said. 'Thinking.'

She turned on the bedside lamp, sat up and looked across at him. 'What is it?'

'Maria, can I ask you something?'

'Of course.'

'Are you absolutely sure that you didn't open the window yesterday before we went out?'

'Absolutely sure.'

'And are you sure that Evans or the maid didn't?'

'Evans doesn't clean the rooms, Donald. And as I told you, I was here when the maid came in to clean.'

'But might she have entered the room for something else later, thought it too hot in here and decided to open the window?'

She shrugged and thrust out her lower lip. 'But why would she have come in here again, Donald?'

'Do you think you could ask her, and Evans, in the morning?'

'Of course I will. But why is it important?'

'Because if you or I didn't open the window – and I'm dashed sure I didn't – and if Evans or the maid didn't, then someone else did. But *why*, Maria? Why would someone have entered our room and opened the bedroom window?'

'I don't know. And to be honest I'm too tired to think properly. Now will you please come to bed?'

He did so, but lay awake for a long time before falling asleep.

In the morning Langham and Maria were the first down for breakfast. He had little appetite, and satisfied himself with a cup of Earl Grey and a slice of toast. He had woken just before seven and lain awake for an hour, contemplating the case and going over the possibilities again and again – and he found the answer he arrived at quite unpalatable.

Evans served them in silence, even more subdued than usual. Langham asked if he knew whether Varla Cartier had returned to the hall last night, or if she were still in police custody in Norwich, but Evans was unable to shed light on the matter.

At one point Maria excused herself and slipped into the kitchen. She returned a minute later, frowning.

She took her seat. 'I asked the maid about the window. She was adamant she didn't enter our room, and she said that Evans didn't either.'

Langham nodded. 'Thank you.'

'Donald . . . you're miles away.'

'I'm sorry. It's just . . .' He smiled and shook his head. 'It's nothing. More tea?'

Chuck Banning joined them as Langham was finishing his second cup. His usual youthful bravado was gone; he seemed diminished, sapped of strength, and responded to Langham's smile with a vacant one of his own, looking around as if he'd just woken up and was wondering where he was.

He sat next to Langham and poured himself a black coffee.

Langham murmured, 'I'm very sorry.'

Banning smiled bleakly. 'Makes you wonder, doesn't it? Do you believe in fate, Mr Langham?'

'No. No, I don't. I think events are random and that nothing is pre-ordained.'

'I dunno, it seems like fate to me. A few months ago I found I had a mother here in the old country, and then I learn about my father. And then they're . . . they're taken away from me.'

Langham smiled in sympathy. 'It's just rotten, tragic misfortune,' he said.

Banning nodded and excused himself. 'I think I'll take this up to my room.'

He left the dining hall, holding the door open as Sir Humphrey entered, closely followed by Terrence Ambler.

'Well,' Sir Humphrey said, slathering a slice of toast with strawberry jam, 'that's that, then. Who would've thought it, eh? Young Banning saw Varla being carted off last night, when we all thought Cynthia had confessed. Bit of a shocker, what? Still, I never liked the woman.'

Maria looked up from blowing on her tea. 'Why was that, Sir Humphrey?'

'Dark horse,' the old man said. 'Man-hater, too. One of *them*, y'know?'

Ambler caught Langham's glance and rolled his eyes.

'One of them?' Maria asked.

'You know,' Sir Humphrey said in a stage whisper. 'Daughter of Sappho. What a waste!'

Langham saw that Maria was about to respond to this, but he shook his head in warning; she bit her lip and attended to her breakfast.

Sir Humphrey opened *The Times*, noisily chewed his toast, and absorbed himself in the news.

Langham murmured to Maria, 'I need to clear my head. How about a stroll after breakfast?'

'That would be nice, yes.'

'I just need to see Ryland for a quick word first. Knowing him, he'll still be snoozing.'

He left the dining hall and made his way upstairs.

He rapped on Ryland's bedroom door and elicited a woozy, 'Who's that?'

'Me, Donald. You decent?'

'As I'll ever be.'

Ryland was pushing himself up in bed, garbed in faded, striped pyjamas, and lighting his first Woodbine of the day.

'Can't a man get some shut-eye?' he whined.

'It's nearly nine,' Langham said, 'and we need to talk.'

Ryland took a long pull on his cigarette. 'That's better. Talk?'

Langham drew up a chair and sat down. 'I remember you saying, years ago, that to be successful in this business, not only did you need to think like a criminal, you had to *act* like one, too.'

'I said that?'

'You did. And you said that in your long and illustrious career you'd acquired many skills: safecracking, pickpocketing, burglarizing . . .'

Ryland laughed. 'What's all this about, Don?'

'I think I know who the killer is,' Langham said, 'but to be sure I need your help.'

Ten minutes later he left Ryland and made his way downstairs. As he was crossing the hallway, Terrence Ambler emerged from the dining room at the far end of the passage.

'Just the man,' Langham said.

He gestured to the entrance and the two men stepped out into the bright morning sunlight. Langham pulled out his pipe, stuffed it and got it going as they ambled up and down in front of the hall.

'I'm shattered,' Ambler said. 'Didn't sleep a wink for thinking about Cynthia.'

'I know what you mean,' Langham said. 'I've been thinking of nothing else. Look here, I wonder if you'd do something for me?'

'Name it.'

'That cine camera of yours you told me about the other day, I wonder if I might borrow it?'

'Of course. I'll give you a quick lesson in how to use it, but it couldn't be simpler. Care to tell me what you're up to?'

'Ah . . . not at the moment, if that's all right. Delicate situation. But I'll tell you everything a little later today. Can you develop the film here?'

'No problem at all. I have all the stuff in the van.'

'How long would it take?'

'An hour or two, no more.'

'Excellent.'

Ambler said he'd deliver the camera to Langham's room at noon and returned inside.

Maria passed the scriptwriter on the threshold and tapped down the steps, frowning. 'What did you need to see Ryland about so urgently?' she asked, linking arms, 'and what were you and Terry talking about?'

He kissed her. 'All will be revealed, as the saying goes, in the fullness of time.'

They strolled across the lawn and through the trees.

TWENTY-NINE

At two o'clock that afternoon, Maria knocked on the bedroom door and, on receiving a reply, turned the handle and stepped inside.

'I hope I'm not interrupting?'

Edward smiled at her from where he was seated before the window. 'Not at all.' He gestured. 'I was just admiring the scenery.'

She joined him and stared out. The view of the rolling greensward, the lake and the distant woodland was idyllic.

'It's odd,' he said, 'but I think one only really appreciates something when one sees it through the eyes of a stranger, or when one is faced with losing that thing . . . or has lost it.'

She looked down at Edward Marling. 'Are you thinking of moving?'

'I can't remain here. There would be too many memories, unpleasant memories, and reminders of what has happened. And anyway, I'd be all alone. Life would be intolerable.'

'I don't think you'll have any difficulty in selling.'

'I had enquiries from the National Trust a couple of years ago. We weren't interested in selling up, then. But now . . .' He sat in silence for a few seconds, gazing through the window, and then resumed, 'I won't get anything approaching what I would like for the place, of course, and after the Inland Revenue have taken their cut . . .'

'What will you do?'

'I think I'll buy a flat in London. I know a lot of people there, friends from the war, ex-army colleagues. I think it would be a good idea to start a new life.'

She nodded. She was about to state her reason for seeing him, to ask if she might take a look at the manuscript of his war memoirs, when he said, 'They took Varla in for questioning last night.'

'Yes, I heard.'

His gaze remained fixed on the view. 'I knew that Cyn didn't take her own life, Maria. It was impossible. She . . . she wasn't the kind of person to do a thing like that. Not only would her religion have proscribed such a violent act, but . . .'

He fell silent. Maria prompted, 'Yes?'

'But she was happier, more optimistic, than at any time for years. You see, she had found her son, at last.'

Maria stared at him. 'You knew?'

'Cyn told me yesterday.' He smiled up at her. 'Must admit that it came as something of a surprise – and a relief, too. You see, I thought she and Chuck Banning were having an affair. Now, that would have hurt.'

He paused, his fingers absently stroking the arm rests of his wheelchair. 'So you see, Cyn had everything to live for. She had been reunited with her long-lost son, and it was as if she were embarking on a new stage of her life, after . . . after being cloistered with an invalid for so long.' He shook his head. 'There's no way that she would have ended her own life.'

The silence stretched, and when Maria began to feel uncomfortable, standing in silence beside him, she said, 'I came to ask if I might take a look at your manuscript? We're probably leaving in the morning, so I wondered if I might take a copy with me?'

'Why, of course. I have a carbon copy you can have.'

'I'll have a quick read through, then show it to my partner at the agency. As I said the other day, there's quite a market for war memoirs these days.'

'That's most kind of you.' He pressed down on the right-hand wheel of his chair, turning it and propelling himself to the door.

Maria followed him from the room.

They made their way along the gallery towards Edward's study. He paused before the door, as if gathering himself, then released a breath and pushed it open.

Maria stepped into the sunlit room. The window at the far end was open. The rug had been removed, along with the chair in which Cynthia had died, and the polished floorboards before the desk scrubbed clean. There was nothing at all to remind Maria of what had taken place here yesterday afternoon, other than the stark recollection of Cynthia Marling's lifeless body.

She moved around the desk and approached the window, taking deep breaths of the fresh, scent-laden air.

When she turned, Edward had taken a carbon copy of the manuscript from a drawer and sat with it on his lap. He murmured, as if to himself, 'I thought I'd seen everything while I was serving in France – the very best of what human beings were capable, and the very worst. I witnessed acts of heroism and sacrifice that were almost beyond belief, and I saw people driven to commit the most barbarous acts of inhumanity that were almost impossible to describe. And the odd thing is . . . the strangest thing is that, on more than one occasion, these two seemingly disparate and mutually exclusive acts were carried out by the very same person.'

Absently, while Edward had been speaking, Maria lifted one of the crossbows from its hook on the wall and caressed its polished stock. She wondered how many lives this relatively unsophisticated weapon had taken down the years, and whether the craftsman who had so carefully put together the weapon had fully realized the misery he was helping to perpetuate.

She smiled to herself; why blame the craftsman, she thought, when the real fault lay in the human heart?

Edward was saying, 'I thought I'd left all that behind, Maria, after the war. Who would have thought that the horror would follow me here?'

'I'm sorry,' she said, setting the crossbow down on a table and rejoining Edward by the desk.

'But Varla?' he said, shaking his head. 'Just as I find it impossible to believe that Cyn took her own life, I find it hard to believe that Varla could be responsible for – for all three killings.'

Maria picked up the small figure of a Roundhead, one of perhaps two dozen different soldiers from down the ages that were ranged along the shelf. They struck her as an odd thing for a grown man to collect.

'I know,' she said. 'I liked – I mean, I *like* Varla, despite her . . .'

'Go on.'

She smiled. 'Despite her cynicism.'

Edward regarded her. 'I could understand how she might have brought herself to kill Douglas in a fit of rage, perhaps. But to kill Suzie . . . and then to kill Cyn in an attempt to shift the blame?' He shook his head.

Maria studied a miniature Cossack, a fierce expression on its painted face. She replaced the figure and turned to Edward. 'Then who . . .?'

He stared down at the bulky manuscript on his lap. He was silent for a time, then looked up at her.

'Who?' he asked. 'Why, the only other person with the where-withal to have killed Cynthia yesterday afternoon.'

Maria found herself picking up another figure, fingering the fine details of its uniform. 'And his motive for the other killings?'

'I think Suzie's killing was a terrible mistake,' Edward said. 'And I think the reason he killed Douglas, and had planned to kill him all along, was for monetary gain.'

She stared at him. 'Monetary . . .?' she echoed.

'Douglas Dennison had no other family,' Edward said, 'so when he died . . .' He shrugged. 'Only one person stood to gain, to inherit.'

Maria's mouth was dry as she said, 'And this person staged Cynthia's death to deflect attention—?'

Edward was shaking his head. 'No,' he said. 'Again, he killed Cynthia for gain.'

Maria replaced the figure on the shelf and gathered herself.

Edward smiled at her. 'But I'm prepared, Maria, for when he comes for me . . .' And he reached into the pocket of his blazer and withdrew a revolver.

Maria nodded, her heart thudding. 'You should make your suspicions known to Inspector MacTaggart,' she said.

'Oh, I fully intend to, Maria.'

He replaced the revolver in his pocket and tapped the manuscript. 'As I said, I thought I had left all the horror behind when I returned from France. How mistaken could one be?'

He held out the manuscript.

Maria took it and hurried from the room.

THIRTY

At five o'clock Langham stood at the library window as MacTaggart's green Humber rolled up the drive. It pulled in beneath the elms and the inspector and Ferrars climbed out, followed by Varla Cartier. Head down, she lost no time in hurrying across the drive and into the hall.

Langham turned. 'MacTaggart's here, along with Varla.'

He'd called Norwich earlier that afternoon and spoken to a desk sergeant, requesting Inspector MacTaggart's presence. He'd also asked what the situation was regarding Varla Cartier, but all the sergeant had said was that she was still being interviewed. Langham was pleased to see that she'd been released.

Maria sat on the sofa, leafing quickly through a copy of *Tatler*. She looked up. 'I'm nervous, Donald. I hope everything goes according to plan.'

'It's just about in the bag,' he said. 'I'm just waiting for confirmation from Ralph.'

At the other end of the room, before the door, Terrence Ambler was setting up a projector on a small table. 'Nearly done here,' he said, looking ashen. 'The image isn't perfect – a bit grainy, but it's clear enough to show what's needed.' He hesitated. 'I still can't believe it, Donald. If I hadn't seen it with my own eyes . . .'

'I know,' Langham said, stepping around the screen on its tripod. 'I found it hard to believe myself, and to be honest when I came to the conclusion . . . I must admit that I felt a bit sick.'

'There,' Ambler said, fitting the second spool of the reel-to-reel in place, 'almost done. Running time three and a half minutes, black-and-white and silent. The only film to be shot at Marling Hall this year.'

Maria said, 'I just want all this to be over and done with.'

The door opened and Ryland almost ran into the room, a big grin on his thin face. 'Bingo!' he said. 'Job done. And you were right, Don. A perfect match.'

'Good man!'

'What now?' Ryland asked.

'I'm going to talk to MacTaggart and Ferrars, then I'll get everyone in here.'

He left the library and found the detectives in the hallway, speaking to Sergeant Briscoe. MacTaggart turned when Langham appeared. 'What's all this about, Langham? You said it was urgent.'

'I'm pleased to see you've released Varla.'

'We had nothing on her,' MacTaggart said. 'Forensics didn't find any blood in her room, or on her person. Now . . .?'

Langham indicated the drawing room. 'If I might have a quick word.'

He led the detectives into the room and, for the next five minutes, outlined the results of his investigations.

'You're sure about this, Langham? You can't just go about accusing people—'

Langham interrupted. 'We have it on film, and we have other evidence.' He outlined this and the killer's motivations.

MacTaggart heard him out. 'My God . . . So, what now?'

'I'll round everyone up and see you in the library in ten minutes. If you two could be in the room with us, and Briscoe stationed in the passage outside, that should ensure the culprit doesn't do a runner.'

He left the drawing room and made his way upstairs.

He hesitated outside Varla Cartier's room, then knocked. The door opened quickly, as if she had been waiting on the other side. She was smoking a cigarette and looked haggard. 'Oh, it's you, Langham. What do you want?'

'If you could make your way down to the library in five minutes . . .'

'Hell, not more questioning? Don't you think they put me through the mill enough last night?'

'I'm sure they did,' he said, 'and I'm pleased to see they released you. But no, there'll be no more questions.'

He made his way along the gallery and knocked on Edward's door.

'Come in.'

Edward Marling was seated in his wheelchair before the window, staring out. When he turned, Langham saw that he appeared gaunt and drawn. 'Donald, how can I help you?'

'We're gathering in the library in five minutes.'

'What's happening?'

Langham hesitated. 'Let's just say there'll be a presentation of the facts of the case,' he temporized.

Edward nodded. 'I'll be along presently.'

Langham looked for Chuck Banning and Sir Humphrey in their rooms, with no success, then made his way downstairs and found the pair in the dining hall enjoying a drink before dinner.

'If you could make your way along to the library, gentlemen.'

Sir Humphrey asked, 'Having a party, are we? Celebrating the end of the . . . the "shoot", as it were!'

'I think it's another round of questions, Sir Humphrey,' Chuck Banning told him. 'I saw Varla arrive back with the cops a few minutes ago.'

'What?' Sir Humphrey looked shocked. 'They've released her?'

'That's the impression I got,' the youth said.

Langham left the dining hall and returned to the library.

'Terry?'

Ambler signalled from his chair beside the projector. 'All set.'

'I'll give you the nod when we're ready to roll,' Langham said.

Maria perched herself on the edge of the sofa. 'I've arranged all the chairs,' she said, indicating the armchairs and dining chairs dotted around the room.

He kissed her. 'Good work.'

He joined Ryland at the far end of the room. His friend had placed a couple of dining chairs on either side of the screen.

Langham took his seat. 'How do you feel, Ralph?'

'Me? Never better. Always wanted to be in on a showdown like this. In at the kill!'

A few minutes later the door opened and Sir Humphrey hobbled in, followed by Chuck Banning. They sat side by side on the sofa and faced the screen. The detectives came next, moving unobtrusively into the room and taking the chairs positioned to either side of the door.

Varla Cartier entered and all eyes turned to her as she slipped into an armchair, her face expressionless. She lit a cigarette and smoked it with quick, nervous movements, then glanced around, and said, 'Can someone tell me what's going on here?'

Ryland said, 'Wait a jiffy and you'll find out.'

Sir Humphrey guffawed. 'All will be revealed,' he said. 'I think this is what they call the denouement!'

Edward Marling was the last person to enter the room. He propelled his wheelchair through the obstacle course of chairs and parked himself before the hearth.

Everyone was present and a silence settled over the gathering.

Langham looked around at the watching faces, took a breath, and then said, 'It's been a gruelling few days for everyone, and more than gruelling for some. It's been a terrible, tragic business, but I'm glad to say that it's almost at an end. Ralph . . .'

He sat back and proceeded to fill and light his pipe.

Ryland stood up, paced back and forth before the screen as if for effect, then faced the audience and began.

'It's been a perplexing case from the very start,' he said. 'We were called in by Suzie Reynard because she was fearful for the safety of her lover, Douglas Dennison. When Don came up here and started digging, he found that Dennison had been sent threatening photos. She was right to be worried.'

Langham glanced around the group. Everyone was watching Ryland intently.

'Don soon discovered that Dennison wasn't well liked. I've heard that people in top positions, those in power, have to be a bit ruthless to get there – I wouldn't know about that, meself, but it was obvious that Douglas Dennison had made quite a few enemies on his way up the Hollywood ladder.' He paused. 'Then, early on Sunday morning, Suzie Reynard was shot dead in Dennison's caravan – and that put the cat among the pigeons.' He paused again, this time to light a half-smoked Woodbine which he kept at the ready behind his right ear. He gestured towards Langham with the cigarette. 'But it didn't take Don long to work out that the killer really intended to murder Dennison.'

He stopped, his weasel gaze raking the audience.

'We weren't short of suspects. Everyone here, more or less, didn't see eye to eye with Douglas Dennison. Some of these gripes were relatively minor – Terry and Sir Humphrey had what might be called "artistic" disagreements with the director – but surely not enough to want to murder the man. Desmond Haggerston wanted Dennison to abandon the film – and he actually confessed to Suzie's murder in what turned out to be drunken guilt for the murder he *did* commit, that of his wife twenty-five years ago. Then there was Varla Cartier . . . who didn't attempt to hide her contempt for the man, and Cynthia Marling, who back in the thirties was just one of the many women who fell under the director's spell. Their affair ended when he walked out on the pregnant Cynthia and returned to the States.

'Then the killer did what he or she originally meant to do, and shot Dennison dead.' Ryland shrugged his thin shoulders. 'Yesterday Cynthia Marling tragically took her own life, and before doing so confessed to the killings. Or so it was assumed.' He looked across at Langham. 'Care to take it from there, Don?' He resumed his seat.

Langham removed his pipe and let his gaze move across the captive audience. There was a hushed anticipation in the air, a sense of expectation. No one moved, and all eyes were fixed on him.

He remained seated, and said evenly, 'Despite Cynthia's death having all the appearances of suicide, it soon became apparent that she did not kill herself. Our initial scepticism that she'd killed Suzie Reynard and Douglas Dennison, and conveniently left a confession before taking her own life, was confirmed by the forensic team's findings. It appeared that she was murdered by someone in a bid to close the case.'

He paused, puffed on his pipe, and regarded the assembly.

'Let's remind ourselves again of the events of yesterday afternoon, at just after four o'clock. Maria and myself were in the hallway, having arrived back from the Seven Sleepers; Ralph and Terry were just behind us. Sir Humphrey was in the library, and Chuck Banning in his room next to Varla's. Edward was in the hallway, and he and I exchanged a few words before he entered the lift. We all heard the fatal shot about fifteen seconds later, while we four were still in the hallway, Sir Humphrey in the library and Edward in the lift. I immediately ran up the stairs to the gallery, to see Edward emerging from the lift to my immediate right and, at the very end of the gallery to my left, perhaps fifteen yards away, Varla Cartier stepping from her room next to Edward's study. Now it would appear pretty obvious that only one person in the house could have shot Cynthia – having first typed out the note confessing to the killings of Reynard and Dennison – and then returned quickly to her room. Varla Cartier was taken away for further questioning last night, and released this morning, the police satisfied that she was not the culprit.'

Varla Cartier fanned smoke from before her face, smiling grimly to herself.

'Therefore it would appear that, if Varla Cartier didn't kill Cynthia Marling, then no one else could have – her murder was impossible. So we must return to the original assumption that she did indeed kill herself. However, the forensic team discovered one very significant fact when they examined Cynthia's body: that the murder weapon was fired at a distance of perhaps two feet from her head. No suicide would hold the gun that far away – in fact it would be physically impossible to do so, and turn one's hand sufficiently to hit one's own head. We can only assume that the killer, though fully intending to position the muzzle of the weapon next to Cynthia's temple, was unable to do so – perhaps Cynthia saw what was happening at the very last second and backed away as the shot was fired . . .' He drew on his pipe, ruminatively, staring from one to the others of those present.

'Suspicion then fell on Chuck Banning, who occupied the room next to Varla's.' He looked at the young man, who stared at him like a rabbit caught in the glare of oncoming headlights. 'Earlier today I conducted a little experiment, moving from Chuck's room to Edward's study and acting out what had to be done in the latter – aiming a weapon, firing, and arranging the confessional note in the typewriter, then returning to his room.'

He shook his head. 'But it just couldn't be done in the fifteen seconds available to Chuck.' On the sofa, Chuck Banning seemed to deflate with relief.

'So there we have it,' Langham said. 'An impossible murder. No one could have killed Cynthia Marling, and she did not kill herself . . . However, immediately after the discovery of Cynthia's body, something happened which at first, though puzzling, had no apparent connection to the killing. I returned to my room and discovered that the window had been opened at some point that afternoon.' He shrugged. '"So what?" I hear you ask. Might either Evans or the maid have opened it to cool down the room? But, when asked, they denied having done so, and neither Maria nor I had opened the window. It was a mystery, apparently inconsequential, that niggled me all evening and kept me awake well into the early hours. By breakfast time, though, I had an inkling who the killer might be – though I must admit I found myself sickened by the idea – and I devised a scheme to prove my suspicions.'

Varla Cartier leaned forward. 'So, who the hell was it, Langham?'

He gestured with his pipe. 'Let's not get ahead of ourselves,' he said. 'I had a good idea who the killer was, but I had to work out a motive. Why did this person want Dennison dead? To understand this, I had to consider the type of person the director was. Put bluntly he was egotistical, power-hungry and abusive. He got what he wanted, always – and he always got the woman he wanted, too. Or he *almost* always got the woman. However, there was one woman who eluded him. Cynthia Marling. Although they'd had an affair in the mid-thirties, and he walked out on her, it's my suspicion that he later came to regret the act, for during the war when he was back in Britain, he resumed his contact with Cynthia and attempted to rekindle their affair. Cynthia, married by this time and converted to Catholicism, was having none of it. And I can only imagine how Dennison, a man accustomed to getting what he wanted and *who* he wanted, found this intolerable. He wanted Cynthia Marling and he was going to get her, by hook or by crook. But as he saw it there was someone, one person, standing in the way of his getting the woman he desired. Edward Marling.'

Langham looked across at Edward, who shook his head. 'But . . . but Douglas hardly ever saw Cynthia during the war. He . . . he never showed the slightest interest.'

'That you were aware of, Edward. Of course he wouldn't have

shown his interest to you, the husband of the woman he coveted. Why would he tip your hand when it was his intention to kill you?'

Gasps sounded around the room.

Edward's mouth opened, and finally he found his tongue. 'What . . .? Kill me? But . . .'

'And he nearly succeeded. What better way of ensuring that you were dead, and that he could not be held accountable, than to shoot you while you were under fire from the enemy during that ill-fated mission in the south of France in 'forty-four? He shot you three times and left you for dead. I can only imagine his shock when he later learned that you had survived, albeit paralysed from the waist down with one of the three bullets lodged close to your spine.'

Into the resulting silence, Sir Humphrey said, 'That's all very well, Langham, but I don't see how what happened then can have any relevance—'

Langham stopped him with a raised hand. 'But it has every relevance, Sir Humphrey, because it provided Edward Marling with the motive to murder Douglas Dennison.'

Langham heard a series of indrawn breaths. Edward leaned forward in his wheelchair.

'This is preposterous!' he snapped. 'Douglas wouldn't have done that . . . and even if he had, how do you suppose that I ever found out?'

Langham smiled. 'Because, Edward, one year ago you had the operation that you hoped might restore your mobility – and the bullet that was removed from next to your spine was *this* one . . . Ralph.'

With assumed weariness, Ryland climbed to his feet and pulled something from his pocket. He stepped forward and held it up between his thumb and forefinger so that everyone could see the bullet. At the same time, Langham noticed Edward reach surreptitiously into his blazer pocket as if to check something.

'This, ladies and gentlemen,' Ryland said, 'is the bullet the surgeons removed from Edward Marling's spinal column. Edward kept it as a talisman, a reminder of Douglas Dennison's treachery. Don here had the bright idea that it might be worthwhile me pick-pocketing the bullet from Edward's blazer while we played billiards earlier today. Then I made my way to Dennison's room where, Don assured me, I'd find the ammunition for the director's Colt service revolver. And what do you know, ladies and gentlemen, but the bullets I found in Dennison's room were identical to the bullet removed from Edward Marling's spine last year.' Ryland shrugged nonchalantly. 'I can only imagine what went through Edward's mind when he was handed the bullet after the op, and realized its significance. Not a German bullet, mind you, but a standard US army issue . . .'

'Thank you, Ralph,' Langham said, and looked across at Edward. 'And when you realized the deceit of your old friend, Edward, you began your plans to kill him.'

Edward flung back his head and laughed. 'This is insane! How on earth might I do that . . .?' He gazed around at the assembled faces as if seeking an ally. He was met by an array of incredulous gazes.

'Last year, after the operation,' Langham said, 'you invited Douglas Dennison to Marling Hall to make the film he'd been planning for years, all the time intending to kill him. On Sunday morning, at a few minutes before six, you made your way to Dennison's caravan.'

Langham paused there, staring at Edward Marling; the man's face was white, his mouth half open. Even at a distance of yards, Langham could see the dew of sweat on his forehead.

'I went over and over the scenario of Suzie Reynard's death,' Langham said, 'attempting to work out *why* someone had killed her. You see, no one knew that Reynard would be in the caravan then – the killer came with the express intention of murdering Dennison. Now I must admit that at first I assumed that the killer had walked into the caravan with the revolver drawn – and it was because Suzie Reynard had seen the weapon that, in a manner of speaking, forced the killer's hand. However, I now believe that that isn't how it happened. I think you, Edward, entered the caravan with the weapon concealed – because you intended to speak with Douglas Dennison before you shot him, tell him why you were killing him, as revenge for his attempt on your life all those years ago. However, when you stepped into the caravan and either found Suzie awake, or woke her, and she saw you . . .' He paused, shaking his head as he envisaged the scene. 'She saw you standing there, *standing* – and in that terrible second you knew that she had to die if your scheme to murder Dennison was to be successful. So you drew your revolver and shot her dead.'

Edward stared at him, shaking his head. 'No . . .' he murmured.

Langham went on, 'You fled the caravan, and on the way back into the hall collided with Desmond Haggerston.' Langham permitted himself a wry smile. 'I can only imagine your horror in those seconds, as you knocked the old man off his feet, then picked yourself up and escaped into the hall. You must have assumed he'd seen you, and I wonder if you considered shooting Haggerston, too, and might very well have done so but for the fact that in the collision you'd dropped the revolver and Haggerston had picked it up.' He smiled. 'When, later, the old man actually confessed to the killing – having left the revolver in the caravan, covered with his fingerprints – you must have thought that all your Christmases had come at once.'

Langham's pipe had gone out. He took his time to relight it, took a few contemplative puffs, and went on, 'And then on Tuesday afternoon you accomplished what you had been planning to do for over a year. As Dennison sat beneath the beech trees, you left Sir Humphrey and Chuck in this very room on the pretext of going into the kitchen. You exited through the window in the gun room and moved to the corner of the house. I can imagine Dennison's incredulity when he saw you. Did you smile, Edward – or even tell him why he had to die – before shooting him three times in the chest? And what twisted satisfaction you must have gained from the act!'

'Ludicrous!' Edward cried. 'How on earth could I—?'

Langham pointed his pipe at the man. 'Now, it just happens that I was on the scene of the shooting seconds before Dennison died, and I heard his very last words: what might have been "No way". Dennison saw you walk around the corner and approach him and he thought it impossible. "*No way*," he said.'

Edward shook his head. 'No!'

'However, it *wasn't* impossible,' he said. 'A year ago the operation to remove the bullet from your spine, and hopefully restore your mobility, was *not* a failure – as you wished everyone to believe. It was a resounding success. After a month of physiotherapy and recuperation in Bournemouth, where Cynthia believed you were attempting to get over the crushing disappointment of the operation's failure, you returned to Marling Hall and played out your deception, feigning your continued incapacity even to your wife . . . while all the while planning your revenge.'

Edward shook his head in silence.

Langham signalled to Terry Ambler, who set the projector running. Ryland stood and drew the curtains, plunging the room into darkness.

'Earlier today,' Langham said, 'I asked Maria to approach Edward about the possibility of reading the manuscript of his wartime exploits. I think,' he went on, 'that everyone will find this interesting.'

He pulled his chair away from the screen and positioned himself so that he could take in both the flickering image on the screen and Edward Marling, seated five yards away in the shadows.

'At two o'clock this afternoon,' Langham said, 'Edward led Maria to his study. They talked for a while, and Maria – on my instructions – moved around the room and took down from the wall one of the crossbows, examined it and left it on a tabletop. She then looked at various military figures in Edward's collection – always careful to replace them at odd angles to each other and so annoying, I hoped, Edward's obsession with symmetry. Now I had entered the study ten minutes before the arrival of Edward and Maria, and set up Terry Ambler's cine camera, concealing it behind a row of books, and set it running to film the subsequent events. This is an edited version of that longer film, the last three and a half minutes, from a second or so after Maria left the room.'

The screen showed a grainy, black-and-white image of Edward's study. In the centre of the screen, beside the desk, was Edward himself, staring at the door and then rotating his wheelchair to look around the room.

'I was relying on Edward's compulsive need for symmetry,' Langham said, 'his drive for order in all things, to betray him. His study, his *sanctum sanctorum*, was a scrupulously neat and tidy refuge, with not a single item out of place. I guessed that Maria's rearranging the objects would be beyond Edward's ability to ignore.' He gestured at the screen. 'And I was right.'

As the audience stared in mesmerized silence, on the screen Edward Marling rolled himself towards the door, reached out and locked it.

Then he eased himself from the chair, stood up, and walked slowly across the room to where a crossbow sat on a small occasional table.

Exclamations and gasps arose from the gathering, and Langham looked across at Edward. In the flickering light from the screen, he stared back at Langham with nothing short of murder in his eyes.

On the screen Edward, a tall, slowly moving figure, walked around the room, replacing the objects moved by Maria, repositioning the figures she had placed at odd angles to each other. After a minute, having gazed around the room and satisfied himself that order had been restored, he returned to his wheelchair, unlocked the door and pushed himself from the study.

Ambler stopped the projection and Ryland drew the curtains,

revealing a gallery of shocked faces as all eyes turned to the accused man.

Langham stared across at Edward. He was clutching the arms of his wheelchair, his face as white as canvas as he stammered, 'You've got it wrong, Langham. Terribly wrong. The operation was – was partially successful in that I gained limited mobility, but that's all it was. I – I can walk a little, for short periods . . . But I didn't murder Reynard, or Dennison, and I certainly didn't – I didn't kill my wife.' He looked around at the staring faces. 'That was impossible! I was in the lift when—'

Langham smiled at Edward. 'But you did kill Cynthia, Edward – and I know how you hoped to get away with it.'

'You're talking rubbish, man!' Edward stared around the room again, frantic appeal in his eyes. 'You saw me, Maria – I was in the hallway – and then in the lift when the shot was fired! Ryland, you saw me enter the lift—'

Langham interrupted, 'I must admit, Edward, that there was a twisted genius in your plan to kill Cynthia. And it so very nearly worked, if it were not for the open window – and the fact that Cynthia jerked her head back as you fired.'

'I don't know what you're talking about,' Edward said in desperation.

'Then I'll explain how you did it, and you can tell me if I'm wrong.' Langham paused, looked around at the expectant faces, and went on, 'Shortly before four o'clock yesterday, you shot your wife with a revolver fitted with a silencer – except that it didn't quite go to plan. Cynthia noticed you draw the gun and instinctively backed off as you fired, killing her from a distance of two feet. You arranged her body, with the revolver on the floor beneath her outstretched fingertips, and inserted her typewritten "confession" into the typewriter. You left the study and took the lift down to the hallway, knowing that we would return at four for the drinks you'd arranged to have with us. You duly met us, exchanged pleasantries, then said you were just going up to the bathroom. You entered the lift and fifteen seconds later we heard the gunshot.'

'But how on earth—?' Sir Humphrey began.

Langham went on, 'What happened, I suspect, was this. Before he came down to meet us in the hallway, Edward entered our bedroom and opened the window. Then he left the bedroom door open and took the lift down to meet us. He had a revolver – this time, importantly, *not* fitted with a silencer – concealed about his person. When he'd spoken to Maria and me in the hallway, he excused himself and took the lift upstairs and, as the lift doors opened onto the gallery, he immediately drew his revolver and fired through the open door into our room and *through the open window*. In a trice he stepped from his wheelchair, crossed the landing and closed the door – but there was not quite enough time to enter the room and close the window. Then he returned to his wheelchair and, as I arrived on the gallery, he appeared to all intents and purposes to be emerging from the lift. To aid his cause, albeit unwittingly, Varla left her room at the sound of the gunshot and so, for a time, incriminated herself. It was an act that Edward must have considered fortunate for himself at the time, for even if the police ruled out suicide, Varla's proximity to the scene of the crime would have pointed to her being the only person in the household who could have possibly been in the right place to have killed Cynthia.'

'No!' Edward cried.

Shaking uncontrollably now, he reached into the pocket of his blazer and pulled out a revolver. He gripped the weapon in both hands and directed it at Langham. Gasps sounded around the room, and Chuck Banning half rose from the sofa.

Edward swung the revolver to cover the actor. 'Sit down! No one make a move . . .'

Banning dropped back onto the sofa. Edward once more turned the weapon on Langham.

'You can have no conception, Langham, of what I went through. To consider someone a loyal friend – more, a comrade in arms – and then to find all that trust and friendship destroyed in a cowardly act of betrayal . . .'

Langham shook his head. 'I think I can understand your feelings, Edward, when the surgeon handed you the bullet and you realized what must have happened on that mission in France. Not only had Dennison shot you in the back and robbed you of a decade of active life, but in shooting you for his own base desires he destroyed what little faith in humanity you had remaining after your wartime experiences. I understand that, and I can sympathize with you . . . But what I find impossible to comprehend is the desire to answer that act of violence with even more violence.'

Edward stared at him, his face ashen. 'Suzie Reynard had to die, Langham. When I entered the caravan and she saw me, standing there . . . I was back in France, on a mission. I – I did what I had been trained to do. Kill . . . or fail. So, instinctively, I killed poor Suzie.'

'And Cynthia?' Langham said. 'Let me guess. Not only would Cynthia's apparent suicide close the case, you hoped – but you'd stand to inherit the hall.'

Edward shook his head. 'You're overlooking a far more basic motive, Langham. Do you have any idea what it was like for me to live with Cynthia for the past ten years? To endure her constant criticism, her snide comments?' His face twisted into a bitter expression. 'For all her piety, Langham, Cynthia was a cold, heartless woman. The look on her face when I raised the revolver and she realized what I was doing . . .'

He gave a strangled laugh. 'It will be worth hanging for,' he said. 'Not that I intend to hang.'

Edward lifted the revolver and aimed it at Langham, smiling.

Then he placed the muzzle of the weapon to his temple and pulled the trigger – and the hammer fell on an empty chamber. He pulled again, and again, and an expression of horror appeared on his face as he took in the fact of his failure and saw Langham smiling at him with satisfaction.

MacTaggart and Ferrars rushed to Edward and wrested the revolver from his grip.

'Edward Marling,' MacTaggart intoned, 'I arrest you for the murder of Suzie Reynard, Douglas Dennison and Cynthia Marling, and warn you that anything you say . . .'

At ten o'clock that evening, Langham and Maria sat around the hearth in the library at Marling Hall. They were joined by Ralph Ryland and Terrence Ambler, and a little later by Varla Cartier, Chuck Banning and Sir Humphrey.

'So much for my making a comeback on the silver screen,' Varla said. 'But I must admit that I was more than impressed by your performance, gentlemen. If I'm ever in need of the services of private eyes, I know where to come.'

'Please,' Ryland said with mock pain. 'It's private *detectives*. Private *eyes* are what you have on the other side of the pond.'

'Forgive me.' Varla smiled and knocked back her gin.

'I must admit,' Chuck Banning said, 'that when Marling pulled the gun and aimed at you, Donald, I thought you'd had your chips.'

'I was never in any danger,' Langham said, 'thanks to Maria and Ralph.'

Sir Humphrey looked puzzled. 'Thanks to . . .? I don't follow, old boy.'

'Ralph, if you'd care to explain.'

The detective laughed. 'Simplicity itself,' he said. 'You see, Maria warned us earlier that Edward was carrying a revolver, so knowing that we had a showdown planned I thought it wise to do something about it. While I was beating him at billiards this afternoon, I lifted his revolver along with the American bullet he carried as a memento.' He shrugged. 'But I must admit that he made it easy for me – he took off his blazer and hung it over a chair while we were playing. As he was concentrating on a shot, I pilfered the bullet and at the same time unloaded the revolver. Not a good idea to take unnecessary risks, you see.'

'Excellent work,' Sir Humphrey declared. 'I think this calls for another drink.'

Terry Ambler lifted his glass. 'I don't know about the rest of you, but I'll be glad to see the back of this place.'

'I'll second that,' Varla Cartier said, looking at Maria. 'Didn't I say that there was something . . . malign about Marling Hall?'

Maria smiled. 'And I disagreed,' she said. 'Places cannot be malign, Varla. Only people can be malign . . . and good.'

'And I'll raise my glass to that,' Langham said.

EPILOGUE

Langham sat with his feet lodged on the corner of the desk and his chair tipped back against the wall. He was going over a short story he'd written earlier that week and trying to work out how it could be improved. No doubt Maria would tell him when she'd cast a critical eye over the manuscript.

It was five o'clock on Friday afternoon, less than a week since the events at Marling Hall – and in three weeks from now he would be married. The idea still seemed a little unreal.

The telephone bell rang and he dislodged his feet from the desk. 'Hello, Ryland and Langham—'

'Donald, Donald! And how does this fine day find you, my boy?'

'Never better, Charles. And you?'

'Tip-top, Donald. Absolutely tip-top!' His agent's fruity tones boomed down the line from Pimlico as if he were in the next room. 'Now, are you sitting comfortably, Donald?'

'Uh-oh, bad news?'

'Far from it. Far, far from it! In fact, quite the reverse. Possibly the finest news I've ever had to impart in my many years of navigating the perfidious depths of the literary ocean! Are you seated?'

'I am, and I'm all ears,' Langham said, smiling to himself and wondering what all this was about.

'Very well. Now, I know that your dealings with the film world have been somewhat fraught of late—'

'That's something of an understatement,' Langham said. 'I'll be happy never to see another thesp for as long as I live.'

'Well, my boy, this little piece of news might cast Tinseltown in a far more favourable light.' Charles paused, as if for effect.

'Out with it, you old ham!' Langham said.

'Very well – I've just put the phone down on an agent from Hollywood who, a week ago, expressed an interest in purchasing the film rights of your novel *Murder at the Mews*. For the past few days I've been in exhaustive negotiations with the fellow, and the upshot is that he's ready to make an offer of two thousand pounds sterling for the film rights. I would advise you, dear boy, to accept.'

Langham opened his mouth, only to find himself speechless.

'Donald? Donald, my boy? Are you still there?'

'Still here, but finding it hard to think straight, never mind speak . . . *Two thousand?*'

'For the initial film rights. What with residuals, and potential publishing tie-ins, I think it might be a good deal more, in the long run.'

'Good heavens . . . I mean, bloody hell! Well, I don't know what to say. Is Maria there?'

'She left just half an hour ago,' Charles said.

'I'll ring her at home and share the good news.'

'I think this calls for a little celebration, Donald. What say I take you out for drink this evening, and then on to the Ivy for dinner, just the four of us: yourself and Maria, Albert and myself?'

'That would be wonderful, yes.'

'Excellent. What say we meet at the Salisbury at eight?'

'Eight it is.'

'And congratulations, my boy, I'm more than delighted – it couldn't happen to a finer fellow.'

Langham thanked him and, a little light-headed, rang off and replaced the receiver.

After staring into space for two minutes, and no doubt grinning fatuously, he picked up the phone and rang Maria's Kensington number.

'Hello.'

'Maria! Are you sitting down?'

'I am.'

'Charles rang a minute ago. You'll never guess? Hollywood has made an offer for one of the early Sam Brooke's . . .'

Maria's trilling laughter sounded down the line. 'So you'll certainly be able to buy me a cottage in the country, Donald!'

He sat up. 'Just a sec . . . You knew? At the Seven Sleepers the other day . . .'

'Oh, Donald . . . Charles mentioned the film interest last Friday, but swore me to secrecy. I so wanted to tell you, but what if it all went wrong?'

'Two thousand,' he said. 'And that's for starters. Charles is taking us out tonight, to celebrate.' He heard footsteps on the stairs, and Ryland's familiar chirpy whistle. 'I'd better dash, Maria. That's Ralph.'

'See you tonight, *mon cher*,' Maria said, and replaced the receiver.

Ryland entered the office and looked at Langham. 'Hope you don't mind me saying, Don, but you look like the cat that's got the cream. You got a promise on for tonight?'

'You might say that, Ralph,' Langham said, and told Ryland about the Hollywood offer.

'Bingo!' the detective said. 'The next round's on you, matey.'

'Oh, and that isn't the only good news,' Langham said, picking up a letter from the desk and flipping it across to Ryland. 'Read this.'

Ryland lit a Woodbine. 'Who's it from?' He pulled a sheet of notepaper from the envelope, along with a cheque. 'Hey . . .' He grinned across at Langham and whistled. 'Two hundred guineas.'

'It's from Chuck Banning,' Langham said. 'Read on, and all will be revealed.'

Ryland dropped into the spindle-backed chair and read the letter, his lips moving as he did so.

'Well, what do you know? Chuck's set to inherit Marling Hall – and "in a gesture of gratitude for bringing the murderer to justice, here is a cheque . . ."' Ryland laughed. 'Fifty-fifty, eh?'

'No, Ralph. You keep it. Buy something for Annie, OK?'

'I'll do that, Don. And thanks. She'll be tickled pink. What say we close up the shop and have a celebratory pint or three?'

'You've read my mind,' Langham said. 'Lead the way.'

He took his jacket from the peg on the wall, locked the door behind him, and followed Ryland down the stairs and around the corner to the Grapes.